The Wiles of the Wicked

The Wiles
of the Wicked

William Le Queux

MINT EDITIONS

The Wiles of the Wicked was first published in 1900.

This edition published by Mint Editions 2021.

ISBN 9781513280967 | E-ISBN 9781513285986

Published by Mint Editions®

 MINT
EDITIONS

minteditionbooks.com

Publishing Director: Jennifer Newens
Design & Production: Rachel Lopez Metzger
Project Manager: Micaela Clark
Typesetting: Westchester Publishing Services

Contents

I

WHY THIS IS WRITTEN

Wilford Heaton is not my real name, for why should I publish it to the world?

The reason I do not give it is, first, because I have no desire to be made the object of idle curiosity or speculation, and secondly, although the explanation herein given will clear the honour of one of the most powerful of the Imperial Houses in Europe, I have no wish that my true name should be associated with it.

I have, however, a reason for writing this narrative—a very strong reason.

The story is an enthralling one; the adventures stranger, perhaps, than ever happened to any other living person. I have resolved to relate the plain unvarnished facts in their sequence, just as they occurred, without seeking to suppress or embellish, but to recount the strange adventures just as they are registered in the small leather portfolio, or secret dossier, which still, at this moment, reposes in the archives of a certain Ministry in one of the European capitals.

There have recently been stories afloat—strange stories. At first I laughed at all the absurd rumours, but very quickly I saw how seriously distorted the real facts had become, for ingenious paragraphs of certain so-called Society papers, grasping the story eagerly, worked it up into a narrative which reflected very seriously upon the honour of one who is dearest in all the world to me.

Well, my tale—or exposure—is written here.

In order that those who read may clearly follow the curious chain of circumstances, it is necessary for me to go back some eight years or so— not a long period as far as time goes, but to me a veritable century. I was young, just turned twenty five. I was decently well-off, having come into an income of nearly a couple of thousand a year left me by my father, a sum which put me beyond the necessity of entering business, pursuing the daily grind, or troubling about the morrow. My career at Oxford had, I fear, been marked by a good many shortcomings and many youthful escapades, but I ended it by taking my degree of Bachelor of Medicine, shortly afterwards pursuing the fashionable habit of "going abroad."

Within two years, however, I returned to London world-weary—like so many other young men who, being left comfortably off, commence to taste the enjoyment of life too early—and settled down in a suite of smoke-begrimed rooms in Essex Street, Strand.

The place was horribly dingy, situated in that *cul-de-sac* which is quiet and almost deserted, even though only a stone's throw from the busiest, noisiest, and muddiest thoroughfare in the world. The ground and first floors of the house were occupied by several firms of solicitors, whose doors were covered with ragged and sadly faded green baize, while the second floor I rented as my abode. The quaint, shabby, bizarre old place had been built at the end of the last century for family residence, in the days when Bloomsbury was an aristocratic quarter and great men lived in Leicester Square; but now, alas! smoke-stained and time-dimmed, it was given over to the dust which the law accumulates. From its exterior, like those of its neighbours, there protruded those great iron extinguishers used by the linkmen of days bygone, while the broad, thin-worn stairs, easy of ascent, the solid mahogany doors, the great carved handrail, and the fine Adams ceilings, like those in the older houses of the Adelphi, told mutely of the prosperity of its long-departed owners.

I had taken over the furniture, a frowsy lot of faded horsehair, which had perhaps done duty there for half a century, together with the rooms, and even though they were so dismal and out-of-date, I must confess that they had one attraction for me, namely, that above, in the low-pitched rooms on the top floor, there lived and worked my old college chum, Dick Doyle, who had, after a good deal of wild-oat sowing, developed into a rising journalist and *litterateur*.

Curious though it may appear, I had returned from the Sunny South and taken up my abode in that dingy, dispiriting place with one sole idea, namely, to be near the man who was practically my only friend in the whole world. I was in sore need of him, for I was utterly heedless of everything past, present, or future.

With the exception of old Mrs. Parker, who had served my family for twenty years, I was absolutely alone and helpless as a child. At the age of twenty-five I had ceased to interest myself in anything, and plunged in eternal gloom, all desire for life having left me, for knowing that its joys could no longer be mine I was, even though in the full possession of all my youthful vigour, mental faculties, and bodily strength, actually looking forward to the grave.

The terrible truth must here be told. The reader will, I feel confident, sympathise. While living abroad, travelling hither and thither through the old Italian towns, where I delighted to roam in the big white piazzas and through the crumbling palaces, every stone of which spoke of a brilliant and historic past, I had been suddenly seized by disease, and for three months lay tossing upon my bed in an English pension in Florence, tended by two calm, sweet-faced sisters of charity, with their grey-blue habits and great white linen head-dresses, which in my hours of fever and delirium seemed always so clean and cool. The two great Italian professors who were called to me shook their heads, believing that, even if they managed to save my life, it would be at a loss of one of my senses. In this, alas! they were not mistaken. My eyes became affected by sclerotitis, a severe inflammation of the sclerotic. Gradually my eyes, those most beautiful structures of the human body which manifest in such small compass the great, the unspeakable, the incomprehensible power of our Creator, grew dim. My sight was slowly but surely failing me. I was recovering from my bodily ailment to be attacked by the ophthalmic disease which the doctors had all along feared.

I implored of them to do something to preserve my sight, but they only dropped into my eye certain liquids from their little brown glass phials, and regarded the effect gravely. A great oculist from Rome came to give his opinion. I saw him but mistily, as though I were looking through a dense fog; and he, too, told me that all that could be done had already been done.

I arose from my bed a fortnight later stone blind.

With this terrible affliction upon me I returned to London with Dick Doyle, who came out to Florence to fetch me home. For me, life had no further charm. The beauties of the world which had given me so much pleasure and happiness were blotted out for me for ever. I lived now only in an eternal darkness which by day, when the sun shone upon my eyes, seemed to assume a dull dark red. At first it struck me that because my sight had been destroyed my personal appearance must have altered, but Dick assured me that it had not. No one, he declared, could tell by looking at my eyes that they were actually sightless.

And so I, Wilford Heaton, lived in those dull old chambers in Essex Street, in rooms that I had never seen.

You, who have sight to read these lines, can you imagine what it is to be suddenly struck blind? Close your eyes for a brief five minutes and see how utterly helpless you become, how entirely dependent you are upon others, how blank would be your life if you were always thus.

Dick gave to me all the time he could spare from his work, and would come and sit with me to chat, for conversation with him was all that was now left to me. He described my rooms and my surroundings with the same minuteness with which he wrote, and tried to interest me by relating scraps of the day's news. Yet when he was absent, away or at work in his rooms above, I sat alone thinking for hours and hours, counting time by the chiming of the clock of St. Clement Danes.

So heavily did time hang upon my hands that at last I engaged a teacher from the Blind School over in Lambeth, and with his books of raised letters he used to visit me each day and teach me to read. I was an apt pupil, I suppose, yet there was something strangely grotesque about a man who had already graduated recommencing to learn his alphabet like a child. Still, it saved me from being driven mad by melancholy, and it was not long before I found that, by the exercise of pains, I could read slowly the various embossed books, standard works manufactured for the recreation of those unfortunates like myself, who would otherwise sit eternally idle with their hands before them. And not only did I learn to read, but also to make small fancy baskets, work very intricate at first, but which, on account of the highly developed sense of touch that I had acquired in reading, soon became quite easy.

The long months of winter darkness went by; but to me, who could not see the sun, what mattered whether the days were brilliant August or black December? Sometimes I went out, but not often. I had not become proficient in finding my way by aid of a stick. I had practised a good deal in my rooms; but for a blind man to go forth into the busy Strand he must have perfect confidence, and be able to guide himself among the bustling throng. Therefore, on my airings I usually went forth upon Dick's arm, and the extent of our wanderings was the end of the Embankment at Westminster Bridge, or around those small ornamental gardens which extend from the Charing Cross station of the Underground Railway up to Waterloo Bridge. Sometimes, on rare occasions, he would take me to dine with him at the Savage Club, in Adelphi Terrace; and men, easy-going Bohemians, whom I could not see, would warmly shake my hand. I heard their voices—voices of artists and *litterateurs* whose names were as household words—sat charmed by their merry gossip of artistic "shop," laughed at their droll stories, or listened to one or other of the members who would recite or sing for the benefit of his "brother Savages." Those evenings, spent amid the tobacco-smoke and glass-jingling of the only Bohemia still existing in London, were the happiest in all that dull, colourless, dismal life of sound and touch.

They were the only recreations left to me. Truly mine was a tristful life.

In April, after I had lived in that dingy den six months or more, Dick came into my room one morning and made an announcement. It was that he had been commissioned by his paper to go as its correspondent with a British punitive expedition on the North-West Frontier of India.

"You'll go, of course," I said, reflecting that such an offer meant both advancement and profit. He had long ago told me that a commission as war correspondent was his greatest ambition.

"No, my dear old fellow," his deep voice answered in a tone more grave than usual. "I can't leave you alone."

"Nonsense!" I exclaimed. "I'm not going to allow you to fling away such a good offer to remain with me. No, you must go, Dick. You'll be back in three months at most, won't you?"

"Perhaps before," and his voice sounded low and strange. "But really, old fellow, I can't go and leave you helpless, like this."

"You'll go," I said decisively. "Mrs. Parker will look after me, and three months will soon pass."

"No," he said. "It's all very well, but you can't sit here month after month, helpless as you are. It's impossible."

"I shall amuse myself with my books and my basket-making," I answered. Truth to tell, this announcement of his had utterly crushed me. His society was the only bright spot in my life. If he left me I should be entirely alone, cheerless and melancholy. Nevertheless, when the sight is destroyed the mind is quickened, and I reflected all that this offer meant to him, and admired his self-denial and readiness to refuse it on my account.

Therefore I insisted that he should go. In the end he was persuaded, and three days later left Charing Cross for India.

When he had gone I became hopelessly depressed. In vain did I try to interest myself in the embossed books, but they were mostly works which I had read long ago, and in vain I toiled at basket-making until my finger-tips were sore and aching. Sometimes at evening Mrs. Parker, herself a sad scholar, would try and read a few of what she considered the choicest morsels of the "extra special." She read very slowly and inaccurately, poor old soul, and many were the words she was compelled to spell and leave me to solve their meaning. Indeed, in those long hours I spent by myself I sank lower and lower in dejection. No longer I heard Dick's merry voice saying—

"Come, cheer up, old chap. Let me tell you all I heard to-day over at the club."

No longer could I lean upon his arm as we descended that steep flight of steps leading from the end of Essex Street to the Embankment; no longer did I hear those playful words of his on such occasions—

"Take care, darling, or you'll fall."

Dear old Dick! Now, when I reflected upon it all, I saw how in my great affliction he treated me as tenderly as he could a woman. Forlorn, hypped, and heart-sick, I lived on from day to day, taking interest in nothing, moping doleful and unmanned.

A single letter came from him, posted at some outlandish place in the North-West. It was read to me by old Mrs. Parker, but as Dick was a sad scribbler, its translation was not a very brilliant success. Nevertheless, from it I gathered how deep were his thoughts of me, and how eager he was to complete his work and return. Truly no man had a more devoted friend, and certainly no man was more in need of one.

As the days grew warmer, and I sat ever with the *taedium vitae* upon me, joyless and dispirited in that narrow world of darkness, I felt stifled, and longed for air. Essex Street is terribly close in July, therefore, finding the heat intolerable, I went forth at evening upon the Embankment with Mrs. Parker, and, with my stick, practised walking alone upon that long, rather unfrequented stretch of pavement between the railings of the Temple Gardens and the corner of Savoy Street.

Try to walk a dozen paces as one blind. Close your eyes, and tap lightly with your stick before you as you walk, and see how utterly helpless you feel, and how erratic are your footsteps. Then you will know how extremely difficult I found my first essays alone. I walked full of fear, as a child walks, stumbling, colliding, halting, and afterwards waiting for my pitying old woman-servant to take my arm and guide me in safety.

Yet evening after evening I went forth and steadily persevered. I had, in the days before the world became shut out from my gaze, seen men who were blind guiding themselves fearlessly hither and thither among the London crowds, and I was determined, in Dick's absence, to master the means of visionless locomotion, so that I might walk alone for health's sake, if for nothing else. And so I continued, striving and striving. When Mrs. Parker had served my dinner, cutting it up for me just as one places meat before a helpless infant, we went forth together, and for an hour each evening I went out upon that wide expanse of the Embankment pavement which formed my practice-ground.

Gradually, by slow degrees, I became proficient in guiding myself with that constant tapping that marks a blind man's progress through the black void which constitutes his own narrow joyless world. At last, after several weeks of constant practice, I found to my great delight that I could actually walk alone the whole length of the pavement, guiding myself by intuition when encountering passers-by, and continuing straight on without stumbling or colliding with any object, a fact which gave me the utmost satisfaction, for it seemed to place me beyond, the need of a constant guide. With this progress I intended to astound Dick upon his return, and so gradually persevered towards proficiency.

II

THE BRACELET AND THE PALM

August was dusty and blazing in London, and I felt it sorely in Essex Street. The frontier war dragged on its weary length, as frontier wars always drag, and Dick was still unable to return. His brilliant descriptions of the fighting had become a feature in the journal he represented. On one of my short walks from end to end of that long even strip of pavement a hand was suddenly placed upon my shoulder, and the voice told me that it was Shadrack Fennell, a charming old fellow, who had been a popular actor of a day long since past, and was now a prominent "Savage," well known in that little circle of London Bohemia. He walked with me a little way, and next evening called and spent an hour over cigars and whisky. He was the only visitor I had had in all those months of Dick's absence.

A blind man has, alas! very few friends.

Once or twice, when the heat became insufferable in my close stuffy rooms, I contemplated going to the country or to the sea. Yet, on reflection, I told myself bitterly that, being unable to see the beauties of God's earth, I was just as well there moping in that gloomy street, and taking my evening airing beside the Thames.

Therefore with all desire for life or enjoyment crushed from my soul, I remained in London, going out each fine evening, sometimes with Mrs. Parker, and at others, with a fearlessness acquired by practice, I carefully guided myself down the steep granite steps leading from Essex Street to the Embankment, and then paced my strip of pavement alone. But how tristful, dispiriting, and soul-sickening was that monotonous world of darkness in which I eternally existed, none can know, only those unfortunate ones who are blind themselves.

About half-past eight o'clock one breathless evening in mid-August, Mrs. Parker being unwell, I went forth alone for my usual stroll. The atmosphere was close and oppressive, the pavement seemed to reflect the heat, and even along the Embankment there was not a breath of air. Alone, plunged in my own thoughts—for the blind think far more deeply than those whose minds are distracted by the sights around them—I went on with those short steps that I had acquired, ever tapping with my stick to discover the crossings. I was afraid of no street traffic; only of cycles, which, by reason of their silence, are veritable ogres to the blind.

Almost unconsciously I passed beyond the limit of my regular track, beneath a railway-bridge which I knew led from Charing Cross station, and then straight on, with only a single crossing, until I came to what seemed the junction of several roads, where I hesitated. It was an adventure to go so far, and I wondered where I was. The chiming of Big Ben, however, gave me a clue. I was at the corner of Bridge Street, for I felt the wall of the St. Stephen's Club. The turning to the left would, I knew, take me over Westminster Bridge; to the right I could cross Palace Yard and Broad Sanctuary, and so gain Victoria Street. Before my affliction I knew well that portion of London around the Houses of Parliament. I decided, therefore, on keeping to the right, and some one whom I know not kindly piloted me over the dangerous crossing from the corner of Parliament Street, for such I judged it to be from the cries of men selling the evening papers. Again, three times in succession, did sympathetic persons, noticing my helplessness as I stood upon the kerb, take my arm and lead me across, but in these constant crossings I somehow entirely lost my bearings. I was, I knew, in a long straight thoroughfare and by the iron railings before the houses guessed it to be that road of flat-dom, Victoria Street.

Amused at my intrepidity, and congratulating myself upon having gone so far alone, I kept on, knowing that even if I lost myself I had only to call a passing hansom and be driven back to Essex Street. Thus for perhaps three-quarters of an hour I wandered on. From a lad who helped me over one of the crossings I learnt that I had passed Victoria Station, and now appeared to be traversing several large squares—at least, such was the impression conveyed upon my mind. It was useless to stop passers-by every moment to inquire where I was, therefore, laughing inwardly at my situation, lost in London, the great city I had known so well, I went on and on, down long straight thoroughfares that seemed endless, in enjoyment of the first real walk I had taken since my crushing affliction had fallen upon me.

Suddenly, in what seemed to be a quiet deserted street, I left the kerb to cross the road alone, but ere I became aware of impending danger a man's voice shouted roughly, and I found myself thrown by violent concussion upon the roadway, struggling frantically beneath a horse's hoofs. I clutched wildly at air to save myself, but next second received a violent kick on the left side of the head, which caused sparks to appear before my sightless eyes, stunned me, and rendered me almost instantly insensible.

How long I remained ignorant of things about me it is impossible to tell. I fancy it must have been a good many hours. On my first return to consciousness I heard strange confused sounds about me, low whispering, the words of which were utterly unintelligible to my unbalanced brain, and the quick rustling of silk. I remember wondering vaguely where I was. The blind quickly develop a habit of extreme caution, and with my senses dulled by the excruciating pain in my skull I lay reflecting without speaking. The throbbing in my head was frightful. When the recollections of my long walk which had ended so disastrously surged through my brain, it struck me that I must have been taken to a hospital after the accident, and that I had most probably remained there some days. Yet in hospitals there is no perfume of *peau d'Espagne*, nor do the nurses wear silken flounces.

I tried to catch the words uttered by those about me, but in vain. It may have been that they were spoken in some foreign tongue, or, what is much more likely, the terrible blow I had received from the horse's hoof had utterly disarranged my sense of hearing. This single thought appalled me. If my hearing had really been injured, then I was rendered absolutely helpless. To the blind the acoustic organs become so sharpened that they can detect sounds where those in full possession of sight and hearing can distinguish nothing. It is the ear that acts for the sightless eye. Therefore the fear that even this had failed me held me appalled.

I stretched forth my hand, and to my surprise felt that I was not in a hospital bed, as I had at first believed, but upon a silken couch, with my head resting upon a soft satin pillow. The covering of the couch was of rich brocade in wide stripes, while the woodwork had a smoothness which caused me to believe that it was gilt. I raised my hand to my head, and found it bandaged with a handkerchief and some apparently improvised compresses.

Although I opened my eyes, all was, of course, an utter blank before me. Yet I felt instinctively, as every blind person does, the presence of some one in my immediate vicinity, and presently, after long reflection, I suddenly asked—

"Where am I? What has happened?"

"You have been run over, and your head is injured," answered a strange harsh voice, hoarse and altogether curious. "But tell me. Your eyes have a curious look in them. Can't you see?"

"No," I responded. "Unfortunately I am totally blind."

"Blind!" gasped the voice, in apparent amazement. "Then that accounts for your accident!"

"But where am I?" I inquired eagerly.

"You need not trouble, I assure you," answered the voice, pleasantly. "You are with friends."

"Then I am not in a hospital?"

"Certainly not. Having witnessed your accident, I am trying to do what little I can for you."

The voice was low-pitched; and, further, it struck me as being disguised.

"May I not know the name of my good Samaritan?" I inquired.

"The name is entirely unnecessary," the voice responded. "From your card-case I see that your name is Heaton, and that you live in Essex Street, Strand."

"Yes," I answered.

"How long have you been blind?" the voice inquired, hoarse and deep. I knew that it was disguised by certain of the syllables being pronounced differently in various words.

"For a year or more," I answered.

"And does your head still pain you very much?" inquired the voice, while at the same moment I felt a cool hand placed upon my throbbing brow.

In an instant I seized it by the wrist. The hand tried to wrench itself free, but not before I had felt the slimness of the fingers, the rings upon them, and the softness of the palm.

It was a woman's. She had cleverly disguised her voice to cause me to believe that it was a man's. I placed my right hand upon her arm and felt it bare. Upon her wrist was a curious bracelet, thin but strangely pliable, evidently made of some ingeniously worked and twisted wire.

The arm was bare; her skirts were of silk. My nurse was evidently in an evening toilette.

"Although I cannot see you, madam, I thank you for your kind attention," I said, a trifle piqued that she should have endeavoured to mislead me by her voice.

She drew her hand away quickly, with a slight cry, as though annoyed at my discovery.

"I witnessed your accident," she explained simply, in a sweet, well-modulated voice, evidently her own. By her tone, she was no doubt young, and I wondered whether she were pretty.

"How did it happen? Tell me," I urged.

"You were crossing the road, and were knocked down by a cab. My doctor has already examined you, and says that you are not seriously hurt. It is a mere scalp-wound, therefore you may rest content, and congratulate yourself upon a very narrow escape."

"I congratulate myself upon failing into the hands of a friend," I said.

"Oh, it is really nothing!" exclaimed my unknown hostess. "In a few hours you will, no doubt, be all right. Rest, and in the morning the carriage shall take you home."

"Then it is not yet morning?" I inquired, vaguely wondering what hour it might be.

"No, not yet."

The response sounded afar off, and I felt somehow that my strength was suddenly failing me. A heavy, drowsy feeling crept over me, and my mind seemed filled with conflicting thoughts, until I fell asleep, the cool, soft, sympathetic hand still upon my brow.

When I awoke it was with a refreshed feeling. No one was, however, in my immediate vicinity. My kind protectress had left me, yet I heard voices in conversation in the adjoining room. The door communicating was closed, but there was the unmistakable pop of a champagne-cork and a jingling of thin glasses that told of festivity. In whose house, I wondered, was I a guest? Already I had inquired, but had been refused information.

Suddenly the voices were hushed, and I could distinguish a woman saying—

"I tell, you he's blind—stone blind. If you doubt me, hold that before his face and see if he flinches." A man's voice sounded in a low growl in response, then all was silent again. Only the ticking of a clock somewhere near me broke the stillness.

Whispers, like low, suspicious exchanges of confidence, soon afterwards reached my ears. The door had opened silently, and a few seconds later I felt the soft hand of my protectress again upon my forehead. My sightless eyes were wide open, and by that she, of course, knew that I was awake.

"Are you better after your sleep?" the well-cultivated voice inquired concernedly.

"Very much," I answered, raising myself upon my elbows. "But I have troubled you far too long, and will go, if you will kindly instruct your servant to call me a cab."

"Oh dear no," the voice answered pleasantly. "I couldn't think of allowing you to go home at this hour, and in your weak state, too. It would be madness. Continue your rest, and you will be quite right again in the morning."

"You are extremely kind," I protested, "but I really couldn't think of remaining longer."

"Would you like to repay me for what you so very generously term my kindness?" she asked. "If so, I would only ask one little favour."

"Certainly. I will grant it if it lies within my power," I responded.

"Well, it is that you would scribble your name here, in this birthday book of mine. It will be a little souvenir of this evening."

"But I cannot write well nowadays. I can't see, you know," I protested.

"But you can write your signature. If the handwriting is uneven I will forgive you, in the circumstances," the voice said merrily; and a moment later she placed a pen with a handle of ivory or pearl within my hand.

"What day of the month?" inquired the sweet voice.

"The second of July," I answered, laughing; and my unknown friend, having opened the book at that page, guided my hand to the paper, whereon I scrawled my name.

She took both pen and book, and by the departing swish of her skirts I knew that she had left me and had passed into the adjoining room.

A strange picture arose in my mind. Was she beautiful? At any rate her surroundings were elegant, and her low musical voice was that of a young and refined girl of twenty or so.

I listened, lying there helpless and sorely puzzled. Again curious whisperings in subdued tones sounded from beyond, but almost at that same moment some one commenced to play upon the piano Chopin's "Andante-Spinato," which prevented me from distinguishing either the words uttered or the trend of the discussion.

For several minutes the sound of the piano filled the room, the touch, light and delicate, seeming to be that of a woman, when, of a sudden, there was a loud smashing of glass, and a woman's shrill, piercing scream rang out, accompanied by the sound of some heavy object falling to the floor.

In an instant the music ceased, and at the same moment I heard a man's voice cry wildly—

"Good God! You've—why, you've killed her!"

Next second there sounded a rapid scuffling of feet, a chair was overturned and broken, and from the quick panting and muttered ejaculations it seemed as though two persons had closed in deadly embrace. In their frantic, desperate struggle they advanced into the room where I was, and I, still utterly helpless, with only a dark void about me, raised myself in horror and alarm. The man's words held me appalled.

Some terrible tragedy had occurred. My kind protectress had been murdered.

The other two persons, whoever they were, fought fiercely quite close to me, and I could distinctly detect from the vain efforts to shout made by the weaker, that the stronger held him by the throat, and was endeavouring to strangle him.

Of a sudden there was a quick, dull thud, the unmistakable sound of a heavy blow, followed by a short agonised cry.

"Ah-h!" shrieked the voice of the person struck; and at the same instant a great weight fell back inertly upon me as I was lying, nearly crushing the breath from me.

I passed my sensitive hands over it quickly. It was the body of a man. Blood ran warm over my fingers.

He had been stabbed to the heart.

III

The House with the Portico

The weight of the inert body oppressed me, and in striving to extricate myself it slipped from the couch and slid to the ground; but such a feeling of dread overcame me that I reached down and pushed the warm body under the couch.

The faint sound of some one moving stealthily across the thick pile carpet caused me to lie rigid, holding my breath. I heard the movement distinctly, and curiously enough it sounded as though it were a woman, for there was just a faint rustling as though her skirts trailed upon the ground. My quick ear told me that the person was approaching. By the panting breath I knew that it was the assassin. Was I, too, to fall a victim?

I tried to call out, but in that moment of agony and horror my tongue refused to articulate. It seemed to cleave to the roof of my mouth.

The sound of movement ceased, and I knew that the person was quite close to me. My eyes were wide open, held fixed in expectant horror.

I felt a warm breath upon my cheeks, and knew that the unknown assassin was peering into my eyes. In a few moments I had an instinctive feeling of something being held a few inches from my face.

Then the words that had been spoken by my protectress recurred to me. She had declared to her companions that I was blind, and urged them to test me by holding something to my head.

This was now being done. The truth of my statement was being proved, possibly by a revolver being held to my brow. If so, my only chance of safety rested in unflinching coolness. My position was certainly a most unenviable one.

For a few moments the panting heart of the assassin thumped close to me; then, apparently satisfied, the unknown person moved off in silence without uttering a single word.

My first impulse was to jump up and arrest the progress of the assassin, but on reflection I saw that to do so would only be to invite death. What could I do, blind as I was?

Only could I sit and listen, trying to distinguish every detail of the mystery.

Yes, I became convinced more than ever that the person leaving the room was not a man—but a woman.

Could it be the same individual whose cool, sympathetic hand had only a quarter of an hour before soothed my brow? The thought held me dumbfounded.

I had all along believed that the assassin had been a man, but it was certain by that swish of silken flounces that it was a woman.

As I listened I heard the click of an electric-light switch at the door of the room, and a couple of minutes later a heavy door closed. From the bang of the knocker I knew that the street door had been shut by some person who had left the house.

I still sat listening. All was silent. Only the low ticking of the clock broke the dead stillness of the night. The mysterious woman who had thus made her exit had evidently switched off the light, leaving me in total darkness with the hideous evidences of her crime.

For some short time longer I listened, my ears open to catch every sound, but, hearing nothing, I now knew that I was alone. Therefore, rising to my feet, I groped about until my hands touched the prostrate body of the man, and as I did so he heaved a long sigh, and a quick shudder ran through his frame. The wound had evidently not caused instant death, but, placing my hand quickly over the heart, I found that it had now ceased its beating with the final spasm.

Slowly, and with utmost care, I passed both my hands over the dead man's face, in order to obtain some mental picture of his appearance. His hair seemed thick and well parted at the side, his features those of a young man shaven save for the moustache, which was long and well trained. He was in evening clothes, and wore in his shirt a single stud, which, to my touch, seemed of very peculiar shape. I tried to make out its design, but in vain, when suddenly I remembered that if I took it, it might afterwards give me some clue to its dead owner's identity. So I took it from the stiff shirt-front and placed it in the pocket of my vest.

His watch-chain was an ordinary curb, I found, with a watch which had the greasy feel of silver. In his pockets were a couple of sovereigns and some loose silver, but no letters nor card-case, nothing indeed to lead me to a knowledge of who he really was. In one pocket I found a small pencil-case, and this I also took for my own purposes.

Half a dozen times I placed my hand upon his heart, whence the blood was slowly oozing, but there was no movement.

My investigations showed that he was about twenty-eight years of age; probably fair, by the softness of the hair and moustache, with even teeth, rather sharp jawbones and cheeks a trifle thin. Having ascertained this much, I groped forward with both hands in the direction of the room wherein the woman had been so swiftly done to death. It was in darkness, I have no doubt, but to me darkness was of no account, for I was ever in eternal gloom. The furniture over which I stumbled here and there was covered with silk brocade, the woodwork being of that smoothness which had led me to believe that it must be gilded. It was without doubt a fine spacious drawing-room where I had been lying, for the dimensions of the place were quite unusual, and the objects with which my hands came into contact were always of a character magnificent, and in keeping with the grandeur of the place. The house was evidently one of those fine mansions with which the West End of London abounds, and certainly this apartment, even though I could not see it, was the acme of comfort and luxury.

I at last found the entrance to the adjoining room, but the door was locked.

This sudden check to my investigations caused me to pause. That a woman had been first struck down by a cowardly blow appeared evident. The loud agonised shriek which had emanated from that inner room was, I felt convinced, that of the tender, sweet-voiced woman who had administered to my wants. It seemed, now that I recollected, as though she had been seated at the piano when the fatal blow was dealt. The scream and the cessation of the music had occurred simultaneously.

The theory impressed itself upon me that a woman was responsible for both crimes. It was a woman who had stood panting near me, who had noiselessly tested me to ascertain whether I could distinguish objects about me, and who had afterwards left the house. My blindness had, no doubt, saved my life.

Before leaving she had, for some unknown reason, locked the communicating door and taken the key. But upon the air, after she had gone, there lingered the subtle fragrance of *peau d'Espagne*, the same perfume used by the woman whose cool palm had soothed my brow. Nevertheless, it seemed impossible that a woman could thus commit a double crime so swiftly and with such force as to drive a knife to the heart of a man and fling him back upon me—all in silence, without the utterance of one single word.

With my eyes only a void of blackness, this mystery was bewildering, and rendered the more tantalising by my inability to gaze about me. I had been present at the enactment of a terrible drama, but had not witnessed it, and could not, therefore, recognise either culprit or victims.

Again I searched the great handsome room, in order to rivet all its details upon my memory. It had three long windows opening down to the floor, which showed that it was situated in the back of the house, otherwise they must have opened upon the street. In one corner was a pedestal, whereon stood a marble bust of a dancing-woman, like those I had seen in the sculptor's at Pisa before the days of my darkness. There were tables, too, with glass tops wherein, I supposed, were curios and bric-a-brac, and before the great fireplace was stretched a tiger-skin, with the paws preserved.

While groping there, however, my hand came into contact with something which I found was a narrow, three-edged knife, so sharp that I cut my finger while feeling it. It had a cross-hilt, and the blade was thin and triangular, tapering to a point. The shape I knew to be Italian, one of those Florentine stilettos used long ago in the Middle Ages, a wound from which was almost certain to be fatal. The Italians have long ago brought the use of the knife to a fine art, and even to-day, murders by stabbing are the most usual occurrences reported in their newspapers. The blade of this antique weapon was about nine inches long, and the handle velvet-covered and bound with wire, probably either gold or silver. The point was sharp as a needle.

My first impulse was to take possession of it; but, on reflection, I saw that if I did so grave suspicion might possibly fall upon me. I might even be charged with the murder, especially as I had already in my pocket the dead's man stud and pencil-case. This thought caused me to throw down the stiletto, and, continuing my search, I at length found the door which gave egress to the place.

I opened it and stood in the hall to listen. There was no sound. The stillness of the night remained quite unbroken, and I believed myself alone with the dead. By coughing, the echo of my voice showed that the hall and staircase were wide and spacious. Then it struck me that I had no stick, without which I feared to walk; but, groping about, I found an umbrella stand, and took therefrom a stout thorn, the handle of which seemed smooth-worn by long usage.

What was my best course? Should I go forth secretly, return home and await the discovery of the terrible affair, which would no doubt be fully reported in those evening newspapers which revel in crime? Or should I go out and inform the first constable I met? The latter, I saw, was my duty, and even though I had no desire to mix myself up in such a mysterious and sensational affair, I resolved to go at once and state all that I heard.

Whether the street door was situated to right or left I knew not, but trying the right first, I found that the door was at the end of the hall. Opening it, I passed out, and having closed it again noiselessly went down the five wide steps into the deserted street.

There were iron railings in front of the house, and before the door was a big stone portico. My hands told me both these details.

I turned to the left, and after walking some little distance crossed a road and kept on down a long road which, although it did not appear to be a main thoroughfare, seemed to run straight as an arrow. For fully a quarter of an hour I walked on without meeting a soul. The only noise that broke the quiet was the dismal howl of a dog, and now and then the distant shriek and low roar of trains. Suddenly I found myself in quite a labyrinth of crooked streets, and after several turns emerged into what I presumed to be one of the great arteries of London.

I stood listening. The air was fresh, and it seemed to me that dawn was spreading. Afar I could hear the measured, heavy tread of a police-constable, and hurried in his direction. As I did so I put out my stick and it struck some iron railings. A few minutes later, in hot haste, I overtook the man of heavy tread, and addressing him, said—

"Tell me, please, are you a constable?"

"Well, I believe I am," answered a rough voice, pleasantly withal. "But can't you see?"

"No, unfortunately I can't," I replied. "Where am I?"

"Outside the South Kensington Museum. Where do you want to go?"

"I want you to come with me," I said.

"With you. What's up?"

"I've been present at a terrible tragedy," I blurted forth. "Two people have been murdered."

"Two people?" exclaimed the voice, quickly interested. "Where?"

"In—in a house," I faltered, for not until that instant did the appalling truth occur to me. I had wandered away from the place, and had no idea of its outward appearance, or in what road it was situated!

"Well, double murders don't often take place in the street, sonny. But—" and the voice hesitated.

"Why, there's blood on your clothes, I see! Tell me all about it. Where's the house?"

"I confess that I've been foolishly stupid, for I've left it, and I could never find my way back again. I'm blind, you see, and I've no idea of its exterior appearance."

"At any rate you've been near enough to the affair to get yourself in a pretty mess," the rough voice said, somewhat suspiciously. "Surely you have some idea of where the affair took place?"

The situation was certainly the most curious in which any man could be placed, for with only one thought in my mind, namely, to raise the alarm, I had gone forth from the house of mystery and failed to mark it. This negligence of mine might, I reflected, result in the affair being hushed up for ever. London is a big place in which to search for the scene of a murder upon which my eyes had never gazed, and the details of which I only knew by my sense of touch. How many thousands of houses there were in the West End each with its smoke-blackened portico and little piece of area railing.

"No," I responded to the officer's inquiry. "I was so bent upon giving information that I forgot to place any mark upon the house by which to know it again."

"Well, I've 'eard a good many funny stories while I've been on night-duty in these eighteen years, but your yarn is about the rummest of the lot," he said bluntly.

"I only know that the house is a large one, very well furnished, and has a portico and railings in front—a double house, with hall in the centre, and rooms on either side."

"That don't 'elp us very much, sonny," the voice observed. "What's the good o' running after me with a yarn like this if you can't take me to the spot? To judge from the state of your clothes, though, you've been in some scrap or another. If your coat was not covered with blood as it is, I'd be inclined to put you down as a chap with a screw loose."

"I'm not demented, I tell you," I cried warmly. "There's a terrible crime been committed, and I have sought your assistance."

"And I'd go and have a look at the premises with you, if you could only tell me where they are. But as you can't—well, what are we to do, sonny?"

IV

The Woman

Take me at once to the police-station," I said firmly. "I must make a statement to your inspector on duty."

"Not much good, is it, if you can't tell us where the affair took place?" queried the man, impertinently.

"It is my duty to make the report, and the duty of the police to investigate it," I answered, annoyed, for it seemed as though he doubted me.

"That's a nasty cut on your hand," he remarked. "How did you get it?"

"I cut it myself by accident with the knife."

"What knife?"

"The knife with which the murders were committed."

"And what were you doing with it?" inquired the constable, utterly regardless of the strict police regulation which forbids an officer to put any such questions.

"I found it," I replied.

"Where?"

"On the floor of the room, while I was searching about."

The man grunted dubiously.

I was well aware of the suspicion which must fall upon me, for I knew there was blood upon my clothes, and that my story possessed a distinct air of improbability.

"Who injured your head like that?" he asked.

In response, I told him how, in crossing a road, I had been knocked down and rendered insensible by a cab, and how, on regaining consciousness, I had found myself under the care of some woman unknown.

He gave vent to a short harsh laugh, as though discrediting my statements.

"You don't believe me," I blurted forth hastily. "Take me to your inspector. We must lose no time."

"Well, you know," observed the man, "your story, you'll admit, is a very extraordinary one. You say that a terrible affair has happened in a house somewhere about here, yet you can't direct us to it. The whole story is so curious that I'm afraid you'll have a difficulty in persuading anybody to believe you."

"If you don't, somebody else will," I snapped. "Come, take me to the police-station."

Thus ordered, the man rather reluctantly took my arm, and crossing the wide main road, we traversed a number of short crooked thoroughfares.

"You don't seem a very good walker, mister," the constable observed presently. "I see a cab in the distance. Would you like to take it?"

"Yes. Call it," I said, for I felt very weak and ill after my terrible night's adventure.

A few minutes later we were sitting together in the hansom, driving towards the address he had given, namely, College Place Police-Station.

On the way I explained to him the whole of the facts as far as I could recollect them. He listened attentively to my curious narrative until I had concluded, then said—

"Well, sir, it's certainly a most mysterious affair, and the only fear I have is that everybody will look upon it with disbelief. I know what I should do if I were a gentleman in your place."

"What would you do?"

"Well, I should keep my knowledge to myself, say nothing about it, and leave the revelation of the crime to chance."

"I am compelled to make a report of it, because I was present at the tragedy," I said. "It is my duty, in the interests of justice."

"Of course, that's all very well, I quite agree that your duty as a citizen is to make a statement to my inspector, but if I may be permitted to say so, my private opinion is, that to preserve a discreet silence is better than making a fool of one's self."

"You're certainly plain-spoken," I said smiling.

"Oh, well, you'll excuse me, sir," the man said, half-apologetically. "I mean no offence, you know. I only tell you how I myself would act. Now, if you could give any real information of value to the detectives, there would be some reason for making the statement, but as you can't, well you'll only give yourself no end of bother for nothing."

"But surely, man, you don't think that with the knowledge of this terrible affair in my mind I'm going to preserve silence and allow the assassin to escape, do you?"

"Well, it seems that the assassin has escaped already, in any case," the man laughed. "You take it from me that they were a cute lot in that house, whoever they were. The wonder is that they didn't kill you."

WILLIAM LE QUEUX

An exactly similar thought had crossed my mind. The drive seemed a long one, but at length the cab stopped, and we alighted.

I heard the conveyance turn and go off, as together we ascended the steps of the station. One thing struck me as curious, namely, that the air was filled with a strong odour like turpentine.

"The station is a long way from your beat," I remarked.

"Yes. A fairish way, but we're used to it, and don't notice the distance."

"And this is College Place—is it?"

"Yes," he responded, conducting me down a long passage. The length of the corridor surprised me, and I humorously remarked—

"You're not going to put me in the cells, I hope?"

"Scarcely," he laughed. "But if we did the darkness wouldn't trouble you very much, I fear. Blindness must be an awful affliction."

He had scarcely uttered these words ere we ascended a couple of steps and entered what seemed to be a spacious place, the charge-room of the police-station.

There was the sound of heavy tramping over bare boards, and suddenly a rather gruff voice inquired—

"Well, four-six-eight? What is it?"

"Gentleman, sir—wants to report a tragedy. He's blind, sir."

"Bring him a chair," said the inspector's voice authoritatively.

My guide drew forward a chair, and I seated myself, saying—

"I believe you are the inspector on duty here?"

"Yes, I am. Will you kindly tell me your name and address?"

I did so, and the scratching of a quill told me that he was about to take down my statement.

"Well?" he inquired at length. "Please go on, for my time is limited. What's the nature of the affair?"

"I've been present to-night in a house where a double murder has been committed," I said.

"Where?"

"Ah! That's unfortunately just the mystery which I cannot solve. Being blind, I could obtain no idea of the exterior of the place, and in my excitement I left it without properly marking the house."

"Tell me the whole of the facts," observed the officer. "Who are the victims?"

"A woman and a man."

"Young or old?"

"Both young, as far as I can judge. At any rate, I examined the body of the man and found him to be about twenty-eight."

"The gentleman has no idea of the street where the tragedy has occurred," chimed in the constable. "He met me outside the Museum, and the blood on his clothes was still wet."

"He's got an injury to the head," remarked the inspector.

"I was knocked down and rendered insensible by a cab," I explained. "When I again became conscious I found myself in a strange house."

"They didn't rob you?"

I felt in my pockets, but I could not discover that I had lost anything. I remembered that I had only a couple of half-sovereigns and some loose silver upon me, and this remained still in my pocket. My fingers touched the stud and pencil-case, and I hesitated whether to give these up to the police. But next second the thought flashed through my mind that if I did, suspicion might be aroused against me, and further that while I kept them in my possession I should possess a secret clue to the victims of the terrible tragedy.

After I had fully explained the whole circumstances, and the inspector had written down with infinite care each word of my remarkable statement, he said—

"It seems as though both the man and woman fell victims to some plot or other. You say that there were no high words, and that all you heard was a woman's shriek, and a man's voice say, 'Why, you've killed her!' Now, have you any idea of the identity of that man?"

"None whatsoever," I answered. "My mind is a perfect blank on everything, save the personal appearance of the man who was afterwards struck to the heart."

"Exactly. But don't you think that the man who expressed horror at the first crime fell the victim of the second?"

"Ah! I never thought of that!" I said. "Of course, it seems most likely."

"Certainly. The second crime was committed undoubtedly in order to conceal the first."

"Then how extraordinary it is that I was spared."

"There was a motive, I believe, for that. We shall no doubt find that later."

"You will communicate with Scotland Yard, I suppose," I remarked.

"Perhaps we shall; perhaps not," answered the inspector, vaguely. "The affair must, of course, be fully investigated. Have you anything to add? You say that some woman treated you kindly. Have you any idea of her personal appearance?"

"None," I answered. "The only fact I know was that she was in evening dress, and that upon her wrist was a curious smooth-worn bangle of a kind of fine plaited wire, very pliable, like those worn by African native women."

"Eh! What—impossible!" gasped the inspector, in a voice which surprised me. But next moment he recovered his self-possession and made a calm remark that this fact did not lead to anything definite. Yet the sudden exclamation of startled surprise which escaped him aroused within me a belief that my words had given him some mysterious clue.

"You have no further statement to make?"

"None," I responded.

There was a few moments' silence during which time the quill continued its rapid scratching.

"You will kindly sign your information," the officer said, whereupon the constable brought me the sheet of foolscap and a pen wherewith I scrawled my name.

"Good," observed the inspector, with a grunt of satisfaction. "And now I must ask you to excuse me further, Mr.—Mr. Heaton, and wish you good morning."

I made my adieu, after obtaining from him a promise to communicate with me if anything transpired, and, accompanied by the constable, made my way out into the long passage again.

I had not walked a dozen paces ere I knew instinctively that some persons were near me, and next instant felt myself seized roughly by both arms and legs.

"What are you doing?" I shouted in alarm; "let me go!"

But only for an instant I struggled. The force used was utterly irresistible, and not a single word was uttered. My arms were in a moment pinioned, rendering me helpless as a child. With my terrible affliction upon me, I could neither defend myself nor could I see my assailants. Whoever the latter were, it was evident that they were determined, and, further, that I had been cleverly entrapped.

My first thought was that I had been arrested, but ere the lapse of a few moments the hideous truth became impressed forcibly upon me.

I tried to fight for life, but my wrists had been seized in grips of steel, and after a few desperate wrenches I stood, bound, and utterly unconscious of where I was.

My real position was, to a certain degree, plain. The man whom I had believed to be a constable was no police-officer at all, but some thief or London ruffian; I, far too confiding, had neglected to take the precaution of feeling his uniform.

A shrewd suspicion overcame me that this trap had been purposely laid for me. The man who had posed as a police inspector had obtained from me a signed declaration of the remarkable occurrence, for what reason I knew not. Did they now intend to silence me for ever? The thought struck a deep and terrible dread within my heart.

To my demands to know where I was, no response was given.

Indistinct whisperings sounded about me, and by the liquid "s's" of one person I felt convinced that a woman was present.

Little time, however, was I given in which to distinguish my surroundings, for two persons gripped my bound arms and drew me roughly through a narrow door, across an uneven floor, and thence down a long, crooked flight of stone steps.

From below came up a dank, mouldy smell, as of some chamber long unopened, and suddenly there broke upon my quick ears the wash of water.

In that moment of mental agony the truth was rendered plain. I was not in a police-station, as I believed, but in some house beside the Thames, and, moreover, I was descending to the water—going to my death.

Once again, as a last effort, I struggled and fought with the fierce desperation begotten of terror, but in a moment the strong hands that held me pushed me violently forward, and I then felt myself falling helplessly from some dizzy height. My head reeled, and weakened as I already was, all knowledge of things became blotted out.

The touch of a cool, sympathetic hand upon my brow was the first thing I subsequently remembered. My arms had apparently been freed, and with a quick movement I grasped the hand. It was a woman's.

Was I dreaming?

I stretched forth my left hand to obtain some idea of my surroundings, and found myself lying upon an uneven stone flooring that seemed covered with the evil-smelling slime of the river.

With my right hand I touched a woman's firm, well-moulded arm, and to my amazement my eager fingers came into contact with a bangle. I felt it.

The hand, the arm, the bangle, the perfume of *peau d'Espagne*, all were the same as those of the woman who had pitied me in my helplessness, and had so tenderly cared for me in that mysterious, unknown house, wherein the tragedy had afterwards occurred.

At first I lay speechless in wonderment, but when I found tongue I spoke, imploring her to make explanation. I heard her sigh deeply, but to all my inquiries she remained dumb.

V

THE UNSEEN

Tell me," I demanded in my helplessness, of the mysterious woman at my side, "what has happened?"

"Rise, and try whether you can walk," said the voice at last, sweet and low-pitched, the same well-remembered voice that had spoken to me in that unknown house of shadows.

I struggled and rose stiffly, assisted tenderly by her. To my joy I found that I could walk quite well.

"Thank God!" she gasped, as though a great weight had been lifted from her mind. "Thank God that I have found you. The tide is rising, and in half an hour you would have been beyond human aid."

"The tide!" I repeated. "What do you mean?"

"At high tide the river floods this place to the roof, therefore nothing could have saved you."

"What place is this?"

The voice was silent, as though hesitating to reveal to me the truth.

"A place wherein, alas! more than one person has found his grave," she explained at last.

"But I don't understand," I said eagerly. "All is so puzzling. I believed that I was inside a police-station, whereas I had actually walked into this mysterious and cleverly-prepared trap. Who are these people who are my enemies?—tell me."

"Unfortunately, I cannot."

"But you, yourself, are not one of them," I declared.

"I may be," answered the voice in a strange, vague tone.

"Why?"

"Ah! no, that is not a fair question to ask."

"But surely, you, who were so kind to me after my accident in the street, will you desert me now?" I argued. Her failure to give me any assurance that she was my friend struck me as peculiar. There was something extremely uncanny about the whole affair. I did not like it.

"I have not said that I intend to leave you. Indeed, from motives of my own I have sought and found you; but before we go further I must obtain from you a distinct and faithful promise."

"A promise—of what?"

There was a brief silence, and I heard that she drew a deep breath as those do who are driven to desperation.

"The situation is briefly this," the voice said, in a tone a trifle harsher than before. "I searched for you, and by a stroke of good fortune discovered where your unknown enemies had placed you, intending that at high tide you should be drowned, and your body carried out to sea, as others have been. From this place there is only one means of egress, and that being concealed, only death can come to you unless I assist you. You understand?"

"Perfectly. This is a trap where a man may be drowned like a rat in a hole. The place is foetid with the black mud of the Thames."

"Exactly," she answered. Then she added, "Now tell me, are you prepared to make a compact with me?"

"A compact? Of what nature?" I inquired, much surprised.

"It will, I fear, strike you as rather strange, nevertheless it is, I assure you, imperative. If I rescue you and give you back your life, it must be conditional that you accept my terms absolutely."

"And what are those terms?" I inquired, amazed at this extraordinary speech of hers.

"There are two conditions," she answered, after a slight pause. "The first is that you must undertake to make no statement whatever to the police regarding the events of last night."

She intended to secure my silence regarding the tragedy. Was it because that she herself was the actual assassin? I remembered that while I had reclined upon the silken couch in that house of mystery this startling suspicion had crossed my mind. Was that same cool, sympathetic palm that had twice soothed my brow the hand of a murderess?

"But there has been a terrible crime—a double crime committed," I protested. "Surely, the police should know!"

"No; all knowledge must be kept from them," she answered decisively. "I wish you to understand me perfectly from the outset. I have sought you here in order to rescue you from this place, because you have unwittingly fallen the victim of a most dastardly plot. You are blind, defenceless, helpless, therefore all who have not hearts of stone must have compassion upon you. Yet if I rescue you, and allow you to go forth again into the world, you may, if you make a statement to the police, be the means of bringing upon me a catastrophe, dire and complete."

Every word of hers showed that guilt was upon her. Had I not heard the swish of her skirts as she crept from the room after striking down that unknown man so swiftly and silently that he died without a word?

"And if I promise to remain mute?"

"If you promise," she said, "I will accept it only on one further condition."

"And what's that?"

"One which I know you will have some hesitation in accepting; yet, like the first, it is absolutely imperative."

Her voice showed traces of extreme anxiety, and the slim hand upon my arm trembled.

She was young, I knew, but was she beautiful? I felt instinctively that she was, and conjured up within myself a vision of a refined face, perfect in its tragic beauty, like that of Van Dyck's Madonna that I had seen in the Pitti Palace at Florence in those well-remembered days when I looked upon the world, and it had given me such pleasure.

"Your words are very puzzling," I said gravely. "Tell me what it is that you would have me do."

"It is not difficult," she answered, "yet the curious character of my request will, I feel, cause you to hold back with a natural caution. It will sound strange; nevertheless, here, before I put the suggestion before you, I give you my word of honour, as a woman who fears her God, that no undue advantage shall be taken of your promise."

"Well, explain what you mean."

"The condition I impose upon you in return for my assistance," she said, in deepest earnestness, "is that you shall promise to render assistance to a person who will ever remain unknown to you. Any requests made to you will be by letter bearing the signature A-V-E-L, and these instructions you must promise to obey without seeking to discover either motive or reason. The latter can never be made plain to you, therefore do not puzzle yourself unnecessarily over them, for it will be all to no purpose. The secret—for secret there is, of course—will be so well guarded that it can never be exposed, therefore if you consent to thus rendering me a personal assistance in return for your life, it will be necessary to act blindly and carry out to the letter whatever instructions you receive, no matter how remarkable or how illogical they may seem. Do you agree?"

"Well," I said hesitatingly, "your request is indeed a most extraordinary one. If I promise, what safeguard have I for my own interests?"

"Sometimes you may, of course, be compelled to act against your own inclinations," she admitted. "I, however, can only assure you that if you make this promise I will constitute myself your protectress, and at the same time give you solemn assurance that no request contained in the letters of which I have spoken will be of such a character as to cause you to commit any offence against the law."

"Then it is you yourself who will be my anonymous correspondent?" I observed quickly.

"Ah, no!" she answered. "That is, of course, the natural conclusion; but I may as well at once assure you that such will not be the case." Then she added, "I merely ask you to accept or decline. If the former, I will ever be at your service, although we must never meet again after to-day; if the latter, then I will wish you adieu, and the terrible fate your unknown enemies have prepared for you must be allowed to take effect."

"But I should be drowned!" I exclaimed in alarm. "Surely you will not abandon me!"

"Not if you will consent to ally yourself with me."

"For evil?" I suggested very dubiously.

"No, for good," she answered. "I require your silence, and I desire that you should render assistance to one who is sorely in need of a friend."

"Financial aid?"

"No, finance has nothing to do with it. The unknown person has money and to spare. It is a devoted personal assistance and obedience that is required."

"But how can one be devoted to a person one has neither seen nor known?" I queried, for her words had increased the mystery.

The shrewd suspicion grew upon me that this curious effort to secure my silence was because of her own guilt; that she intended to bind me to a compact in her own nefarious interests.

"I am quite well aware of the strangeness of the conditions I am imposing upon you, but they are necessary."

"And if I accept them will the mystery of to-night ever be explained?" I inquired, eager to learn the truth.

"Of that I know not," she answered vaguely. "Your silence is required to preserve the secret."

"But tell me," I said quickly, "how many persons were there present in that house beside yourself?"

"No, no!" she exclaimed in a tone of horror. "Make no further inquiry. Try and forget all—everything—as I shall try and forget. You cannot know—you will never know—therefore it is utterly useless to seek to learn the truth."

"And may I not even know your identity?" I inquired, putting forth my hand until it rested upon her well-formed shoulder. "May I not touch your face, so as to give me an impression of your personal appearance?"

She laughed at what, of course, must have seemed to her a rather amusing request.

"Give me permission to do this," I urged. "If there is to be mutual trust between us it is only fair that I should know whether you are young or old."

She hesitated. I felt her hand trembling.

"Remember, I cannot see you," I went on. "By touch I can convey to my mind an impression of the contour of your features, and thus know with whom I am dealing."

"Very well," she said at last. "You have my permission."

Then eagerly, with both my hands, I touched her face, while she stood rigid and motionless as a statue. I could feel by the contraction of the muscles that this action of mine amused her, and that she was laughing.

Her skin was soft as velvet, her lashes long, her features regular and finely cut like those of some old cameo. Her hair was dressed plainly, and she had about her shoulders a large cape of rich fur—sable I believed it to be. There was no doubt she was young, perhaps not more than twenty-one or so, and certainly she was very handsome of countenance, and dressed with an elegance quite unusual.

Her mouth was small, her chin pointed, and her cheeks with a firm contour which spoke of health and happiness. As I carefully passed my hands backwards and forwards, obtaining a fresh mental impression with each movement, she laughed outright.

Of a sudden, however, she sprang aside quickly, and left me grasping at air.

"Ah!" she cried, wildly horrified at a sudden discovery. "There is blood upon your hands—*his blood*!"

"I had forgotten," I apologised quickly. "Forgive me; I cannot see, and was not aware that my hands were unclean."

"It's too terrible," she gasped hoarsely. "You have placed those stained hands upon my face, as though to taunt me."

WILLIAM LE QUEUX

"With what?" I inquired, breathlessly interested.

But she did not reply. She only held her breath, while her heart beat quickly, and by her silence I felt convinced that by her involuntary ejaculation she had nearly betrayed herself.

The sole question which occupied my thoughts at that moment was whether she was not the actual assassin. I forgot my own critical position. I recollected not the remarkable adventures that had befallen me that night. I thought not of the ghastly fate prepared for me by my unknown enemies. All my thoughts were concentrated upon the one problem—the innocence or guilt of that unseen, soft-spoken woman before me.

"And now," she said at last—"now that you have satisfied yourself of my personal appearance, are you prepared to accept the conditions?"

"I confess to having some hesitation in doing so," I answered, quite frankly.

"That is not at all surprising. But the very fact of your own defencelessness should cause you to ally yourself with one who has shown herself to be your protectress, and seeks to remain your friend."

"What motive can you possibly have for thus endeavouring to ally yourself with me?" I inquired, without attempting to disguise my suspicion.

"A secret one."

"For your own ends, of course?"

"Not exactly. For our mutual interests. By my own action in taking you in when you were knocked down by the cab I have placed your life in serious jeopardy; therefore, it is only just that I should now seek to rescue you. Yet if I do so without first obtaining your promise of silence and of assistance, I may, for aught I know, bring an overwhelming catastrophe upon myself."

"You assure me, upon your honour as a woman, that no harm shall befall me if I carry out the instructions in those mysterious letters?"

"If you obey without seeking to elucidate their mystery, or the identity of their sender, no harm shall come to you," she answered solemnly.

"And regarding the silence which you seek to impose upon me? May I not explain my adventures to my friend, in order to account for the blood upon my clothes and the injury to my head?"

"Only if you find it actually necessary. Recollect, however, that no statement whatever must be made to the police. You must give an undertaking never to divulge to them one single word of what occurred last night."

There was a dead silence, broken only by the lapping of water, which had already risen and had flooded the chamber to the depth of about two inches. The place was a veritable death-trap, for, being a kind of cellar and below high-water mark, the Thames flood entered by a hole near the floor too small to permit the escape of a man, and would rise until it reached the roof.

"Come," she urged at last. "Give me your undertaking, and let us at once get away from this horrible place."

I remained silent. Anxious to escape and save my life, I nevertheless entertained deep suspicions of her, because of her anxiety that I should give no information to the police. She had drawn back in horror at the sight of the blood of the murdered man! Had she not, by her hesitation, admitted her own guilt?

"You don't trust me," she observed, with an air of bitter reproach.

"No," I answered, very bluntly; "I do not."

"You are at least plain and outspoken," she responded. "But as our interests are mutual, I surely may presume to advise you to accept the conditions. Life is better than death, even though one may be blind."

"And you hold back from me the chance to escape from this slow but inevitable fate unless I conform to your wishes?"

"I do."

"Such action as yours cannot inspire confidence."

"I am impelled by circumstances beyond my own control," she answered, with a momentary touch of sadness. "If you knew the truth you certainly would not hesitate."

"Will you not tell me your name?"

"No. It is useless."

"At least, you can so far confide in me as to tell me your Christian name," I said.

"Edna."

"And you refuse your surname?"

"I do so under compulsion."

The water had by this time risen rapidly. My legs had become benumbed, for it now reached nearly to my knees.

"Why do you longer hesitate?" she went on. "Give me your word that you will render the assistance I require, and we will at once escape. Let us lose no time. All this seems strange to you, I know; but some day, when you learn the real reason, you will thank me rather than think ill of my present actions."

Her determination was, I saw plainly, the outcome of some terror which held her fettered, and I knew that, in order to save myself, I must give her the promise she had so persistently desired to extract from me.

Therefore, with sudden determination, prompted by the natural, instinct of self-preservation than by any desire to assist her, I gave her my bond of secrecy.

Again she sighed deeply, as though released of some oppressive weight by my words. Then our hands clasped in mutual trust, and without further word she led me to the opposite side of the noisome cellar into which my enemies had cast me.

"You shall never regret this decision," she assured me in a strained voice, trembling with emotion—"never, never!"

And with a sudden movement she raised my hand and touched it lightly with her dry, fevered lips.

VI

HAND AND HEART

This impulsive action of hers was as though she were deeply indebted to me. I stood motionless in wonderment.

But only for an instant. She left my side for a moment, and from the sound that escaped her lips appeared to be struggling to open some means of egress from the place.

"Remain where you are," she said, "and I will return to you in a moment. The way out is rather difficult, and I shall be compelled to assist you." Her voice sounded above me, as though she had somehow climbed to the roof of the place.

I heard the drawing of a bolt and the clang of iron; then she climbed down again to where I anxiously awaited her. The river flood had risen alarmingly, and was still entering rapidly.

"Come, let me guide you," she said, taking my arm and leading me to the wall. "Lift your foot, so!" and taking my foot, she placed it in a kind of narrow step in the rough stone wall, at the same time placing my hand upon a piece of iron that seemed to be a large nail driven into the masonry. "Now climb very carefully," she went on.

Without hesitation, I raised myself from the ground slowly, and with infinite care commenced to scale the wall, while she remained below, wading almost up to her waist in water.

"Take care that you don't strike your head," she cried warningly. "Above you is a small hole just large enough for you to get through. Be very careful, and take your time."

The one hand at liberty I stretched above my head, and found, as she described, a square hole in the roof of the place, and, grasping the stone, I eventually managed to escape through it, finding myself at last standing upon a boarded floor.

A few moments later she was again at my side, and by the clang of iron I knew that the aperture of that fatal place was closed again.

I inquired of her where we were, but she only replied—

"I've already explained to you that to seek to elucidate the mystery of these adventures of yours is entirely useless. We have promised to each other mutual faith. That is, in itself, sufficient."

Then, taking my arm, she hurriedly led me across the room, up some steps, and along two long passages that ran at right angles to each other, until at length we emerged into the street.

Where we were I had not the slightest idea. I only knew that we were beside the river bank, for upon my ears there fell the shrill whistle of a steam-tug.

With her arm linked in mine, and heedless of the water dripping from her skirts, she led me forward through a number of narrow turnings, until by the bustle about me I knew that we must have reached a main road.

I heard the approaching hoot of a taxi, and the vehicle, at her demand, pulled up at the kerb.

"We must now part," she said, in a low, earnest voice. "Remember that in this remarkable affair our interests are absolutely identical. Any order that you receive you will obey without seeking to discover the why or wherefore, and above all, silence to the police."

"I have promised," I answered.

"And whatever may occur in the future, recollect that I am still your protectress, as I have been to-day. I have forced you to your promise, but for that I ask your forgiveness, because it is essential, if the mystery is ever to be solved."

"Are you, too, seeking the truth?"

"Yes," she responded. "But we must not talk here. The condition of our clothes is attracting attention."

"I shall think always of the mysterious Edna who refuses all information," I laughed.

"And I, too, shall not easily forget you—and all I owe to you. Farewell."

Her soft hand grasped mine for an instant, that same cool hand that had soothed my brow. Afterwards she assisted me into the cab.

"Good-bye," she cried. Then she became lost to me.

I told the driver where to go, and sat back in the vehicle, plunged in my own thoughts. I was like a man in a dream. The mystery was most tantalising. Feeling weak, I stopped at a public-house and had some brandy. Indeed, I felt so unwell that I sat in the bar-parlour fully half an hour before resuming my drive.

Suddenly I recollected that I might gather something from the driver, and I inquired where he had taken me up.

"In Albert Road, Battersea, sir."

This surprised me, for I had no idea that I had been on the Surrey side of the river.

I explained to the man my blindness, and asked him to describe the lady who had put me into this cab.

"Well, sir," he said, "she was very pretty indeed, with grey eyes and darkish hair."

"She was good-looking—eh?"

"Yes, sir. I don't think I've ever seen a much prettier young lady."

I sighed. How tantalising it was that my poor sightless eyes had been unable to gaze upon her.

"Describe her more closely," I urged. "I'm anxious to know exactly what she's like."

"She had lovely eyes, sir. Her hair seemed a bit untidy, but it was a pretty shade of dark-brown. Her face seemed innocent-looking, like a child's. I was surprised to see her like that."

"Like what?"

"Half-drowned like. She had on a black skirt that seemed soaking wet through, and covered with mud. She looked in an awful plight, and yet her face was merry and smiling. She took another cab as soon as she parted from you, and drove after us across the Albert Bridge, and then down Oakley Street. There she stopped the cab to speak to some one."

"Who was it?" I asked eagerly.

"A woman. But I couldn't see distinctly. They were too far away, and turned down Cheyne Walk, so I didn't see 'em any more."

"You say that her clothes were very dirty?"

"Yes, worse than yours, and, great Scott! sir, they're bad enough. You'll want to send 'em to the cleaners when you get 'ome."

What the man said was perfectly true. The slime of the river emitted a sickening stench, but it fortunately served to conceal one thing, namely, the blood-stains upon my coat.

I laughed at this remark of his, but I had no intention to enter upon explanations.

"From her appearance did my companion lead you to believe that she was a lady?"

"Oh yes, sir. By her manner you'd tell her as a lady among ten thousand."

"There was nothing noticeable about whereby I might recognise her again? Try and recollect."

WILLIAM LE QUEUX

"No, sir," answered the man. "She was a very beautiful young lady, and that's all I noticed."

"You'd know her again if you saw her?"

"I should just say I would," laughed the man. "When a chap sees a woman as lovely as she is it ain't likely he'll forget her, even though he may have a wife and 'arf a dozen kids at 'ome."

"You're smitten by her beauty, it seems," I laughed. "What's your name?"

"West, sir—Tom West. Number L.C.432. I stand on the rank at Hyde Park Corner."

"Well, West," I said, taking a card out of my case, and handing it to him, "if you ever see that lady again, and can find out who and what she is, and where she lives, I'll give you a present—say twenty pounds."

"Twenty quid!" the man echoed with a whistle. "I'd like to touch the oof, sir, and you bet I'll keep my weather eye open."

"As soon as you've found her, let me know, and the money is yours. You understand that's a bargain."

"Right you are, sir. I'll do my very best."

"If you only knew the driver of the cab she took after we parted you might, perhaps, learn something."

"That's just what I'm thinking," he said. "The man who drove her was, I believe, an old fellow that we know as 'Doughy' but I'm not at all sure. However, as soon as I set you down I'll go and find him. A driver is difficult to recognise if he wears another overcoat, you see. That's why I'm not certain that it really was 'Doughy'."

By the sharp descent of the roadway I knew that we were already in Essex Street, and a few moments later I had paid the man West and was ascending the stair to my own chambers.

The enlistment into my service of this man, the only person who had seen the mysterious Edna, was, I congratulated myself, a very shrewd and clever commencement of the investigation which I intended, at all hazards, to carry out.

Indeed, my only means of tracing her was through the intermediary of this one man, who had seen her and remarked upon her marvellous beauty. He seemed a sharp, witty fellow, and I therefore entertained every confidence in his efforts to earn the promised reward. He was now on his way to find his colleague, the old driver "Doughy," and if Edna had actually taken his cab I should, without doubt, soon be in possession of some information.

Thus, with a light step and reassured feeling, I ascended the stairs, wondering what old Mrs. Parker would say to my protracted absence, and how I should explain it to her. I took out my latch-key and opened the door.

As I entered the tiny lobby that served the dual purpose of hall and a place in which to hang coats, a startling sound broke upon my ears—the sound of a woman's cry.

In an instant I drew back. Fresh mystery greeted me. I stood there rigid, speechless, aghast.

VII

The Mystery is Increased

The voice which greeted me was that of a woman surprised by my sudden entrance; and walking swiftly forward to investigate, I passed into my own dingy sitting-room.

"I have a visitor, it seems," I exclaimed, stopping short. "May I not know your name?"

There was no response. Instinctively I knew that the woman I had thus disturbed was still present in that room wherein I spent so many lonely hours. Her startled cry was sufficient to convince me that she was there for some secret purpose. What, I wondered, could it be?

"Speak," I urged. "Kindly explain your business with me, and the reason of your presence here."

Yet she uttered no word of response, and apparently did not move.

I advanced, crossing towards the window, where I believed she must be standing, but with a quick movement my mysterious visitor eluded me, passing me by so near that her warm breath fanned my cheek, and next instant she had escaped and slammed the outer door of my chambers.

I stood wondering. Her presence there was most extraordinary. The faithful Parker, too, was absent, a circumstance which aroused misgivings within me. Could this strange female visitor have entered the place with a false key; or was she a mere pilferer whom I had disturbed in her search for plunder? Numbers of female thieves haunt the London streets, and it seemed more than likely that she was one who had ascended the stairs on pretence of selling something or other.

At any rate, I had returned at an unexpected moment, or she would not have given vent to that involuntary cry of dismay. I groped about the familiar room in order to ascertain whether it were disordered, but could find nothing whatsoever out of place. I called Parker loudly by name, but all was silence save the quick ticking of the timepiece upon the mantelshelf.

The clock of St. Clement Danes chimed merrily, then slowly struck the hour. I counted, and found that it was eleven o'clock in the morning.

How much had happened during the past fifteen hours! I had twice nearly lost my life.

Having cast aside my hat, I sank into my armchair, muddy and dirty, just as I was. My head, where it had been struck in the accident, pained me considerably, and I felt that I had a touch of fever coming on. Yet all my thoughts were concentrated upon the future and what the curious alliance with my strange protectress might bring upon me. Surely no man had ever found himself in a more remarkable situation than I was at that moment; certainly no man could be more mystified and puzzled. Deeply I pondered again and again, but could make nothing of that tangled web of startling facts.

By no desire or inclination of my own I had fallen among what appeared to be very undesirable company, and had involuntarily promised to become the assistant of some person whom I could not see. The strange oppression that fell upon me seemed precursory of evil.

My wet clothes sticking to me chilled me to the bone, and, with a sudden resolve to shake off the gloomy apprehensions that seemed to have gripped my heart, I rose and passed into my own room to wash and get a change of clothing.

The prolonged absence of Parker caused me much wonder. She never went out unless to go into the Strand to purchase the diurnal steak or tri-weekly chop which constituted my chief sustenance; or, perhaps, on Sunday afternoon she would, on rare occasions, go "to take a cup o' tea" with her daughter, who was a music-hall artiste, and lived somewhere off the Kensington Road.

Having cleaned myself, I proceeded to dress the wound on my head, my own medical knowledge standing me in good stead, and when I had satisfactorily bandaged it and put on a dry suit of clothes, I groped about through the several small rooms which were my home. Nothing seemed disarranged, nothing missing—only the woman who had ever been so faithful to me and had treated me as tenderly in my helplessness as though I had been her own son.

In impatience I took a cigar, lit it, and sat down to wait. No doubt, when she returned I should find that she had been absent upon some errand connected with her not-over-extensive *cuisine*. The thought grew upon me that my promise to the mysterious Edna, whoever she might be, was a rashly foolish one, and must result in some very serious *contretemps* for me. I had willingly given up my liberty of action and become the instrument of a person who had, without doubt, imposed upon me.

WILLIAM LE QUEUX

It seemed most probable, now that I reflected, that she was acting in concert with the man who had so cleverly practised deception upon me and led me to believe that he was a police-constable. That man, it now seemed plain, had followed me from the house of mystery, allowed me to wander sufficiently far to lose my bearings, and then got on in front of me so that I might approach and accost him. The whole affair had been carried out with amazing ingenuity, and every precaution had apparently been taken to conceal the remarkable tragedy. Yet the chief feature of the affair which puzzled me was the motive in endeavouring to take my life in that cellar beside the Thames. I had surely harmed no one, and, being utterly ignorant of the house wherein the affair had taken place, and also knowing me to be blind, they certainly could not fear any revelations that I might make. It was an enigma which I strove in vain to solve.

My gloomy thoughts were suddenly interrupted by the sound of a latch-key in the outer door, and as I rose old Mrs. Parker entered with an expression of profound surprise.

"Why, sir?" she cried. "I understood that you'd gone away into the country!"

"Into the country?" I echoed. "Who told you so?"

"The lady you sent to tell me."

"Lady? What lady?" I inquired, amazed. "Surely, Parker, you've taken leave of your senses?"

"The lady came about an hour ago, sir, and said that you had sent her to tell me that you would be absent for perhaps a week or so—that you had gone down to your uncle's in Hampshire."

"I've sent no one," I responded, astounded at this fresh phase of the affair. "What kind of lady was she—old or young?"

"Middle-aged."

"Well-dressed?"

"Yes, sir. She spoke with a funny kind of lisp, which made me think she might be a foreigner. She said she knew you quite well, being a friend of your aunt's, and that you were travelling down to Hampshire this morning, your uncle having been taken ill. I remarked that it was strange that you shouldn't come home for your bag and things, but she gave me a message from you to send a bag packed with your clothes by train from Waterloo to Christchurch Station marked 'To be called for.'"

"But didn't you think her story a very lame one, Parker?" I asked, angry that my old serving-woman should have thus been misled and deceived.

"Of course I did, sir, especially as you were absent all night. I told her that, and she said that you had called upon her, and finding your aunt, Lady Durrant, there on a visit, remained to supper. While at supper a telegram had arrived summoning your aunt home, as your uncle had been taken dangerously ill, and at once you had resolved to accompany her. But you've hurt your head, sir, haven't you?" she added, noticing my bandages.

"Yes," I answered. "I fell down. It is nothing—my own carelessness."

The story was, to say the least, a most ingenious one. Whoever the mysterious woman was she apparently knew that my uncle, Sir Charles Durrant, lived in the neighbourhood of Christchurch; that he was at that moment in a very critical state of health, suffering from paralysis, and further, that I had considerable expectations from him, and would not hesitate to travel down to see him if I knew him to be worse. One thing, therefore, was quite plain, namely, that my family affairs were perfectly well known to these persons whose movements were so mystifying.

"It was foolish of you, Parker, very foolish indeed, to have given credence to such an absurd tale as that," I said, annoyed. "You are usually a shrewd woman, but you have displayed no discretion in this affair—none whatever."

"I'm very sorry, sir," the woman answered. "But I knew that if Sir Charles were worse you'd go down to the Manor at once. Did you really send nobody, sir?"

"No; nobody at all. There's some underhand business in all this, Parker, so keep your wits about you."

"And haven't you seen her ladyship at all, sir?" she inquired, in her turn astonished.

"No, and, moreover, I know nothing of this mysterious woman who came to you with this cock-and-bull story. Did she say where she lived, or give any card?"

"No, she didn't, sir."

"I suppose you'd know her again if you saw her?"

"Well," she answered with considerable hesitancy, "I don't know as I should, sir. You see, she wore one of them white lace veils which makes it difficult to distinguish the features."

"But what object could any one have in coming to you and telling a falsehood in that manner?" I cried, my anger increased by the knowledge of Parker's inability to again recognise the bearer of the false message.

"I don't know, I'm sure, sir," was the woman's reply, in a voice which showed how deeply she regretted the occurrence.

"How long was she here?" I inquired.

"About five minutes. She asked me to let her see your sitting-room and the reading-books with the embossed letters, as she was much interested in you, and had heard so much of you from Lady Durrant."

"And you showed them to her?"

"Yes, sir."

"Then you had no right to do so without my permission, Parker," I said angrily. "You are an old and trusted servant, and should have known better."

"I'm very sorry, sir. The truth was that she seemed such a well-spoken lady, and her manner was so perfect that I thought you would not like to offend her."

"Recollect that if any other persons call they are not to enter my rooms on any pretext," I said decisively.

"Very well, sir. I acknowledge that I was entirely in the wrong in allowing her to pry about the place."

"And when she had gone?"

"Then I went over to the butcher's in the Strand to get a bit of steak."

"And saw nothing more of her?"

"Yes, sir. I did see her again. As I was coming back I met her in the Strand, at the corner of Arundel Street, walking with a gentleman who looked like a City man. She said something to him, and he turned and had a good look at me."

"Then it must have been this same woman who was in my chambers here when I returned," I said.

"A woman here?" she exclaimed.

"Yes; when I entered there was a woman here, and she escaped as though she were a thief. She must have gone out and rejoined the man, who was awaiting her somewhere in the vicinity. That would bear out the fact that you encountered her again."

"But how could she get in? I'm always careful to see that the door is properly closed."

"Probably she stole the extra latch-key while prying about the place. See whether it is still on the nail." She crossed the room, and next moment gasped—"It's gone, sir!"

"Ah!" I said. "Just as I thought! The story she told you was a mere excuse to obtain admittance to the place, and, if possible, to get possession of the key. This she obtained, and, having watched you out, returned and continued her search for something she desired to secure. We must at once examine the whole place, and seek to discover what's been stolen."

"Do you think she was a common thief, sir?" inquired Parker, dumbfounded by the ingenuity with which the latch-key had been secured.

"I don't know what to believe at present," I answered. "We must investigate first, and form our conclusions afterwards. Now, make a thorough search and see what has been disturbed and what is missing."

I had no intention of entering into a long explanation with Parker regarding the events of that fateful night, or to disturb her peace of mind by relating any of the tragic circumstances. Therefore, I went to my room and locked away my muddy, blood-stained clothing, and afterwards returned, and with my hands felt the various objects in my sitting-room, to assure myself that none was displaced or missing.

VIII

The Stranger

The visit of this mysterious woman in the white lace veil—at that time a fashionable feminine adornment—was, I felt assured, more than a coincidence. That it had some connexion with the strange events of the past night seemed certain, yet, try how I would, I could form no definite idea of either the motive of the visit or the object of her search. As far as Parker could discover, nothing whatever had been taken. A writing-table, the drawers of which contained some family papers, had apparently been hastily examined, but no object of value, nor any paper, had been extracted. Therefore I concluded that I had returned before the intruder had had time to make the complete examination of my effects which she had intended.

A curious thought occurred to me. Was the intruder in the white veil none other than the mysterious Edna herself?

As the day wore on I became more and more impressed by the belief that my surmise was the actual truth. Yet the cabman West had declared that she was young and pretty, while Parker expressed herself positive that she was middle-aged. But of the two statements I accepted that of the cabman as the more reliable. He had seen her in the broad daylight without the veil.

The fact of her concealing her features in a species of fine window-curtain proved an attempt at disguise, therefore what more likely than that she should contrive to render her features older, and thus impose upon Parker, whose sight was not over good? In any case, however, if it were really Edna, she had certainly lost no time in carrying out her design, and further, she must have been fully aware of my intended return.

Days passed, hot blazing days and stifling nights, when the dust of throbbing, ever-roaring London seemed over my heart. Each morning, with Parker's assistance, I searched the newspapers, but nothing appeared to show that that strange midnight crime had been discovered. Were there two victims, or only one? How strange it was that although I had been present I could not tell I only knew that the male victim was young and well-dressed, probably a gentleman, and that he had been stabbed by a cowardly blow which had proved almost instantly fatal. That woman's scream that had sounded so shrill and agonised in the dead stillness of the night I remembered plainly as though it were but an hour ago—indeed, I remember it now as distinctly as ever. Was it the cry of Edna herself?

In my helplessness I could do nothing but remain silent, and keep my terrible secret to myself. Unable either to communicate with the police or seek the assistance of my friend, I found that any endeavour to seek a solution of the problem was mere sowing of the wind. My thoughts hour by hour, as I sat alone in my dingy room, my poor blind eyes a black void, were of the ghastly affair, and in all its phases I considered it, trying to find some motive in the subsequent actions of the unscrupulous persons into whose hands I had had the misfortune to fall.

I heard of Dick through the office of his journal. He was down with fever at some outlandish place on the Afghan frontier, and would certainly not be home for a couple of months or so.

At first I was puzzled how to get rid of my soiled and blood-stained clothes so that Parker should not discover them, and at last hit upon the expedient of making them into a bundle and going forth one night when she was over at Kennington with her daughter Lily, the dancing-girl, and casting them into the Thames from the Embankment. It was a risky operation, for that part of London is well guarded by police after dark; nevertheless I accomplished it in safety, and was much amused a few days later by reading in an evening paper that they had been found near London Bridge and handed over to the river police, who, of course, scented a mystery. The blood-stains puzzled them, and the journal hinted that Scotland Yard had instituted inquiries into the ownership of the discarded suit of clothes. The paragraph concluded with that sentence, indispensable in reporting a mystery, "The police are very reticent about the matter."

Fortunately, having cut out the maker's name, and taken everything from the pockets which might serve as a clue to ownership, I felt perfectly safe, and eagerly read the issue of the same journal on the following evening, which told how the stains had been analysed, and found to be those of human blood.

A little more than a week had passed since my remarkable midnight adventure, when one morning I received a brief note by post, which Parker read to me. It consisted of only two typewritten lines stating that at mid-day I would receive a visitor, and was signed with the strange word "AVEL."

It was, I knew, a message from Edna, and I dressed myself with greater care in expectation that she herself would visit me. In this, however, I was disappointed, for after existing some three hours on tiptoe with anxiety I found my visitor to be a well-spoken, middle-aged man, whose slight accent when introducing himself betrayed that he was an American.

When we were alone, with the door closed, he made the following explanation—

"I have called upon you, Mr. Heaton, at the request of a lady who is our mutual friend. You have, I presume, received a letter signed 'Avel'?"

"Yes," I said, remembering how that I had promised to blindly and obediently render my protectress whatever assistance she desired. "I presume you desire some service of me. What is it?"

"No," he said. "You are mistaken. It is with regard to the terrible affliction from which I see you are suffering that I have been sent."

"Are you a medical man?" I inquired, with some astonishment.

"I am an oculist," was his reply.

"And your name?"

"Slade—James Slade."

"And you have been sent here by whom?"

"By a lady whose real name I do not know."

"But you will kindly explain, before we go further, the circumstance in which she sought your aid on my behalf," I said firmly.

"You are mutual friends," he answered, somewhat vaguely. "It is no unusual thing for a patient to seek my aid on behalf of a friend. She sent me here to see you, and to examine your eyes, if you will kindly permit me."

The man's bearing irritated me, and I was inclined to resent this enforced subjection to an examination by one of whose reputation I knew absolutely nothing. Some of the greatest oculists in the world had looked into my sightless eyes and pronounced my case utterly hopeless. Therefore I had no desire to be tinkered with by this man, who, for aught I knew, might be a quack whose sole desire was to run up a long bill.

"I have no necessity for your aid," I answered, somewhat bluntly. "Therefore any examination is entirely waste of time."

"But surely the sight is one of God's most precious gifts to man," he answered, in a smooth, pleasant voice; "and if a cure is possible, you yourself would, I think, welcome it."

"I don't deny that," I answered. "I would give half that I possess—nay, more—to have my sight restored, but Sir Leopold Fry, Dr. Measom, and Harker Halliday have all three seen me, and agree in their opinion that my sight is totally lost for ever. You probably know them as specialists?"

"Exactly. They are the first men in my profession," he answered. "Yet sometimes one treatment succeeds where another fails. Mine is entirely and totally different to theirs, and has, I may remark, been successful in quite a number of cases which were pronounced hopeless."

Mere quackery, I thought. I am no believer in new treatments and new medicines. The fellow's style of talk prejudiced me against him. He actually placed himself in direct opposition to the practice of the three greatest oculists in the world.

"Then you believe that you can actually cure me?" I remarked, with an incredulous smile.

"All I ask is to be permitted to try," he answered blandly, in no way annoyed by my undisguised sneer.

"Plainly speaking," I answered, "I have neither inclination nor intention to place myself at your disposal for experiments. My case has been pronounced hopeless by the three greatest of living specialists, and I am content to abide by their decision."

"Oculists are liable to draw wrong conclusions, just as other persons may do," he remarked. "In a matter of this magnitude you should—permit me to say so—endeavour to regain your sight and embrace any treatment likely to be successful. Blindness is one of man's most terrible afflictions, and assuredly no living person who is blind would wish to remain so."

"I have every desire to regain my sight, but I repeat that I have no faith whatever in new treatment."

"Your view is not at all unnatural, bearing in mind the fact that you have been pronounced incurable by the first men of the profession," he answered. "But may I not make an examination of your eyes? It is, of course, impossible to speak with any degree of authority without a diagnosis. You appear to think me a charlatan. Well, for the present I am content that you should regard me as such;" and he laughed as though amused.

He seemed so perfectly confident in his own powers that I confess my hastily formed opinion became moderated and my prejudice weakened. He spoke as though he had detected the disease which had deprived me of vision, and knew how to successfully combat it.

"Will you kindly come forward to the window?" he requested, without giving me time to reply to his previous observations. I obeyed his wish.

Then I felt his fingers open my eyelids wide, and knew that he was gazing into my eyes through one of those glasses like other oculists had used. He took a long time over the right eye, which he examined first, then having apparently satisfied himself, he opened the left, felt it carefully, and touched the surface, of the eyeball, causing me a twinge of pain.

"As I thought!" he exclaimed when he had finished. "As I thought! A slight operation only is necessary. The specialists whom you consulted were wrong in their conclusions. They have all three made an error which is very easy to make, yet it might have deprived you of sight for your whole life."

"What!" I cried, in sudden enthusiasm. "Do you mean to tell me solemnly that you can perform a miracle?—that you can restore my sight to me?"

"I tell you, sir," he answered quite calmly, "that if you will undergo a small operation, and afterwards subject yourself to a course of treatment, in a fortnight—or, say three weeks—you will again open your eyes and look upon the world."

His words were certainly startling to me, shut out so long from all the pleasures of life. This stranger promised me a new existence, a world of light and movement, of colour, and of all the interests which combine to make life worth living. At first I was inclined to scorn this statement of his, yet so solemnly had he uttered it, and with such an air of confidence, that I became half convinced that he was more than a mere quack.

"Your words arouse within me a new interest," I said. "When do you propose this operation?"

"To-morrow, if you will."

"Will it be painful?"

"Not very—a slight twinge, that's all."

I remained again in doubt. He noticed my hesitation, and urged me to submit.

But my natural caution asserted itself, and I felt disinclined to place myself in the hands of one of whose *bona fides* I knew absolutely nothing.

As politely as I could I told him this, but he merely replied—

"I have been sent by the lady whom we both know as Edna. Have you no confidence in her desire to assist you?"

"Certainly I have."

"She has already explained to me that you have promised to carry out her wishes. It is at her urgent request that I have come to you with the object of giving you back your sight."

"She wishes me to submit to the experiment?"

"Pardon me. It is no experiment," he said. "She desires you to submit yourself to my treatment. If you do, I have entire confidence that in a week or so you will see almost as well as I do."

I hesitated. This stranger offered me the one great desire of my life—the desire of every person who is afflicted with blindness—in return for a few moment's pain. Edna had sent him, prefaced by the mysterious letter signed "Avel." It was her desire that I should regain my sight; it was my desire to discover her and look upon her face.

"If I find your name in the *Medical Register* I will undergo the operation," I said at last.

"To search will be in vain," he responded, in the same even tone.

"Then your name is assumed?"

"My practice is not a large one, and I have no need to be registered," he said evasively.

His words again convinced me that he was a mere quack. I had cornered him, for he was palpably confused.

"As I have already told you," I said, with some warmth, "your attempts at persuasion are utterly useless. I refuse to allow my eyes to be tampered with by one who is not a medical man."

He laughed, rather superciliously I thought.

"You prefer your present affliction?"

"Yes," I snapped.

"Then, now that you force me to the last extremity," he said firmly, "I have this to present to you."

And next moment I felt within my hand a paper neither the nature of which, nor the writing thereon, could I distinguish; yet from his voice I knew instinctively that this stranger, whoever he was, held triumph over me.

❦

IX

From the Unknown

I have no knowledge of what this is," I said, puzzled, holding the paper he had given me.

"Then I will read it to you," he responded; and taking it from my hand, he repeated the words written there. Even then I doubted him, therefore I took the paper into the kitchen and bade Parker read it. Then I knew that he had not deceived me, for Parker repeated the very same words that he had read, namely—

> "The first request made to you, Wilford Heaton, is that you shall repose every confidence in Doctor Slade, and allow him to restore your sight. Obey.
>
> Avel

The note was very brief and pointed, written, I learnt, like the first note, with a typewriter, so that no clue might be afforded by the calligraphy. It was an order from the unknown person whom I had promised to blindly and faithfully obey. At the time I had given the mysterious Edna that promise I was in deadly peril of my life. Indeed, the promise had been extracted from me under threat of death, and now, in the security of my own home, I felt very disinclined to conform with the wishes of some person or persons whom I knew not. I saw in what a very serious position I had placed myself by this rash promise, for I might even be ordered to commit a crime, or, perhaps, for aught I knew, have unwittingly allied myself with some secret society.

The one desire which ever possessed me, that of being able to look upon the unseen woman with the musical voice, who had at one time been my protectress and my captor, urged me, however, in this instance, to accede. There was evidently some object in making this attempt to give me back my sight, and if it really succeeded I alone would be the gainer.

Understand that I had no faith whatever in the stranger who had thus come to me with a promise of a miraculous cure; on the other hand, I felt that he was a mere charlatan and impostor. Nevertheless, I could not be rendered more blind than I was, and having nothing to lose in the experiment, any gain would be to my distinct advantage.

Therefore, after further argument, I very reluctantly promised to allow him to operate upon me on the morrow.

"Good," he answered. "I felt sure that your natural desire for the restoration of your sight would not allow your minor prejudices to stand in the way. Shall we say at noon to-morrow."

"Any hour will suit me," I answered briefly, with a rather bad grace.

"Then let it be at noon. I and my assistant will be here by eleven-thirty."

"I should prefer to come to your surgery," I said, with the idea of obtaining some knowledge of the stranger's address. If I knew where he lived I could easily find out his real name.

"That is, unfortunately, impossible," he answered blandly. "I am staying at an hotel. I do not practise in London."

He seemed to have an ingenious answer always upon the tip of his tongue.

So, after some further conversation, in which he continually foiled any attempt I made to gain further knowledge of Edna or of himself, he rose and bade me adieu, promising to return on the morrow with the necessary instruments.

With a rather unnecessary show of punctuality he arrived next day, accompanied by a younger, sad-voiced man, and after some elaborate preparations, the nature of which I guessed from my own medical knowledge, I sat in my big armchair, and placed myself entirely at his disposal. From the first moment that he approached me and examined me prior to producing anaesthesia of the part to be operated upon I knew that my prejudice had been hastily formed. He was no quack, but careful, confident, and skilled, with a firm hand evidently used to such cases.

To fully describe what followed can be of no interest to any save medical men, therefore suffice it to relate that the operation lasted about an hour, after which my eyes were carefully bandaged, and my attendant and his assistant left. Slade called each day at noon, and carefully dressed my eyes, on each occasion expressing satisfaction at my progress, but always impressing upon me the absolute necessity for remaining with the blinds closely drawn, so that no ray of light should reach me. Darkness did not trouble me, yet Parker found it rather difficult to serve my meals in the gloom, and was very incredulous regarding the mysterious doctor's talents. She viewed the whole affair just as I had once done, and, without mincing words, denounced him as a quack, who was merely running up a long bill for nothing.

For nearly three weeks I lived with the Venetian blinds of my sitting-room always down, and with a thick curtain drawn across them, shutting out all light, as well as a good deal of air, until the summer heat became stifling. Hour after hour I sat alone, my hands idly in my lap, ever wondering what the success of this experiment would be. Should I ever again see, after those grave and distinct pronouncements of Fry and the rest, who had plainly told me that my sight was for ever destroyed? I dared not to hope, and only remained inert and thoughtful, congratulating myself that I had at least obeyed the dictum of my mysterious and unknown correspondent, under whose influence I had so foolishly placed myself.

At last, however—it was on a Sunday—Slade came, and as usual raised the bandages and bathed my eyes in a solution of atropine. Then, having made a careful examination, he went to the window, drew aside the curtains, and slightly opened the Venetian blinds.

In an instant I cried aloud for joy.

My sight had been restored. The desire of my life was an accomplished fact. I could actually see!

Dimly I could distinguish his short, burly form between myself and the faint light of the half-opened blinds, but even though all was as yet misty and indistinct, I knew that what had been averred was the actual truth—the specialists had been mistaken. With care and continued treatment my sight would strengthen until I became like other men.

"I can see!" I cried excitedly. "I can see you, doctor—and the light—and the blinds!"

"Then you acknowledge that what I told you was the truth—that I did not lie to you when I told you that your case was not beyond recovery?"

"Certainly. You told me the truth," I said hastily. "At the time it seemed too improbable, but now that you have shown me proof, I must ask your pardon if any words of mine have given you offence."

"You've not offended me in the slightest, my dear sir," he answered pleasantly. "Persevere with the treatment, and continue for another few days in darkness, and then I feel confident that a perfectly satisfactory cure will have been effected. Of course, we must not expect a clear vision at once, but by degrees your sight will slowly become stronger."

And with those words he closed the blinds and drew the curtain close, so that the room was again darkened.

Imagine the thankfulness that filled my heart! It was no illusion. I had actually seen the narrow rays of sunlight between the half-opened blind and the dark silhouette of the short, stout, full-bearded man who was effecting such a marvellous cure.

I gripped his hand in the darkness, and thanked him.

"How can I sufficiently repay you?" I said. "This service you have rendered me has opened up to me an absolutely new life."

"I desire no repayment, Mr. Heaton," he answered in his deep, hearty voice. "That my treatment of malignant sclerotitis is successful, and that I have been the means of restoring sight to one of my fellow-men, is sufficient in itself."

"But I have one question I wish to ask you," I said. "The mode in which you were introduced to me is extremely puzzling. Do you know nothing of the lady named Edna?"

"I know her—that is all."

"Where does she live?"

"I regret that I am not able to answer your question."

"You are bound to secrecy regarding her?"

"I may as well admit the truth—I am."

"It's extraordinary," I exclaimed. "Very extraordinary!"

"Not so extraordinary as the recovery of your vision," he observed. "Remain perfectly quiet, and don't take upon yourself any mental problems. A great deal now depends upon your own calmness."

The fact that my sight was gradually returning to me seemed too astonishing to believe. This man Slade, whoever he was, had performed a feat in surgery which seemed to me miraculous.

Again and again I thanked him, but when he had gone and I told Parker she only gave vent to a grunt of incredulity. Yet had I not actually seen the silhouette of Slade, and the streaks of sunlight beyond? Had I not already had ocular proof that a cure was being effected?

What would Dick, dear old Dick, say on his return when he found me cured? I laughed as I pictured to myself his amazement at finding me at the railway-station on his arrival—looking for him.

Through a whole month Slade came regularly each day at noon, and surely, by slow degrees, my vision became strengthened, until at length I found that, even though I wore smoke-darkened glasses, I could see almost as well as I had done in the days of my youth. The glasses destroyed all colour, it was true, yet I could now go forth into the busy Strand, mingle with the bustling crowds, and revel in their life and movement. Indeed, in those first days of the recovery of my vision I went about London in taxis and omnibuses, hither and thither, with all the enthusiasm of a country cousin or a child on his first visit to the Metropolis. All was novel and interesting on my return to a knowledge of life.

Slade, I found, was a gentlemanly fellow with the air of a clever physician, but all my efforts to discover his abode proved unavailing, and, moreover, just as the cure was complete he one day failed to call as usual. Without word he relinquished me just as suddenly as he had come; but he had restored to me that precious sense which is one of God's chief gifts.

In those September days, when all the world seemed gay and bright, I went forth into the world with a new zest for life. I took short trips to Richmond and Hampton Court, so that I might again gaze upon the green trees, the winding river, and the fields that I loved so well; and I spent a day at Brighton, and stood for a full couple of hours watching the rolling sea beating upon the beach. Six weeks before I was a hopeless misanthrope, whose life had been utterly sapped by the blighting affliction upon me. Now I was strong and healthy in mind and in body; prepared to do anything or to go anywhere.

It was a fancy of mine to go down to the home of my youth, Heaton Manor, a place well known to those acquainted with the district around Tewkesbury. The great old mansion, standing in the centre of a wide, well-wooded park that slopes down to the Severn close to the Haw Bridge, had long been closed, and in the hands of the old servant Baxter and his wife. Indeed, I had never lived there since, on my father's death, it had passed into my possession. The rooms were opened for my inspection, and as I wandered through them and down the long oak-panelled gallery, from the walls of which rows of my time-dimmed ancestors, in their ruffles, velvets, and laces looked down solemnly, a flood of recollections of my sunny days of childhood crowded upon me.

Seven years had passed since my last visit there. The old ivy covered manor was, indeed, dilapidated, and sadly out of repair. The furniture and hangings in many of the rooms seemed rotting with damp and neglect, and as I entered the nursery, and was shown my own toys, it seemed as though, like Rip Van Winkle, I had returned again to life after a long absence.

Alone, I wandered in the park down the avenue of grand old elms. The wide view across the brimming river, with Hasfield Church, and the old Tithe Barn at Chaceley standing prominent in the landscape, had, I saw, in no way changed. I looked back upon the house—a grand old home it was, one that any man might have been proud of, yet of what use was it to me? Should I sell it? Or should I allow it to still rot and decay until my will became proved, and it passed into the hands of my heirs and assigns?

I felt loth to part with it, for the old place had been built soon after the fierce and historic battle had been fought at Tewkesbury, and ever since Richard Heaton had commanded one of the frigates which went forth to meet the Armada, it had been the ancestral home of the Heatons.

How strange it all was! At every turn I peered upon the world through my grey glass spectacles, and took as keen an interest in it as does a child. All seemed new to me; my brain, like a child's, became filled with new impressions and fresh ideas. After my dull, colourless existence of sound and touch, this bright life of movement filled me with a delight that pen cannot describe. Imagine, however, what joy it is to one who has been pronounced incurably blind to look upon the world again and taste of its pleasures. It was that joy which gave lightness to my heart.

Yet over all was one grim shadow—the remembrance of that fateful night with its grim tragedy. Who was Edna? Where was she? What was she?

Through her instrumentality I had regained my sight, but her identity and her whereabouts still remained hidden, as she had plainly told me they would be before we had parted.

Hither and thither I went, feted and feasted by my friends at the Savage, the Devonshire, and other clubs, yet my mind was ever troubled by the mystery of the woman who had, from motives that were entirely hidden, exerted herself on my behalf, first in saving my life from unscrupulous assassins, and, secondly, in restoring my vision.

I entertained a strong desire to meet her, to grasp her small hand, to thank her. I longed to see her.

X

The Girl in Blue

The man who abandons all hope is constantly haunted by fears. This is as strange as it is unjust, like much else in our everyday life. Even though there had returned to me all the joys of existence, yet I was still haunted by an ever-present dread—a terror lest some terrible mandate should suddenly be launched upon me by the unknown director of my actions.

My situation was, to say the least, a most extraordinary one. Valiantly I strove to rid myself of the obsession which constantly crept upon me whenever my attention was not actually distracted by the new existence that had so mysteriously been opened up to me. For a little while I would let my mind dwell upon the terrifying thought that I was entirely helpless in the hands of one who was, without doubt, unscrupulous. I had pledged my honour to keep secret that appalling midnight crime, and to act always as directed. Edna herself, the woman whose voice sounded so tender, whose hands were so small and soft to the touch, had forced me to this. To her alone was due this state of constant anxiety as to what might next be demanded of me. The thought would creep upon me, now pausing, now advancing, until at length it wrapped me round and round, and stifled out my breath, like a death-mask of cold clay. Then my heart would sink, my sight seemed to die, even sound would die until there seemed an awful void—the void of death for ever and for ever dumb, a dreadful, conquering silence.

A thousand times I regretted that I had in that moment of my utter helplessness given my promise to conceal the mysterious crime. Yet, when I recollected with what extraordinary ingenuity I had been deceived by the man whom I had believed to be a police-constable, the deep cunning which had been displayed in obtaining from my lips a statement of all the facts I knew, and the subsequent actions of the cool-headed Edna, my mind became confused. I could see no solution of the extraordinary problem, save that I believed her to be deeply implicated in some plot which had culminated in the murder of the young man, and that she herself had some strong personal motive in concealing the terrible truth.

With the return of my vision my sense of hearing had, curiously enough, become both weakened and distorted. Sounds I had heard when blind presented quite a different impression now that I could see. The blind hear where those with eyesight can detect nothing. The ears of the former train themselves to act as eyes also, yet the moment the vision is recovered the sharpened sense of hearing again assumes its normal capacity. Hence I found that I could not distinguish voices and sounds so quickly as before; indeed, the voices of those about me sounded some how different now I had recovered my sight.

My friends, into whose circle they declared I had returned like one from the grave, welcomed me everywhere, and I confess that, notwithstanding the oppression constantly upon me, I enjoyed myself to the top of my bent. I still remained in my dingy, smoke-grimed rooms in Essex Street, really more for Parker's sake than for my own, and also, of course, in order to be near Dick when he returned, but nearly every evening I was out somewhere or other, going here and there about town.

In the middle of October, when most men I knew were away on the moors, I had a dinner engagement one evening with the Channings, in Cornwall Gardens. Colonel Channing, a retired officer of the Guards, was a man I had known during greater part of my lifetime. His service had been mainly of a diplomatic character, for he had served as British military *attache* at Berlin and Vienna, and now lived with his wife and daughter in London, and seemed to divide his time mainly between the St. James's and the United Service Clubs. He was a merry old fellow, with white hair and moustache and a florid complexion, the dandified air of *attache* still clinging to him.

As he sat at the head of his table, his habitual monocle in his eye, and the tiny green ribbon of the order of the Crown of Italy in the lapel of his dining-jacket, he looked a perfect type of the *ex-attache*. His wife, a rather spare woman of fifty, who seemed to exist externally in a toilette of black satin and lace, was pleasant, though just a trifle stiff, probably because of her long association with other diplomatists' wives; while Nellie Channing was a happy, fair-haired girl, who wore pretty blouses, motored, golfed, flirted and shopped in the High Street in the most approved manner of the average girl of South Kensington.

Nellie and I had always been good friends. She had been at school in England while her parents had been abroad, but on completing her education she had lived some five years or so in Vienna, and had thus acquired something of the cosmopolitan habit of her father. She looked charming in her pink blouse, a trifle *decollete*, as she sat on my left at dinner, and congratulated me upon my recovery.

If, however, Nellie Channing was pretty, her beauty was far eclipsed by that of my neighbour on my right, a tall, dark-haired girl in blue, a Miss Anson, who with her mother, a quiet, white-haired elderly lady, were the only other guests in addition to myself. From the moment we were introduced I saw that Mrs. Anson's daughter possessed a face that was absolutely perfect, rather oval in shape, with large, beautiful eyes, that seemed to shine as they looked upon me, and to search me through and through. Her complexion was good, her cheeks well-moulded, her mouth small and perfectly formed; her teeth gleamed white ever and anon as she smiled at the Colonel's humorous remarks, and her nose was just sufficiently tip-tilted to give her countenance a piquant air of coquetry.

Her costume, rich and without any undue exaggeration of trimming or style, spoke mutely of the handiwork of a first-class *couturiere*. The shade of turquoise suited her dark beauty admirably, and the bodice, cut discreetly low, revealed a neck white and firmly moulded as that of the Venus of Milo. Around her throat, suspended by a golden chain so fine as to be almost imperceptible, was a single diamond set in a thin ring of gold, a large stone of magnificent lustre. It was her only ornament, but, flashing and glittering with a thousand fires, it was quite sufficient. She wore no rings. Her hands, white and well-formed, were devoid of any jewels. The single diamond gleamed and glittered as it rose and fell upon her breast, an ornament assuredly fit to adorn a princess.

Mrs. Anson sat opposite me, chatting pleasantly during the meal, and now and then her daughter would turn, raise her fine eyes to mine for an instant, and join in our conversation. That she was exceedingly clever and well-informed I at once detected by her terse and smart criticism of the latest play, which we discussed. She compared it, with a display of knowledge that surprised me, to a French play but little known save to students of the French drama, and once or twice her remarks upon stage technicalities caused me to suspect that she was an actress.

Mrs. Anson, however, dispelled this notion by expressing her disapproval of the stage as a profession for women, an opinion with which her daughter at once agreed. No, she could not be an actress, I felt assured. Both mother and daughter bore the unmistakable hallmark of gentlewomen.

I sat beside Mabel Anson in rapt admiration. Never before in all my life had my eyes fallen upon so perfect an incarnation of feminine grace and marvellous beauty; never before until that moment had a woman's face held me in such enchantment.

Presently the conversation turned, as it so often does at dinner-tables, upon certain engagements recently announced, whereupon the Colonel, in the merry, careless manner habitual to him, advanced the theory that most girls married with a view to improve their social position.

"As to a husband's fortune," remarked his wife, with that stiff formality which was her peculiar characteristic, "it really isn't so important to a woman as the qualities which lead to fortune—ambition, determination, industry, thrift—and position such a man may attain for himself."

"And in education?" inquired Miss Anson, softly, apparently interested in the argument.

"In education a man certainly should be his wife's equal," answered Mrs. Channing.

"And is not good temper essential with a husband?—come, now. Let's hear your ideas on that point," said the Colonel, chaffingly, from behind the big epergne.

Mabel Anson hesitated. For an instant her lustrous eyes met mine, and she at once lowered them with a downward sweep of her long dark lashes.

"I don't argue that a girl thinking seriously of her future husband should lay any great stress on good temper," she answered, in a sweet musical voice. "A soldierly form, a pair of good eyes, a noble profile— any of these might easily outweigh good temper."

"Ah! there, I fear, I disagree with you," I remarked smilingly. "It has always appeared to me that after the first year or so married people rarely think of each other's features, because they are always in each other's presence. They become heedless of whether each other's features are classical or ugly; but they never fail to be cognisant of one another's temper or shortcomings."

"You speak as though from experience," she laughed, without, however, attempting to combat my argument.

Another outburst of laughter greeted this bantering remark of hers.

"No," observed Nellie, on my other hand. "Mr. Heaton is the most confirmed bachelor I know. I believe he's a woman-hater—if the truth were told."

"Oh, really, Miss Channing!" I protested. "That's certainly too bad of you. I assure you I'm no hater of the sex, but an admirer."

"Heaton's about to make a pretty speech," observed the jovial, red-faced Colonel. "Go on, Wilford, my dear fellow, we're all attention."

"No," I said, laughing. "I've been drawn quite unfairly into this controversy. Therefore I'll preserve a masterly silence."

"Mr. Heaton is, I think, diplomatic," laughed the dark, handsome girl next to me. "He has cleared his character of the aspersion cast upon it, and preserves a dignified attitude." And she turned and smiled gaily upon me in triumph.

She was exquisitely charming. I sat at her side gossiping merrily, while to my dazzled gaze she presented a beautiful picture of youthful airy delicacy—feminine sweetness combined with patrician grace. For the first time in all my life that petticoated paradox, woman, conveyed to me the impression of perfect beauty, of timidity and grace, combined with a natural, inborn dignity. There was nothing forced or unnatural in her manner as with other women I had met; none of that affected mannishness of deportment and slangy embellishments of conversation which are so characteristic of girls of to-day, be they daughters of tradesmen or of peers.

She gave me the impression—why, I cannot tell—of one who had passed under the ennobling discipline of suffering and self-denial. A melancholy charm tempered the natural vigour of her mind; her spirit seemed to stand upon an eminence and look down upon me as one inferior to her in intellect, in moral principle—in fact, in everything. From the very first moment when I had bowed to her on our introduction she held me spell-bound in fascination.

When the ladies had left, and I sat alone with the Colonel, smoking over a liqueur, I inquired about her.

"Mrs. Anson is the widow of old General Anson," he said. "He died about twelve years ago, and they've since lived a great deal abroad."

"Well off?" I inquired, with affected carelessness.

"Very comfortably, I should say. Mrs. Anson has a fortune of her own, I believe. They have a house at present in The Boltons."

"Mabel is extremely good-looking," I remarked.

"Of course, my dear boy," laughed the Colonel, with his liqueur-glass poised in his hand, a twinkle in his eye. "Between us, she's the prettiest girl in London. She creates a sensation wherever she goes, for beauty like hers isn't met with twice in a lifetime. Lucky chap, whoever marries her."

"Yes," I said reflectively, and then diligently pursued the topic in an endeavour to learn further details regarding her. My host either knew very little, or purposely affected ignorance—which, I was unable to determine. He had known her father intimately, having been in his regiment long ago. That was about all I learnt further.

So we tossed away our cigars, drained our glasses, and rejoined the four ladies who were awaiting us in the drawing-room, where later, at Mrs. Channing's urgent persuasion, my divinity in blue seated herself at the piano, and in a sweet, clear contralto sang in Italian a charming solo from Puccini's *Boheme*, the notable opera of that season.

Then, with the single diamond glittering at her throat, she came back to where I stood, and sinking into the cosy-corner with its pretty hangings of yellow silk, she accepted my congratulations with a delicate grace, a charming dignity, and a grateful smile.

At last, however, the hour of parting came, and reluctantly—very reluctantly—I took her small hand, bent over it, and handed her into her carriage beside her mother.

"Good-night," she cried merrily, and next instant the fine pair of bays plunged away into the rainy night.

I returned into the hall, and my host helped me into my overcoat.

We were alone, for I had made my adieux to his wife and daughters.

"Wilford," he said very gravely, as he gripped my hand prior to my departure, "we are old friends. Will you permit me to say one word without taking offence at it?"

"Certainly," I answered, surprised. "What is it?"

"I've noticed to-night that, like many another man, you are entranced by the beauty of Mabel Anson. Be careful not to make a fool of yourself."

"I don't understand," I said quickly.

"Well, all I would say is, that if you desire happiness and peace of mind, steel your heart against her," he answered with a distinct air of mystery.

"You speak in enigmas."

"I merely give you a timely warning, that's all, my dear fellow. Now, don't be offended, but go home and think it over, and resolve never again to see her—never, you understand—never."

XI

The Fourteenth of October

Long and deeply I pondered over the Colonel's words. That he had some underlying motive in thus warning me against the woman by whom I had become so fascinated was vividly apparent, yet to all my demands he remained dumb. On the afternoon following I found him in the St. James's Club—that club of diplomatists—and reverted to the subject. But all the response he vouchsafed was—

"I've merely warned you, my dear fellow. I shall say no more. I, of course, don't blame you for admiring her, I only tell you to pull yourself up short."

"But why?"

"Because if you go further than admiration you'll be treading dangerous ground—devilish dangerous, I can assure you."

"You mean that she has a jealous lover?" I suggested.

"She has no lover, as far as I'm aware," he answered.

"Then, speaking candidly, Channing," I said, "I don't see why you should turn prophet like this without giving me any reason."

"My reason is briefly told," he said with unusual gravity. "I don't wish to see you upset and unhappy, now that you've recovered your sight."

His words seemed very lame ones.

"Why should I be unhappy?"

"Because Mabel Anson can never be more to you than an acquaintance; she can never reciprocate your love. I tell you plainly that if you allow yourself to become entranced and all that sort of thing, you'll only make a confounded ass of yourself."

"You certainly speak very plainly," I observed, annoyed that he should interfere so prematurely in a matter which was assuredly my affair alone.

"I speak because I have your welfare at heart, Wilford," he answered in a kindly tone. "I only regret now that I asked you to my table to meet her. It is my fault—entirely my fault."

"You talk as though she were some genius of evil," I laughed. "Let me act as I think fit, my dear Channing."

"Let you go headlong to the devil, eh?" he snapped.

"But to love her is not to go on the downward path, surely?" I cried incredulously.

"I warn you, once and for all, to have nothing whatever to do with her," he said. "I know her—you do not."

But I laughed him to scorn. His words seemed utterly absurd, as though his mind were filled by some strong prejudice which he dared not to utter for fear of laying himself open to an action for slander. If her acquaintance were so extremely undesirable, why did he invite her and her mother to his table? His words were not borne out by his own actions.

So I bade him farewell rather coolly, and left the club abruptly, in anger with myself at having sought him, or bestowed a single thought upon his extraordinary warning.

In the days that followed my mind was fully engrossed by recollections of her charm and beauty. Like every other man, I had had, before my blindness, one or two minor affairs of the heart, but never before had I experienced the grand passion. I had, indeed, admired several other women of various ages and various stations, but none had ever approached in grace, beauty, or refinement the woman who had so suddenly come into my life, and so quickly gone out of it.

Yes, I openly confess that I, who had of later years determined to remain a bachelor, was deeply in love with her. Indeed, for the time, I actually forgot the grim shadow of evil which had in my blindness fallen upon me.

Hither and thither in the great world of London I went with my eyes ever open in eagerness to catch a glimpse of her. I lounged in the Row at the fashionable hour; went to the opera, and swept boxes and stalls with my glasses; and strolled about Regent Street, Oxford Street, and High Street, Kensington, in the vicinity of those great drapery emporiums so dear alike to the feminine heart and to the male pocket. For ten days or so I spent greater part of my time in searching for her slim, erect figure among the bustling London crowds. I knew her address, it was true, but my acquaintance was not sufficient to warrant a call, therefore I was compelled to seek a chance encounter.

All, however, was in vain. I had firmly resolved to take no heed of the Colonel's extraordinary premonition, and laughed at his dehortatory suggestions; for I meant at all costs to meet her again. One day I suddenly recollected that in conversation Mrs. Anson had mentioned that her daughter was a student at the Royal Academy of

Music. If so, then she would undoubtedly go there alone on certain days to take her lessons. By carefully watching I might, I thought, meet her as if by accident. So I at once set to work to make inquiries, and discovered through tipping one of the hall-porters of the institution that Miss Anson came there every Tuesday and Friday at two o'clock in the afternoon. The next day chanced to be Tuesday, therefore I went to Hanover Square and waited for her at the corner of Tenterden Street. As I watched I saw quite a number of smart-looking lady students pass into the institution but, although I remained on the alert for nearly two hours, she did not come, and at length I was compelled to return home wearied, unsuccessful, and dispirited.

That night, however, a blow fell upon me. An incident which I had constantly dreaded occurred, for by the last post was delivered one of those strange typewritten mandates from the unknown. The envelope was a blue-grey one, such as lawyers use, and the postmark showed that it had been dispatched from the Lombard Street office, in the City. I tore it open in fear and trepidation, and glanced at the few even lines it contained. The lines I read were signed by the word "Avel," traced with a heavy hand in rough Roman capitals, and were as follows:—

"To-morrow, the fourteenth of October, enter the Park at Grosvenor Gate at four o'clock, and wait at the third seat on the path which leads to the band-stand."

I stood silent, with the mysterious missive in my hand. Some secret service was evidently required of me. The shadow of that fateful night had again fallen, crushing me beneath its weight of mystery and crime. I thought of the unknown Edna, and pictured her in comparison with Mabel. In my helplessness I had become an unwilling tool in the hands of the former, and now I hated and despised her. This galling servitude which she had imposed upon me under penalty of death was doubly irksome now that I loved; yet so mysterious and tragic were all the circumstances that I feared to break the bond that I had given.

In ordinary circumstances I think I should have been eager to obey this sudden demand to go to the Park on the following day. There was a distinct air of adventure in the appointment, and, eager to fathom the mystery surrounding Edna, I saw that this meeting might furnish me with some clue. But I recollected Mabel, all sweetness and purity, and hated it all. Edna had declared that she herself was not the mysterious "Avel," yet I had no reason to disbelieve her statement. To me it seemed as though she were acting under instructions which had for their object the preservation of the secret of the midnight crime.

Who was the young man who had fallen victim? His identity puzzled me always, until the problem had become so perplexing as to drive me to despair. Although time after time I had searched the newspapers, I had found no one answering to his description mentioned as missing. He had evidently been done to death and his body disposed of without a single inquiry, while the crime had been concealed with an ingenuity which appalled me. Might I, myself, not fall victim in a similar manner if I refused to obey these strange mandates of an unknown hand?

These thoughts were the reverse of reassuring, for even if I went to the police they would be unable to assist me. A detective might keep the appointment in the Park, but it was certain on seeing a stranger in the vicinity the person who intended to meet me would give him a very wide berth.

That hot night I lay awake through many hours calmly reviewing the whole situation. On the last occasion when I had obeyed the order of my mysterious correspondent—sent undoubtedly at Edna's instigation—I had profited considerably. Was the present order for good or for evil?

Naturally, I had always been fond of adventure, for I came of a family of sailors. But the gruesome incidents of that single night when I had wandered alone in London had utterly unnerved me. I had become so surrounded by mystery that each effort of mine to elucidate it caused me to sink deeper and deeper into the complex quagmire of uncertainty.

Perhaps Edna herself desired to speak with me, now that I could see. This suggestion took possession of me, and next morning I was anxious and interested in the appointment. Soon after three I took an omnibus from the Strand to the corner of Park Lane, and on the stroke of four entered the Park at Grosvenor Gate and glanced eagerly around. No one was in the vicinity save one or two loungers of the "unemployed" type and two or three nursemaids with children. Without difficulty I soon found the seat indicated, and sat down to wait. It was a pleasant spot beneath a large chestnut tree, quiet and more secluded than any of the others. Evidently my correspondent knew the Park well.

I lit a cigarette and possessed myself in patience. After some five minutes or so a female figure entered the gate and approached in my direction. It was that of an elderly woman of rather common type, and as she came straight towards me I waited her with some curiosity, but she passed me by without a look, and continued on her way. Then

I knew that she was not the person who intended to meet me, and laughed within myself.

My position was one of curiosity, sitting there prepared to meet some person unknown. We have all of us, at one time or another, sat awaiting persons we have never before seen, and we have invariably found mental pictures of their appearance utterly different from their real aspect. It was so with me at that moment. I sat waiting and wondering for half an hour or so, watching narrowly all who chanced to approach, until I began to suspect that for some reason or other the appointment would not be kept.

A glance at my watch showed it to be already twenty minutes to five. My patience was exhausted, and I felt annoyed that I should be thus brought here on a purposeless errand. Of one man who had passed, a dark-faced, ill-dressed lounger, I had had my suspicions. He had idled past, feigning to take no notice of my presence, yet I saw that he was covertly watching me. Perhaps he had been sent to see whether I had come there alone. I waited and waited, but in vain.

The shadows had lengthened, the sun was sinking behind the trees in Kensington Gardens, and at length I cast away the end of my last remaining cigarette and rose to depart. Perhaps some untoward incident had occurred, and I should receive a further communication from my unknown correspondent. I had, at least, carried out my part of the compact, and was therefore free. So I took my stick and set forth towards Grosvenor Gate at a brisk pace, for I was tired of waiting, and my limbs were cramped by my long and fruitless vigil.

I had almost reached the gate leading out to Park Lane when of a sudden, at a sharp bend of the path, a dark figure loomed up before me.

In an instant I drew up speechless, aghast, amazed. The mystery was absolutely dumbfounding.

XII

"It is his!"

The figure before me was that of a woman, calm, sweet-faced, her countenance rendered piquant by its expression of surprise.

It was none other than Mabel Anson.

Dressed in a tight-fitting tailor-made gown of some dark cloth, and a neat toque, she looked dignified and altogether charming. The slight severity of attire became her well, for it showed her marvellous figure to perfection, while the dash of red in her hat gave the necessary touch of colour to complete a tasteful effect. Her countenance was concealed by the thinnest of gauze veils, and as she held forth her well-gloved hand with an expression of pleasure at the unexpected meeting, her bangles jingled musically.

"This is indeed a most pleasant surprise, Miss Anson," I said, when I recovered speech, for so sudden had been our encounter that in the moment of my astonishment my tongue refused to utter a sound.

"And to me also," she laughed.

"I've been wondering and wondering when we should meet again," I blurted forth. "I'm so very glad to see you."

For the first few moments after she had allowed her tiny hand to rest for an instant in mine we exchanged conventionalities, and then suddenly, noting a roll of music in her hand, I asked—

"Are you going home?"

"Yes, across the Park," she laughed. "Mother forbids it, but I much prefer the Park to those stuffy omnibuses."

"And you've been to your music, I suppose?" I inquired.

"Yes. I've not been well for the past few days, and have missed several lessons. Now, like a good pupil, I'm endeavouring to make them up, you know." And she laughed merrily.

"How many times a week do you go to the Academy?" I asked, surprised that she should have gone there that day, after what the hall-porter had told me.

"Twice, as a general rule," she remarked; "but just now I'm rather irregular."

"And so you prefer to cross the Park rather than ride by omnibus?"

"Certainly. Mother doesn't approve of girls riding on the tops of 'buses, and says it's fast. Therefore I'd much rather walk, for at this hour half London seems to be going from Piccadilly Circus to Hammersmith. I go right across, past the Serpentine, through Kensington Gardens to the Broad Walk, and out by the small gate next the *Palace Hotel*," she added, with a sweep of her gloved hand.

Her eyes were lovely. As she stood there in the fading sunlight she seemed the fairest vision I had ever seen. I stood spell-bound by her marvellous beauty.

"And may I not act as your escort on your walk to-day?" I asked.

"Certainly. I have no objection," she answered with graceful dignity, therefore I turned and walked beside her, carrying her music.

We took the road, which leads straight away to the Magazine, and crosses the Serpentine beyond. There in the yellow glow of the October sunset I lounged at her side and drank my fill of her loveliness. Surely, I thought, there could be no more beautiful woman in all the world. The Colonel's strange warning recurred to me, but I laughed it to scorn.

As we passed beneath the rustling trees the sun's last rays lit up her beautiful face with a light that seemed ethereal and tipped her hair until there seemed a golden halo about her. I was no lovesick youth, be it remembered, but a man who had had a bitter experience of the world and its suffering. Yet at that hour I was fascinated by the grace of her superb carriage, the suppleness of her figure, the charm of her sweet smile, and the soft music of her voice as she chatted to me.

She told me of her love for music; and from the character of the pieces which formed her studies I knew that she must be a musician of a no mean order. The operatic melody which she had sung at the Colonel's was, she declared, a mere trifle. We discussed the works of Rossini and Massent, of Wagner and Mendelssohn, and of Verdi, Puccini, Mascagni, Perosi, and such latter-day composers. I had always prided myself that I knew something of music, but her knowledge was far deeper than mine.

And so we gossiped on, crossing the Park and entering Kensington Gardens—those beautiful pleasure grounds that always seem so neglected by the majority of Londoners—while the sun sank and disappeared in its blood-red afterglow. She spoke of her life abroad, declaring that she loved London and was always pleased to return to its wild, turbulent life. She had spent some time in Paris, in Vienna, in Berlin, but no one was half as interesting, she declared, as London.

"But you are not a Londoner, are you?" I asked.

"No, not exactly," she responded, "although I've lived here such a long time that I've become almost a Cockney. Are you a Londoner?"

"No," I answered; "I'm a countryman, born and bred."

"I heard the Colonel remark that other night that you had been afflicted by blindness for some time. Is that so?"

I responded in the affirmative.

"Terrible!" she exclaimed, glancing at me with those wonderful dark eyes of hers that seemed to hold me in fascination and look me through and through. "We who possess our eyesight cannot imagine the great disadvantages under which the blind are placed. How fortunate that you are cured!"

"Yes," I explained. "The cure is little short of a miracle. The three greatest oculists in London all agreed that I was incurable, yet there one day came to me a man who said he could give me back my sight. I allowed him to experiment, and he was successful. From the day that I could see plainly he, curiously enough, disappeared."

"How strange! Did he never come and see you afterwards?"

"No. He took no reward, but simply discontinued his visits. I do not even know his real name."

"How extraordinary!" she observed, greatly interested. "I really believe that there is often more romance and mystery in real life than in books. Such a circumstance appears absolutely bewildering."

"If to you, Miss Anson, then how much more to me! I, who had relinquished all hope of again looking upon the world and enjoying life, now find myself actually in possession of my vision and able to mix with my fellow-men. Place yourself for a moment in my position, and try to imagine my constant thankfulness."

"You must feel that a new life is opened to you—that you have begun a fresh existence," she observed with a true touch of sympathy in her sweet voice. Then she added, as if by afterthought. "How many of us would be glad to commence life afresh!"

The tone in which she uttered that sentence seemed incongruous. A few moments before she had been all brightness and gaiety, but in those words there vibrated a distinctly gloomy note.

"Surely you do not desire to commence your life again?" I said.

She sighed slightly.

"All of us have our burden of regrets," she answered vaguely, raising her eyes for an instant to mine, and then lowering them.

We appeared in those moments to grow confidential. The crimson and orange was fast fading from the sky. It was growing dark beneath the shadow of the great elms, and already the line of street lamps out in Kensington Gore were twinkling through the foliage on our left. No one was in the vicinity, and we were walking very slowly, for, truth to tell, I desired to delay our parting until the very last moment. Of all the leafy spots in giant London, there is none so rural, so romantic, or so picturesque in summer as that portion of Kensington Gardens lying between Queen's Gate and the Broad Walk. Save for the dull roar of distant traffic, one might easily fancy one's self far in the country, a hundred miles from the sound of Bow Bells.

"But you are young, Miss Anson," I observed philosophically, after a brief pause. "And if I may be permitted to say so, you have scarcely begun to live your life. Yet you actually wish to commence afresh!"

"Yes," she responded briefly, "I do. Strange, is it not?"

"Is the past, then, so full of bitterness?" I asked, the Colonel's strange warning recurring to me at the same moment.

"Its bitterness is combined with regrets," she answered huskily, in a low voice.

"But you, young, bright, happy, and talented, who need not think of the trials of everyday life, should surely have no regrets so deep as to cause you this anxiety and despair," I said, with a feeling of tenderness. "I am ten years older than you, therefore I may be permitted to speak like this, even though my words may sound presumptuous."

"Continue," she exclaimed. "I assure you that in my present position I appreciate any words of sympathy."

"You have my deepest sympathy, Miss Anson; of that I assure you," I declared, detecting in her words a desire to confide in me. "If at your age you already desire to recommence life, your past cannot have been a happy one."

"It has been far from happy," she answered in a strange, mechanical voice. "Sometimes I think that I am the unhappiest woman in all the world."

"No, no," I hastened to reassure her. "We all, when in trouble, imagine that our burden is greater than that of any of our fellows, and that while others escape, upon us alone fall the graver misfortunes."

"I know, I know," she said. "But a pleasant face and an air of carelessness ofttimes conceal the most sorrowful heart. It is so in my case."

"And your sorrow causes you regret, and makes you wish to end your present life and commence afresh," I said gravely. "To myself, ignorant of the circuit stances, it would seem as though you repented of some act or other."

"What do you mean?" she gasped quickly, looking at me with a strange expression in her dark eyes. "I do not repent—I repent nothing!"

I saw that I had made a grave mistake. In my fond and short-sighted enthusiasm I had allowed myself to speak a little too confidentially, whereupon her natural dignity had instantly rebelled. At once I apologised, and in an instant she became appeased.

"I regret extremely that you should have such a weight of anxiety upon your heart," I said. "If I can do anything to assist you, rely upon me."

"You are extremely kind," she answered in a gloomy tone; "but there is nothing—absolutely nothing."

"I really can't understand the reason why, with every happiness around you, you should find yourself thus plunged in this despair," I remarked, puzzled. "Your home life is, I presume, happy enough?"

"Perfectly. I am entirely my own mistress, save in those things which might break through the ordinary conventionalities of life. I must admit to you that I am rather unconventional sometimes."

I had wondered whether, like so many other girls, she had some imaginary grievance in her home; but now, finding that this was not so, it naturally occurred to me that the cause of her strange desire to live her life over again arose through the action of some faithless lover. How many hundreds of girls with wealth and beauty, perfectly happy in all else, are daily wearing out their lives because of the fickleness of the men to whom they have foolishly given their hearts! The tightly-laced corsets of every eight girls in ten conceals a heart filled by the regrets of a love long past; the men smile airily through the wreaths of their tobacco-smoke, while the women, in those little fits of melancholy which they love to indulge in, sit and reflect in silence upon the might-have-beens. Is there, I wonder, a single one of us, man or woman, who does not remember our first love, the deep immensity of that pair of eyes; the kindly sympathy of that face, which in our immature years we thought our ideal, and thereupon bowed the knee in worship? If such there be, then they are mere unrefined boors without a spark of romance in their nature, or poetry within their soul. Indeed, the regrets arising from a long-forgotten love ofttimes mingle pleasure with sadness, and through one's whole life form cherished memories of those flushed days of a buoyant youth. To how many of those who read these lines will be recalled vivid recollections of a summer idyll of long ago; a day when, with the dainty or manly object of their affections, they wandered beside the blue sea, or on the banks of the tranquil, willow-lined river, or perhaps hand-in-hand strolled beneath the great old forest trees, where the sunlight glinted and touched the gnarled trunks with grey and gold! To each will come back the sweet recollection of a sunset hour now long, long ago, when they pressed the lips of the one they loved, and thought the rough world as rosy as that summer afterglow. The regret of those days always remains—often only a pleasant memory, but, alas! sometimes a lamentation bordering upon despair, until the end of our days.

"And may I not know something, however little, of the cause of this oppression upon you?" I asked of her, after we had walked some distance in silence. "You tell me that you desire to wipe out the past and commence afresh. The reason of this interests me," I added.

"I don't know why you should interest yourself in me," she murmured. "It is really unnecessary."

"No, no," I exclaimed hastily. "Although our acquaintance has been of but brief duration, I am bold enough to believe that you count me among your friends. Is it not so?"

"Certainly, or I would not have given you permission to walk with me here," she answered with a sweetness which showed her unostentatious delicacy of character.

"Then, as your friend, I beg of you to repose whatever confidence in me you may think fit, and to be assured that I will never abuse it."

"Confidences are unnecessary between us," she responded. "I have to bear my grief alone."

"Your words sound strange, coming from one whom I had thought so merry and light-hearted," I said.

"Are you, then, ignorant of the faculty a woman has of concealing her sorrows behind an outward show of gaiety—that a woman always possesses two countenances, the face and the mask?"

"You are scarcely complimentary to your own sex," I answered with a smile. "Yet that is surely no reason why you should be thus wretched and downhearted." Her manner puzzled me, for since the commencement of our conversation she had grown strangely melancholy—entirely unlike her own bright self. I tried to obtain from her some clue to the cause of her sadness, but in vain. My short acquaintance with her did not warrant me pressing upon her a subject which was palpably distasteful; nevertheless, it seemed to me more than strange that she should thus acknowledge to me her sorrow at a moment when any other woman would have practised coquetry.

"I can only suffer in silence," she responded when I asked her to tell me something of the cause of her unhappiness.

"Excuse my depression this evening. I know that to you I must seem a hypochondriac, but I will promise you to wear the mask—if ever we meet again."

"Why do you speak so vaguely?" I inquired in quick apprehension. "I certainly hope that we shall meet again, many, many times. Your words would make it appear as though such meeting is improbable."

"I think it is," she answered simply. "You are very kind to have borne with me like this," she added, her manner quickly changing; "and if we do meet, I'll try not to have another fit of melancholy."

"Yes, Miss Anson," I said, halting in the path, "let us meet again. Remember that we have to-day commenced a friendship—a friendship which I trust will last always."

But she slowly shook her head, as though the heavy sadness of her heart still possessed her.

"Friendship may exist between us, but frequent meetings are, I fear, impossible."

"Why? You told me only a moment ago that you were your own mistress," I observed.

"And so I am in most things," she answered. "But as far as meeting you, we can only leave that to chance."

"Why?"

"Please do not endeavour to force me to explanations," she answered with firmness. "I merely tell you that frequent meetings with you are unlikely—that is all."

We had walked on, and were nearing the gate leading out into the High Street, Kensington.

"In other words, then, you are not altogether pleased with my companionship?"

"No, really," she laughed sweetly. "I didn't say that. You have no reason to jump at such a conclusion. I thank you very much indeed for your words of sympathy."

"And you have no desire to see me again?" I interrupted, in a tone of bitter disappointment.

"If such were the case, ours would be a very extraordinary friendship, wouldn't it?" and she lifted her eyes to mine with a kindly look.

"Then I am to take it that my companionship on this walk has not been distasteful to you?" I asked anxiously.

She inclined her head with dignified air, saying. "Certainly. I feel that this evening I have at least found a friend—a pleasant thought when one is comparatively friendless."

"And as your friend—your devoted friend—I ask to be permitted to see you sometimes," I said earnestly, for, lingering at her side, I was very loth to part from her. "If I can ever be of any assistance, command me."

"You are very kind," she answered, with a slight tremor in her voice. "I shall remember your words always." Then, putting forth her well-gloved hand, as we stood upon the kerb of the High Street, she added, "It is getting late. We've taken such a long time across the Park that I must drive home;" and she made a gesture to a passing hansom.

"Before we part," I said, "I will give you a card, so that should you require any service of me you will know where to write;" and, as we stood beneath the street lamp, I drew out a card and, with a pencil I took from my vest-pocket, scribbled my address.

In silence she watched, but just as I had finished she suddenly gripped my hand, uttering a loud cry of amazement.

"What's that you have there?" she demanded. "Let me see it!"

Next instant—before, indeed, I could be aware of her intention— she had snatched the pencil from my grasp, and was examining it closely beneath the gaslight.

"Ah!" she gasped, glaring at me in alarm. "It is—yes, it is his!"

The small gold pencil which I had inadvertently used was the one I had taken from the pocket of the dead unknown on that fateful August night.

XIII

The Enchantment of a Face

The face of Mabel Anson, my new-found friend and idyll, had in that instant changed. Her countenance was pale as death, while the hand holding the small pencil trembled.

"Whence did you obtain this?" she demanded in an awe-stricken tone, which showed plainly that she recognised it. She held her breath in expectancy.

What could I reply? To explain the truth was impossible, for I had pledged my honour to Edna to preserve the secret. Besides, I had no wish to horrify her by the strange story of my midnight adventure. Hence a lie arose involuntarily to my lips.

"I found it," I stammered.

"Found it? Where?"

"I found it when groping about during the time I was blind, and I've carried it ever since, wondering whether one day I should discover its owner."

"It is extraordinary?" she gasped—"most extraordinary."

"You appear to recognise it," I observed, much puzzled at her attitude. "If you can tell me to whom it belongs I will return it."

She hesitated, and with a quick effort regained her self-control.

"I mean it possesses an extraordinary resemblance to one I have seen many times before—but I suppose there are lots of pencil-cases of the same shape," she added with affected carelessness.

"But there is a curious, unintelligible cypher engraved upon it," I said. "Did you notice it?"

"Yes. It is the engraving which makes me doubt that I know its owner. His initials were not those."

"You speak in the past tense," I observed. "Why!"

"Because—well, because we are no longer friends—if you desire to know the truth;" and she handed me back the object, which, with the dress-stud, formed the only clue I had to the identity of the unfortunate victim of the assassin.

There was something in her manner which was to me the reverse of convincing. I felt absolutely certain that this unimportant object had, in reality, been identified by her, and that with some hidden motive she was now intentionally misleading me.

"Then you do not believe that this really belonged to your friend?" I asked, holding it up to her gaze.

"No," she answered quickly, averting her face as though the sight of it were obnoxious. "I feel certain that it did not. Its resemblance is striking—that's all."

"It would have been a remarkable coincidence if it really were the property of your friend," I said.

"Very remarkable," she admitted, still regarding me strangely. "Yet the trite saying that 'The world is small' is nevertheless very true. When I first saw it I felt certain it belonged to a gentleman I knew, but on closer examination I find it is older, more battered, and bears initials which have evidently been engraved several years."

"Where did your friend lose his?" I inquired, reflecting upon the lameness of her story. The mere recognition of a lost pencil-case would never have affected her in the manner that sight of this one had if there were not some deeper meaning attached to it.

"I have no idea. Indeed, I am not at all sure that it is not still in his possession."

"And how came you to be so well acquainted with its aspect?" I asked, in eagerness to ascertain the truth.

She hesitated for a few moments. "Because," she faltered—"because it was a present from me."

"To an admirer?"

She did not answer, but even in that dim lamplight I detected the tell-tale flush mounting to her cheeks.

Then, in order, apparently, to cover her confusion, she added—

"I must really go. I shall be late for dinner, and my mother hates to wait for me. Good-bye."

Our hands clasped, our eyes met, and I saw in hers a look of deep mystery, as though she held me in suspicion. Her manner and her identification of that object extracted from the pocket of the dead man were very puzzling.

"Good-bye," I said. "I hope soon to have the pleasure of meeting you again. I have enjoyed this walk of ours immensely."

"When we meet—if ever we do," she answered with a mischievous smile, "remember that I have promised to wear the mask. Good-bye." And she twisted her skirts gracefully, entered the cab, and a moment later was driven off, leaving me alone on the kerb.

I hesitated whether to return home by 'bus or Underground Railway, but, deciding on the latter, continued along the High Street to the station, and journeyed to the Temple by that sulphurous region of dirt and darkness known as the "Inner Circle."

The reader may readily imagine how filled with conflicting thoughts was my mind on that homeward journey. Although I adored Mabel Anson with a love beyond all bounds, and would on that evening have declared my passion for her had I dared, yet I could not disguise from myself that sight of the pencil-case I had taken from the dead unknown had wrought an instant and extraordinary change in her.

She had identified it. Of that fact there was no doubt. Her lame explanation that it bore a resemblance to the one she had given to her friend was too palpably an afterthought. I was vexed that she should have thus attempted a deception. It was certainly true that one gold pencil-case is very like another, and that a Birmingham maker may turn out a thousand of similar pattern, yet the intricate cypher engraved on the one in question was sufficient by which to identify it. It was these very initials which had caused her to deny that it was really the one she had purchased and presented; yet I felt convinced that what she had told me was untrue, and that those very initials had been placed upon it by her order.

Again, had she not spoken of its owner in the past tense? This, in itself, was a very suspicious circumstance, and led me to the belief that she was aware of his death. If he were dead, then certainly he would no longer be her friend.

Her sudden and abject amazement at seeing the pencil in my hand; her exclamation of surprise; her eagerness to examine it; all were facts which showed plainly that she knew that it remained no longer in his possession, and was yet dumbfounded to find it in my hand. Had she not also regarded me with evident suspicion? Perhaps, having identified her present, she suspected me of foul play?

The thought held me petrified. For aught I knew she might be well aware of that man's tragic end, and the discovery of part of his property in my possession was to her evidence that I had committed murder.

My position was certainly growing serious. I detected in the rather formal manner in which she took leave of me a disinclination to shake my hand. Perhaps she believed it to be the hand of the murderer. Indeed, my declaration that I had found that incriminating object was in itself sufficient to strengthen her suspicion if, as seemed quite probable, she

WILLIAM LE QUEUX

was aware of her friend's tragic end. Yet I had really found it. It was no lie. I had found it in his pocket, and taken it as a clue by which afterwards to identify him.

Now, if it were true that the man who had been struck dead at my side was actually Mabel's friend, then I was within measurable distance of elucidating the mystery of that fateful night and ascertaining the identity of the mysterious Edna, and also of that ruler of my destiny, who corresponded with me under the pseudonym of "Avel."

This thought caused me to revert to that hour when I had sat upon the seat in the Park, keeping a tryst with some person unknown. Seated in the corner of the railway-carriage I calmly reflected. More than a coincidence it seemed that at the moment my patience became exhausted, and I rose to leave the spot my mysterious correspondent had appointed for the meeting, I should have come face to face with the woman whose grace and beauty held me beneath their spell. For some purpose—what I knew not—I had been sent to that particular seat to wait. I had remained there in vain, smoking a dozen cigarettes, reading through my paper even to the advertisements, or impatiently watching every person who approached, yet the moment I rose I encountered the very person for whom I had for days past been in active search.

Had Mabel's presence there any connexion with the mysterious order which I had obeyed? Upon this point I was filled with indecision. First, what possible connecting link could there be between her natural movements and the letter from that unknown hand? As far as I could discern there was absolutely none, I tried to form theories, but failed. I knew that Mabel attended at the Royal Academy of Music, and what was more natural than that she should cross the Park on her way home? Her way did not lie along the path where I had kept such a watchful vigil, and had I not risen and passed towards Grosvenor Gate at that moment we should not have met. There, indeed, seemed no possible combination between the request I had received from my unknown correspondent and her presence there. In my wild imaginings I wondered whether she were actually the woman whom in my blindness I had known as Edna, but next instant flouted the idea.

The voice, the touch, the hand, all were different. Again, her personal appearance was not at all that of the woman described by West, the cabman who had driven me home after my strange adventures.

No; she could not be Edna.

As the train roared through the stifling tunnels City-wards, I strove to arrive at some decision. Puzzled and perplexed at the various phases presented by the enigma which ever grew more and more complicated, I found any decision an extremely difficult matter. I am not a man given to forming theories upon insufficient evidence, nor jumping to immature conclusions, therefore I calmly and carefully considered each fact in its sequence as related in this narrative. The absence of motives in several instances prevented any logical deduction. Nevertheless, I could not somehow prevent a suspicion arising within me that the appointment made by my anonymous correspondent had some remote connexion with my meeting with the woman who had so suddenly come into my life—a mere suspicion, it is true, but the fact that no one had appeared to keep the appointment strengthened it considerably.

Whenever I thought of Mabel, recollections of Channing's strange admonition arose within me. Why had he uttered that warning ere I had been acquainted with her a few hours? To say the least, it was extraordinary. And more especially so as he refused to give any explanation of his reasons.

The one dark spot in my life, now that I had recovered my sight, was the ever-present recollection of that midnight tragedy. Its remembrance held me appalled when I thought of it. And when I reflected upon my own culpability in not giving information to the police, and that in all probability this neglect of mine had allowed the assassin to escape scot free, I was beside myself with vexation and regret. My thoughts for ever tortured me, being rendered the more bitter by the reflection that I had placed myself in the power of one who had remained concealed, and whose identity was inviolable.

As I declared in the opening of the narrative, it seems almost incredible that in these end-of-the-century-days a man could find himself in such a plight, surrounded by mysterious enemies, and held in bondage by one unknown and unrevealed. Laboriously I tried to unravel the tangled skein of events and so extricate myself, but, tired with the overtask, I found that the mystery grew only more inscrutable.

The woman I loved—the woman to whom I had fondly hoped some day ere long to make the declaration of the secret of my heart—had discovered in my possession an object which might well be viewed as evidence of a foul and cowardly crime. I feared—indeed, I felt assured—that her sweet sympathy had, in an instant, been turned to hatred.

I loved her. I adored her with all the strength of my being, and I knew that without her my life, in the future must only be an aimless blank. In the sweetest natures there can be no completeness and consistency without moral energy, and that Mabel possessed it was plainly shown. In her confidences with me as we traversed the Park and Kensington Gardens she had shown, with the most perfect artfulness, that she had that instinctive unconscious address of her sex which always renders a woman doubly charming. Persons who unite great sensibility and lively fancy possess unconsciously the power of placing themselves in the position of another and imagining rather than perceiving what is in their hearts. A few women possess this faculty, but men never. It is not inconsistent with extreme simplicity of character, and quite distinct from that kind of art which is the result of natural acuteness and habits of observation—quick to perceive the foibles of others, and as quick to turn them to its own purpose; which is always conscious of itself, and if united with strong intellect, seldom perceptible to others.

In her chat with me she had no design formed or conclusion previously drawn, but her intuitive quickness of feeling, added to her imagination, caused her to half-confide in me her deep sorrow. Her compassionate disposition, her exceeding gentleness, which gave the prevailing tone to her character, her modesty, her tenderness, her grace, her almost ethereal refinement and delicacy, all showed a true poetic nature within, while her dark, fathomless eyes betrayed that energy of passion which gave her character its concentrated power.

Was it any wonder, even though she might have been betrayed into a momentary tergiversation, that I bowed down and worshipped her? She was my ideal; her personal beauty and the tender sweetness of her character were alike perfect. Therefore my love for her was a passion— that headlong vehemence, that fluttering and hope, fear and transport, that giddy intoxication of heart and sense which belongs to the novelty of true love which we feel once, and but once, in our lives.

Yet I was held perplexed and powerless by her unexpected and unacknowledged identification of that clue to the unknown dead.

XIV

A Revelation

Although many days passed, no word of apology came from my mysterious correspondent for not having kept the appointment. I watched every post for nearly a fortnight, and as I received no explanation, my suspicion regarding Mabel's connexion with the strange affair became, of course, strengthened.

With heart-sinking I had taken leave of her on the kerb in Kensington High Street on that well-remembered evening, feeling that the likelihood of our frequent meeting was very remote, especially now that she apparently held me in suspicion. In this case, however, I was mistaken, for within a week we met again quite accidentally in Bond Street, and, finding her disposed to accept my companionship, I accompanied her shopping, and spent an extremely pleasant afternoon. Her mother was rather unwell, she explained, and that accounted for her being alone.

She was dressed entirely in black, but with a quiet elegance that was surprising. I had never known before that day how smart and *chic* a woman could appear in a gown of almost funereal aspect. Her manner towards me retained nothing of its previous suspicion; she was bright and merry, without that cloud of unhappiness that had so strangely overshadowed her on the last occasion we had been together. She possessed a clever wit, and gossiped and joked amusingly as we went from shop to shop, ordering fruit for dessert, and flowers for table-decoration. That her mother was wealthy appeared certain from the extravagant prices which she gave for fruits out of season and choice hothouse flowers. She bought the best she could procure, and seemed utterly regardless of expense.

I remarked how dear were some grapes which she had ordered, but she only smiled and gave her shoulders a little shrug.

This recklessness was not done to impress me, for I was quick to detect that the shopkeepers knew her as a good customer, and brought forward their most expensive wares as a matter of course.

Although at first she declined my invitation, as though she considered it a breach of the *convenances*, I at length persuaded her to take some tea with me at Blanchard's, and we continued our gossip as we sat together at one of the little tables surrounded by other ladies out shopping with their male encumbrances.

I had, rather unwisely, perhaps, passed a critical remark regarding a lady who had entered in an unusually striking toilette, in which she looked very hot and extremely uncomfortable, and laughing at what I had said, she replied—

"You are certainly right. We women always overweigh ourselves in our garments, to say nothing of other and more fatiguing things. Half of life's little worries accrue from our clothes. From tight collar to tight shoe, and not forgetting a needlessly befeathered hat, we take unto ourselves burdens that we should be much happier without."

"I agree entirely," I said, smiling at her philosophy. "Some blatant crank bent on self-advertisement might do worse than found an Anti-ornamental Dress League. Just think how much of life's trials would at once slip off a man if he wore neither collar nor tie—especially the dress-tie!"

"And off a woman, if she wore neither belt, gloves, nor neck arrangement!"

"Exactly. It would be actually making us a present for life of nearly an hour a day. That would be seven hours a week, or nearly a fortnight a year," I said. "It's worth consideration."

"Do you remember the derision heaped upon that time-saving arrangement of our ancestors, the elastic-side boot?" she observed, with a merry smile. "But just fancy the trouble they must have saved in lacing and buttoning! Sewing on shoe-buttons ought always to be done by criminals condemned to hard labour. Button-sewing tries the conscientiousness and thoroughness of the work more than anything else, and I'm certain oakum-picking can't be worse. It also tries the quality of the thread more than anything else; and as to cottons, well, it treats them as Samson did the withs."

The carriage met her outside the Stores in the Haymarket at five o'clock, and before she took leave of me she mischievously asked—

"Well, and how do you find me when I wear my mask?"

"Charming," I responded with enthusiasm. "Mask or no mask, you are always the same to me, the most charming friend I have ever had."

"No, no," she laughed. "It isn't good form to flatter. Good-bye."

And she stretched forth her small hand, which I pressed warmly, with deep regret at parting. A moment later the footman in his brown livery assisted her into the carriage. Then she smiled merrily, and bowed as I raised my hat, and she was borne away westward in the stream of fine equipages, hers the smartest of them all.

A week later, having seen nothing further of her, I wrote and received a prompt response. Then in the happy autumn days that followed we contrived to meet often, and on each occasion I grew deeper and deeper in love with her. Since that evening when we had stood together beneath the street lamp in Kensington, she had made no mention of the pencil-case or of its owner. Indeed, it seemed that her sudden identification of it had betrayed her into acknowledging that its owner had been her lover, and that now she was trying to do all she could to remove any suspicion from my mind.

Nevertheless, the remembrance of that crime and of all the events of that midnight adventure was ever within my mind, and I had long ago determined to make its elucidation the chief object of my life. I had placed myself beneath the thrall of some person unknown, and meant to extricate myself and become again a free agent at all costs.

On several occasions I had seen the cabman West on the rank at Hyde Park Corner, but although he had constantly kept his eyes open in search of Edna, his efforts had all been in vain. I had seen also the old cab-driver who bore the nickname "Doughy," but it turned out that it had not been his cab which my mysterious protectress had taken after parting from me. One point, however, I settled satisfactorily. On one of our walks together I contrived that, the man West should see Mabel, but he afterwards declared that the woman of whom he was in search did not in the least resemble her. Therefore, it was certain that Mabel and Edna were not, as I had once vaguely suspected, one and the same person.

Sometimes I would meet my idol after her studies at the Royal Academy of Music, and accompany her across the park; at others we would stroll together in the unfrequented part of Kensington Gardens, or I would walk with her shopping and carry her parcels, all our meetings being, of course, clandestine ones.

One morning in the middle of November I was overfed at receiving an invitation from Mrs. Anson to dine at The Boltons, and a couple of days later the sum of my happiness was rendered complete by finding myself seated beside Mabel in her own home.

The house possessed an air of magnificence and luxury which I scarcely expected. It was furnished with great elegance and taste, while the servants were of an even more superior character than the house itself. Among the homes of my many friends in the West End this was certainly the most luxurious, for money seemed to have been literally squandered upon its appointments, and yet withal there was nothing whatever garish nor any trace of a plebeian taste. There was a combined richness and quietness about the whole place which impressed one with an air of severity, while the footman who ushered me in was tall, almost a giant in stature, and solemn as a funeral mute.

Mrs. Anson rose and greeted me pleasantly, while Mabel, in a pretty gown of coral-pink, also shook my hand and raised her fine dark eyes to mine with a glance of pleasure and triumph. It was, no doubt, due to her that I had been bidden there as guest. A red-headed, ugly-faced man named Hickman, and a thin, angular, irritating woman, introduced to me as Miss Wells, were my only fellow-guests. The man regarded me with some suspicion as I entered, and from the first I took a violent dislike to him. It may have been his forbidding personal appearance which caused my distrust. Now that I reflect, I think it was. His face was bloated and deeply furrowed, his eyes large, his lips thick and flabby, his reddish beard was ill-trimmed and scanty. He was thick-necked; his face was further disfigured by a curious dark-blue scar upon the left jaw, and I could not help remarking within myself, that if some faces resembled those of animals, his was closely allied to that of a savage bulldog. Indeed, I had never before seen such an eminently ugly face as his.

Yet he spoke with the air and perfect manner of a gentleman. He bowed with refined dignity as I was introduced, although I thought his smile seemed supercilious, while I was almost certain that he exchanged a curious, contemptuous look with Mabel, who stood behind me.

Was he aware of our little exchanges of confidences? Had he secretly watched us in our walks along the leafy byways of Kensington Gardens, and detected that I loved her? It seemed very much as though he had, and that he had endeavoured to disparage me in her eyes.

At Mrs. Anson's invitation, I took Mabel in to dinner, and sat next her, while opposite us sat the dog-faced man with the irritating spinster. The latter was a fitting companion for him, bony of countenance, her back straight as a board, her age uncertain, and her voice loud, high-pitched, and rasping. She wore a number of bangles on her left wrist; one of them had pigs and elephants hanging on it, with hearts, crosses, bells, and framed and glazed shamrock leaves mixed in. That would not have mattered much had she not been eating, but as dinner progressed the room grew a trifle warm, and she unfortunately had a fan as well as those distressing bangles, which fan she rhythmically waved to and fro, playing the orchestra softly when fanning herself, or loudly as she plied her knife and fork "click-clack, jingle-jingle, tinkle-tinkle, click-clack!" until the eternal music of those pigs, elephants, crosses, hearts and bells prevented anything beyond a jerky conversation. She turned and twisted and toyed with her *menu*, tinkling and jingling the whole time like a coral consoler or an infant's rattle. Little wonder, I thought, that she remained a spinster. With such an irritating person to head his household, the unfortunate husband would be a candidate for Colney Hatch within a month. Yet she was evidently a very welcome guest at Mrs. Anson's table, for my hostess addressed her as "dear," and seemed to consider whatever positive opinion she expressed as entirely beyond dispute.

I liked Mrs. Anson. Although of that extremely frigid type of mother, very formal and unbending, observing all the rules of society to the letter, and practically making her life a burden by the conventionalities, she possessed, nevertheless, a warm-hearted affection for her child, and seemed constantly solicitous of her welfare. She spoke with the very faintest accent with her "r's," and I had, on the first evening we had met at the colonel's, wondered whether she were of Scotch, or perhaps foreign, extraction. The general conversation in the interval of the Irritating Woman's orchestra turned upon foreign travel, and incidentally, in answer to an ingenious question I put to her, she told me that her father had been German, but that she had nearly all her life lived in England.

The Irritating Woman spoke of going to the Riviera in December, whereupon Mabel remarked—

"I hope mother will go too. I'm trying to persuade her. London is so dull and miserable in winter compared with Cannes or Nice."

"You know the Riviera well, I suppose?" I inquired of her.

"Oh, very well," she responded. "Mother and I have spent four winters in the south. There's no place in Europe in winter like the Cote d'Azur—as the French call it."

"I much prefer the Italian Riviera," chimed Miss Wells's high-pitched voice. She made it a point of honour to differ with everybody. "At Bordighera, Ospedaletti, San Remo, and Alassio you have much better air, the same warmth, and at about half the price. The hotels in

Nice and Cannes are simply ruinous." Then, turning to Mrs. Anson, she added, "You know, dear, what you said last year."

"We go to the Grand, at Nice, always," answered Mrs. Anson. "It is dear, certainly, but not exaggeratedly so in comparison with the other large hotels."

"There seems of late to have been a gradual rise in prices all along the Riviera," remarked Hickman. "I've experienced it personally. Ten or twelve years ago lived in Nice for the season for about half what it costs me now."

"That exactly bears out my argument," exclaimed the Irritating Woman, in triumph. "The fact is that the French Riviera has become far too dear, and English people are, fortunately for themselves, beginning to see that by continuing their journey an extra twenty miles beyond Nice they can obtain just as good accommodation, live better, breathe purer air, and not be eternally worried by those gaudy tinsel-shows called Carnivals, or insane attempts at hilarity miscalled Battles of Flowers."

"Oh, come, Miss Wells," protested Mabel, "surely you won't condemn the Battles of Flowers at Nice! Why, they're acknowledged to be amongst the most picturesque spectacles in the world!"

"I consider, my dear, that they are mere rubbishy ruses on the part of the Nicois to cause people to buy their flowers and throw them into the roadway. It's only a trick to improve their trade."

We all laughed.

"And the Carnival?" inquired Hickman, much amused.

"Carnival!" she snorted. "A disgraceful exhibition of a town's lawlessness. A miserable pageant got up merely to attract the unsuspecting foreigner into the web spread for him by extortionate hotel-keepers. All the so-called fun is performed by paid mountebanks; the cars are not only inartistic, but there is always something extremely offensive in their character, while the orgies which take place at the masked balls at the Casino are absolutely disgraceful. The whole thing is artificial, and deserves no support at all from winter visitors."

Mrs. Anson, for once, did not agree with this sweeping condemnation, while Mabel declared that she always enjoyed the fun of the battles of flowers and paper confetti, although she admitted that she had never had the courage to go out on those days when the pellets of lime, or "harp confetti," are permitted. Both Hickman and myself supported Mabel in defence of the annual fetes at Nice as being unique in all the world.

But the Irritating Woman was not to be convinced that her opinions were either ill-formed or in the least distorted. She had never been present at a Carnival ball, she admitted, but it had been described to her by two estimable ladies who had, and that was, for her, sufficient. They were a pair of pious souls, and would, of course, never exaggerate to the length of a lie.

Dinner over, the ladies retired, and Hickman and myself were left to smoke and gossip. He was certainly a very ugly man, and at times asserted an overbearing superiority in conversation; but having watched him very closely, I at length arrived at the conclusion that this was his natural manner, and was not intended to be offensive. Indeed, ever since that first moment when I had entered and been introduced, he had shown himself to be very pleasant and affable towards me.

"Poor Miss Wells!" he laughed, after the door had closed. "She's so infernally positive about everything. It would be as good as an entertainment to induce her to expound her views upon religious matters."

"Any argument seems utterly useless," I remarked.

"Do you know Nice well?" he inquired, after reflecting a moment.

"I've spent three winters there," I answered.

"And at Monte Carlo, I suppose?"

"Yes, of course," I responded, laughing. "I suppose scarcely any man goes to Nice without going over to Monty and risking a few louis."

"Were you lucky?"

"So, so. One season I won five thousand francs. In fact, I've never lost on the whole season. I've always left the Riviera with some of the bank's money."

"Then you can heartily congratulate yourself," he said, "I'm the reverse. I generally lose. Do you believe in any system at roulette?"

"No; they are all frauds," I answered promptly. "Except one," he interposed. "There's one based on the law of averages, which must turn up in your favour if you're only patient enough. The reason why it is so difficult is because it's such a long and tedious affair."

"Explain it," I urged, for a new system that was infallible was, to me, of greatest interest. I had, in the days before my blindness, made a study of the chances at roulette, and had played carefully upon principles which had, to me, appeared most natural. The result had been that with care I had won—not much, it was true—but it was better than leaving one's money to swell the company's dividends.

"The system," he said, tossing off his glass of curacoa at one gulp, "is not at all a complicated one. If you study the permanences of any table—you can get them from the *Gazette Rose*—you'll find that each day the largest number of times either colour comes up in succession is nine. Now, all you have to do is to go to a table at the opening of the play, and taking one colour, red or black it makes no difference, stake upon it, and allow your money to accumulate until it is swept away. If the colour you stake upon comes up eight times in succession, and you have originally staked twenty francs, your gains lying on the table will amount to two thousand five hundred and sixty francs. Even then, don't touch it. The colour must, in the law of averages, come up nine times in succession each day, taking the week through. If it comes up, you'll win five thousand and twenty francs for the louis you staked, and then at once leave the table, for it will not come up nine times again that day. Of course, this may occur almost at the opening of the play, or not until the table is near closing, therefore it requires great patience and constant attendance. To-day it may not come up nine times, but it will probably come up nine times on two occasions to-morrow, and so the average always rights itself."

His theory was certainly a novel one, and impressed me. There might, I thought, be something in it. He had never had patience to try it, he admitted, but he had gone through a whole year's "permanences," and found that only on three or four occasions had it failed.

For half an hour or so he sat lucidly explaining the results of his studies of the game with the air of a practised gambler. In these I became at once interested—as every man is who believes he has found the secret of how to get the right side of the bank; but we were at length compelled to put down our cigars, and he led the way into the drawing-room, where the ladies awaited us.

The room was a large, handsome one, elegantly furnished, and lit by two great lamps, which shed a soft, subdued light from beneath their huge shades of silk and lace. Mabel was sitting at the open grand piano, the shaded candlelight causing the beautiful diamond star in the coils of her dark-brown hair to flash with a dazzling iridescence, and as I entered she turned and gave me a sweet smile of welcome.

A second time I glanced around that spacious apartment, then next instant stood breathless—transfixed.

I could not believe my own eyes. It seemed absolutely incredible. Yet the truth was beyond all doubt.

In the disposition of the furniture, and in the general appointments of that handsome salon, the home of the woman I so dearly loved, I recognised the very room which I had once explored with my keen sense of touch—the room in which had been committed that ghastly, mysterious, midnight crime!

XV

What I Saw

"How you men gossip!" Mabel exclaimed, tingling upon the piano-stool, and laughing merrily.

"I wasn't aware that we had been very long," I answered, sinking into a low armchair near her. "If so, I'm sure I apologise. The fact is, that Mr. Hickman was explaining a new system of how to break the bank at Monte Carlo."

"Oh, Mr. Hickman!" she cried, turning at once to him. "Do explain it, and I'll try it when we go to the Riviera."

"Mabel, my dear," exclaimed her mother, scandalised, "you'll do nothing of the kind. You know I don't approve of gambling."

"Oh, I think it's awfully good fun," her daughter declared.

"If you win," I added.

"Of course," she added; then, turning again to Hickman, she induced him to explain his new and infallible system just as he had explained it to me.

The trend of the conversation was, however, lost to me. My ears were closed to all sound, and now that I reflect I am surprised that I succeeded in retaining my self-possession. I know I sat there rigid, as one held motionless in terror; I only replied in monosyllables to any remark addressed to me, and I knew instinctively that the colour had left my countenance. The discovery was as bewildering as it was unexpected.

Every detail of that handsome room was exactly as I had pictured it. The blind, with their keen sense of touch, are quick to form mental impressions of places and things, and the general character of this apartment I had riveted upon my mind with the fidelity of a photograph.

The furniture was of gilt, just as I had detected from its smoothness, and covered with a rich brocade in wide stripes of art green and dull red-brown—an extremely handsome pattern; the carpet was dark, with a pile so thick that one's feet fell noiselessly; the three long windows, covered by heavy curtains of brocade to match the furniture, reached from the high-painted ceiling to the ground, exactly as I had found them in my blind gropings. About the room were two or three tables with glass tops, in trays beneath which were collections of choice *bric-a-brac*, including some wonderful Chinese carvings in ivory, while before the fireplace was spread the great tiger-skin, with paws and head preserved, which I so well remembered.

I sat there speechless, breathless. Not a single detail was there wanting. Never before, in all my life, had amazement held me so absolutely dumbfounded.

Close to where I saw was a spacious couch, over the centre of which was thrown an antimacassar of silken crochet-work. It was covered with the same brocade as the rest of the furniture, and I stretched forth my hand, with feigned carelessness and touched it. Its contact was the same, its shape exact; its position in the room identical.

Upon that very couch I had reclined while the foul tragedy had been enacted in that room. My head swam; I closed my eyes. The great gilt clock, with its pendulum representing the figure of a girl swinging beneath the trees, standing on the mantelshelf, ticked out low and musically, just as it had done on that fateful night. In an instant, as I sat with head turned from my companions and my eyes shut, the whole of that tragic scene was re-enacted. I heard the crash, the woman's scream, the awe-stricken exclamation that followed in the inner room. I heard, too, the low swish of a woman's skirts, the heavy blow struck by an assassin's hand, and in horror felt the warm life-blood of the unknown victim as it trickled upon my hand.

Mabel suddenly ran her white fingers over the keys, and the music brought me back to a realisation of my true position. I had at length discovered the actual house in which the mysterious tragedy had been enacted, and it became impressed upon me that by the exercise of greatest care I might further be enabled to prosecute secret investigations to a successful issue, and at length solve the enigma.

My eyes fixed themselves upon the couch. It was the very spot where I had rested, sightless, helpless, while those strange events had taken place about me. Was it any wonder that I became filled with apprehensions, or that I sat there petrified as one turned to stone?

The square, dark-green antimacassar had been placed in the exact centre of the couch, and sewed down in order to keep it in its place. Where I was sitting was fortunately in the shadow, and when Mabel commenced playing I rose—unsteadily I think—and reseated myself upon the couch, as being more comfortable. Then, while the woman who held me entranced played a selection from the "Trovatore," I, unnoticed by the others, succeeded in breaking the stitches which tacked the antimacassar to the brocade. The feat was a difficult one, for one does not care to be detected tearing the furniture of one's hostess. Nevertheless, after ten minutes or so I succeeded in loosening it, and then, as if by the natural movement of my body, commenced to work aside.

The music ceased, and even though all my attention was now centred upon my investigations, I congratulated Mabel upon her accurate execution. Hickman was standing beside her, and together they began to search for some piece he had requested her to play, while Miss Wells, with her hearts and elephants jingling, turned to me and commenced to talk. By this I was, of course, interrupted; nevertheless, some ten minutes later, I rose, and naturally turned back to straighten the rumpled antimacassar. In doing so I managed to lift it and glance beneath.

In an instant the truth was plain. Concealed beneath that square of green crochet-work was a large dark-brown stain upon the brocade. It was the mark of the life-blood of that thin, well-dressed, unknown victim, who had, in an instant, been struck to the heart!

The shock at its discovery caused me to start, but next instant I smoothed out the antimacassar into its former place without attracting any attention, and passed across the room with the motive of inspecting an object which I well remembered discovering when I had made my blind search. Upon a pedestal of black marble stood an exquisite little statuette of a Neapolitan dancing-woman, undoubtedly the work of some Italian master. Without pausing to examine it, I took in its every detail as I passed. It was exactly as I had felt it, and in the self-same spot as on that fatal night.

Beside the couch, as I turned again to look, I saw that a large skin rug had been thrown down. Without doubt it had been placed there to conceal the ugly stain of blood upon the carpet.

And yet there, on the scene of one of the foulest and most cowardly assassinations, we were actually spending the evening quietly, as became a respectable household. The thing seemed absolutely incredible. A dozen times I endeavoured to persuade myself that the whole discovery was but a chimera, arising from my disordered imagination. Nevertheless, it was impossible to disguise from myself the fact that in every detail the truth was borne out. In that very room the unknown man had been struck dead. The marks of his blood still remained as evidence of the truth.

I saw that beside the high lamps at that moment in use, there was a magnificent candelabra suspended from the ceiling, and in this were electric lamps. Then, at the door, I noticed the switch, and knew that it was the same which I had heard turned off by the assassin before leaving the house.

At the end of the room, too, were the folding doors, now concealed by curtains. It was through those very doors that Edna, my mysterious protectress, had passed and repassed to that inner room whence had come the sound of champagne being uncorked and the woman's piercing scream.

Mabel leaned over and spoke to me, whereupon I sank again into the chair I had previously occupied. She began to chat, but although her beautiful eyes held me fixed, and her face seemed more handsome than any I had ever seen, the diamonds in her hair dazzled my eyes, and I fear that my responses were scarcely intelligible.

"You are not quite yourself to-night, I think," she remarked at last, rising from the piano, and taking the low chair that I drew up for her. "Are you unwell?"

"Why?" I asked, laughing.

"Because you look rather pale. What's the matter?"

"Nothing," I answered, as carelessly as I could. "A slight headache. But it has passed now."

My eyes wandered to those curtains of green plush. How I longed to enter that room beyond!

At that moment she took out her handkerchief. Even that action added to the completion of the mental picture I had formed. Her tiny square of lawn and lace exhaled a sweet odour. It was that of *peau d'Espagne*, the same subtle perfume used by the mysterious Edna! It filled my nostrils until I seemed intoxicated by its fragrance combined with her beauty.

Her dress was discreetly *decollete*, and as she sat chatting to me with that bright vivaciousness which was so charming, her white neck slowly heaved and fell. She had, it seemed, been striving all the evening to get a tete-a-tete chat with me, but the chatter of that dreadful Irritating Woman and the requests made by Hickman had prevented her.

As she gossiped with me, now and then waving her big feather fan, she conveyed to my mind an impression of extreme simplicity in the midst of the most wonderful complexity. She seemed to take the peculiar traits from many characters, and so mingle them that, like the combination of hues in a sunbeam, the effect was as one to the eye. I had studied her carefully each time we had met, and had found that she had something of the romantic enthusiasm of a Juliet, of the truth and constancy of a Helen, of the dignified purity of an Isabel, of the tender sweetness of a Viola, of the self-possession and intellect of a Portia—combined together so equally and so harmoniously that I could scarcely say that one quality predominated over the other. Her dignity was imposing, and stood rather upon the defensive; her submission, though unbounded, was not passive, and thus she stood wholly distinct in her sweetness from any woman I had ever met.

The following day was one on which she was due to take her music-lesson, and I inquired whether I might, as usual, meet her and escort her across the Park.

"You are really very kind," she responded; "but I fear I take up far too much of your time."

"Not at all," I hastened to assure her. "I always enjoy our walks together."

She smiled, but a moment later said—

"I fear that I shall be prevented from going to Hanover Square to-morrow, as I shall be making calls with mother. We've been neglecting to call of late, and have such a host to make."

"Then I shan't see you at all to-morrow?" I said in deep disappointment.

"No, I fear not," she answered. "As a matter of fact, my movements for the next few days are rather uncertain."

"But you'll write and tell me when you are free?" I urged earnestly.

"If you wish," she responded, smiling sweetly. Apparently she was in no wise averse to my companionship, a fact which had become to me more apparent now that she had induced her mother to invite me to their table.

I endeavoured to extract from her some appointment, but she only whispered—

"Remember that our meetings are clandestine. Don't let them overhear us. Let's change the subject." And then she began to discuss several of the latest novels.

She had apparently a wide knowledge of French fiction, for she explained how a friend of hers, an old schoolfellow, who had married a French baron and lived in Paris, sent her regularly all the notable novels. Of English fiction, too, she was evidently a constant reader, for she told me much about recent novels that I was unaware of, and criticised style in a manner which betrayed a deep knowledge of her subject.

"One would almost think you were a lady novelist, or a book-reviewer," I remarked, in response to a sweeping condemnation which she made regarding the style of a much-belauded writer.

"Well, personally, I like books with some grit in them," she declared. "I can't stand either the so-called problem novel, or a story interlarded with dialect. If any one wants nasty problems, let them spend a few shillings in the works of certain French writers, who turn out books on the most unwholesome themes they can imagine, and fondly believe themselves realists. We don't want these *queue-de-siecle* works in England. Let us stick to the old-fashioned story of love, adventure, or romance. English writers are now beginning to see the mistake they once made in trying to follow the French style, and are turning to the real legitimate novel of action—the one that interests and grips from the first page to the last."

She spoke sensibly, and I expressed my entire accord with her opinion. But this discussion was only in order to hide our exchange of confidences uttered in an undertone while Hickman and the two ladies were chatting at the further end of the room.

All the time I was longing to get a sight of the interior of the adjoining apartment, the room whence had burst forth that woman's agonised cry in the stillness of the night. I racked my brain to find some means of entering there, but could devise none. A guest can hardly wander over his hostess's house on the first occasion he receives an invitation. Besides, to betray any interest in the house might, I reflected, arouse some suspicion. To be successful in these inquiries would necessitate the most extreme caution.

The fragrant odour of *peau d'Espagne* exhaled by her chiffons seemed to hold me powerless.

The gilt clock with its swinging girl had already struck eleven on its silver bell, and been re-echoed by another clock in the hall playing the Westminster chimes, when suddenly Mrs. Anson, with a book in her hand, looked across to her daughter, saying—

"Mabel, dear, I've left my glasses on the table in the library. Will you kindly fetch them for me?"

In an instant I saw my chance, and, jumping to my feet, offered to obtain them. At first she objected, but finding me determined, said—

"The library is the next room, there. You'll find them on the writing-table. Mother always leaves them there. It's really too bad to thus make a servant of you. I'll ring for Arnold."

"No, no," I protested, and at once went eagerly in search of them.

XVI

The Inner Room

The adjoining room was, I found, in the front part of the house—a rather small one, lined on one side with books, but furnished more as a boudoir than a library, for there were several easy-chairs, a work-table, and a piano in a corner. At this instrument the mysterious player had on that night sat executing Chopin's "Andante-Spinato" the moment before it became interrupted by some tragic and unexpected spectacle. I glanced around and noted that the furniture and carpet were worn and faded, that the books were dusty and evidently unused, and that the whole place presented an air of neglect, and had nothing whatever in keeping with the gorgeousness of the other handsome apartments.

The glasses were, as Mrs. Anson had said, lying beside the blotting-pad upon a small rosewood writing-table. I took them up, and, having made a tour of inspection, was about to leave the place, when suddenly, on the top of some books upon a shelf close to the door, I espied a small volume.

The curious incident of the birthday book occurred to me; therefore I took down the little volume and found that it really was a birthday book. No name was inscribed on the title-page as owner, but there were many names scribbled therein. In swift eagerness I turned to the page of my own birthday—the 2nd of July. It was blank.

I stood pondering with the book still in my hand. The absence of my name there proved one or two things, either I had not signed a birthday book at all, or, if I had, it was not the one I had discovered. Now, there are frequently two birthday-books in one house, therefore I resolved, ere I gave the matter reflection, to prosecute my investigations further and ascertain whether there was not a second book.

With this object I made a second tour around the room, noting the position of every article of furniture. Some music lay scattered beside the piano, and, on turning it over, I found the actual copy of Chopin's "Andante" which had been played on the night of the tragedy. The cover had been half torn away, but, on examining it closely beneath the light, I detected plainly a small smear of blood upon it.

Truly the house was one of mystery. In that room several persons had drunk champagne on that memorable night when blind Fate led me thither; in that room a woman had, according to the man's shout of alarm, been foully done to death, although of this latter fact I was not altogether sure. At any rate, however, it was plain that some tragic event had previously taken place there, as well as in that room beyond where I had reclined blind and helpless. It was strange also that the apartment should remain neglected and undusted, as though the occupants entertained some dislike to it. But I had been absent long enough, and, returning to the drawing-room with the missing glasses, handed them to Mrs. Anson.

Hickman had, in my absence, crossed to Mabel, and was sitting beside her in earnest conversation, therefore I was compelled to seat myself with my hostess and the Irritating Woman and chat with them. But ere long I contrived again to reach the side of the woman whom I adored, and to again press her for an appointment.

"It is far better forme to write to you," she answered, beneath her breath. "As I've told you, we have so many calls to make and cards to leave."

"Your mother tells me that you have a box for the Prince of Wales's on Saturday night, and has asked me to join you," I said. Her eyes brightened, and I saw that she was delighted at the prospect. But she expressed a hope that I wouldn't be bored.

"Bored!" I echoed. "Why, I'm never bored when in your company. I fear that it's the other way about—that I bore you."

"Certainly not," she responded decisively. "I very soon contrive to give persons who are bores their *conge*. Mother accuses me of rudeness to them sometimes, but I assure you I really can't help being positively insulting. Has mother asked you to dine on Saturday?"

"Yes," I answered. "But shan't I see you before then?"

"No; I think it is very unlikely. We'll have a jolly evening on Saturday."

"But I enjoy immensely those walks across the Park," I blurted forth in desperation.

"And I also," she admitted with a sweet frankness. "But this week it is utterly impossible to make any arrangements."

Mention of the theatre afforded me an opportunity of putting to her a question upon which, during the past couple of hours, I had reflected deeply.

"You've, of course, been to the Exhibition at Earl's Court, living here in the immediate vicinity," I said.

"I've only been once," she answered. "Although we've had this house nearly two years, exhibitions don't appeal to me very much. I was there at night, and the gardens were prettily illuminated, I thought."

"Yes," I said. "With the exception of the gardens, there is far too much pasteboard scenic effect. I suppose you noticed that serrated line of mountains over which the eternal switchback runs? Those self-same mountains, repainted blue, grey, or purple, with tips of snow, have, within my personal knowledge, done duty as the Alps, the Pyrenees, the Rockies, and the Atlas, not counting half a dozen other notable ranges."

She laughed, slowly fanning herself the while.

By her reply I had obtained from her own lips a most important fact in the inquiry I intended now to prosecute, namely, that this house had been her home for nearly two years. Therefore it had been in Mrs. Anson's possession at the time of the tragedy.

Since the moment when I had first recognised that; room as the one in which I had been present on the night of the mysterious assassination, the possibility had more than once occurred to me that Mrs. Anson might have; unwittingly taken it ready furnished after the committal of the crime. Such, however, was not the fact. Mabel had asserted that for nearly two years she had lived, there.

Again, even as I sat there at her side, deep in admiration of her magnificent figure in that striking toilette of coral-pink, with its soft garniture of lace and chiffons, I could not help reflecting upon the curious fact that she should have recognised the dead man's pencil-case. And she had, by her silence, assented to my suggestion that he had been her lover. That little gold pencil-case that I had found in his pocket when he lay dead at that very spot where we were now sitting had been one of her love-gifts to him.

The mystery hourly grew more puzzling and bewildering. Yet so also each hour that I was at her side I fell deeper and deeper in love with her, longing always for opportunity to declare to her the secret of my heart, yet ever fearing to do so lest she should turn from me.

Our unexpected meeting at Grosvenor Gate, after I had received that letter from my anonymous correspondent, combined with the startling discovery that it was actually in her house that the mysterious tragedy had been enacted; that in that very room the smart, refined young man who had been her lover had fought so fiercely for life, and had yet been struck down so unerringly, formed an enigma inscrutable and perplexing.

The mystery, however, did not for one moment cause me to waver in my affection for her. I had grown to love her fondly and devotedly; to adore her as my idol, as the one who held my whole future in her hands, therefore whatever suspicion arose within my mind—and I admit that grave suspicion did arise on many occasions—I cast it aside and fell down to worship at the shrine of her incomparable beauty.

Miss Wells's carriage was announced at last, and the Irritating Woman, tinkling and jingling, rose with a wearied sigh and took her leave, expressing her thanks for "a most delightful evening, my dear."

Mabel, mischievous as a school-girl, pulled a grimace when the music of the bangles had faded in the hall outside, at which we laughed in merry chorus.

With Hickman I remained ten minutes or so longer, then rose, also declaring that it was time we left. The grave man-servant Arnold served us with whiskies and sodas in the dining-room, and, Mabel having helped me on with my covert-coat, we shook hands with our hostess and her daughter, and left in company.

The night was bright and starlit, and the air refreshing. Turning to the left after leaving the house, we came immediately to a road which gave entrance to that secluded oval called The Boltons. I looked at the name-plate, and saw it was named Gilston Road. It must have been at this corner that I had been knocked down by a passing cab when, on my first adventurous journey alone, I had wandered so far westward.

I turned to look back, and noticed that from the dining-room window of the house we had just left any occurrence at the corner in question could be distinctly seen. Edna had explained that she had witnessed my accident from that window, and in this particular had apparently told me the truth.

The remarkable and unexpected discoveries of that evening had produced a veritable tumult of thoughts within my brain, and as I walked with Hickman I took no note of his merry, irresponsible gossip, until he remarked—

"You're a bit preoccupied, I think. You're pondering over Mabel's good looks, I suppose?"

"No," I answered, starting at this remark. Then, to excuse myself, I added, "I was thinking of other things. I really beg your pardon."

"I was asking your opinion of Mabel. Don't you consider her extremely handsome?"

"Of course," I answered, trying to suppress my enthusiasm. "She's charming."

"A splendid pianist, too."

"Excellent."

"It has always been a wonder to me that she has never become engaged," he remarked. "A girl with her personal charms ought to make an excellent match."

"Has she never been engaged?" I inquired quickly, eager to learn the truth about her from this man, who was evidently an old friend of the family.

"Never actually engaged. There have been one or two little love-affairs, I've heard, but none of them was really serious."

"He'd be a lucky fellow who married her," I remarked, still striving to conceal the intense interest I felt.

"Lucky!" he echoed. "I should rather think so, in many ways. It is impossible for a girl of her beauty and nobility of character to go about without lots of fellows falling in love with her. Yet I happen to know that she holds them all aloof, without even a flirtation."

I smiled at this assertion of his, and congratulated myself that I was the only exception; for had she not expressed pleasure at my companionship on her walks? But recollecting her admission that the victim of the assassin's knife had been her lover, I returned to the subject, in order to learn further facts.

"Who were the men with whom she had the minor love-affairs—any one I know?" I inquired.

"I think not, because it all occurred before they returned to live in England," he answered.

"Then you knew them abroad?"

"Slightly. We met in a casual sort of way at Pau, on the Riviera, and elsewhere."

"Both mother and daughter are alike extremely pleasant," I said. "In high spirits Mrs. Anson is sometimes almost as juvenile as Mabel."

"Quite so," he laughed. "One would never believe that she's nearly sixty. She's as vivacious and merry as a woman half her age. I've myself been surprised at her sprightliness often and often."

Again and again I endeavoured to turn the conversation back to the identity of Mabel's former lover, but he either did not know or purposely refused to tell me. He spoke now and then with an intentional vagueness, as though his loyalty to the Ansons prevented him from betraying any confidences reposed in him as a friend of the family. Indeed, this cautiousness showed him to be a trustworthy man, and his character became thereby strengthened in my estimation. On first acquaintance I had instantly experienced a violent aversion to him, but now, on this walk together along the Fulham Road, I felt that we should probably end by becoming friends.

He walked with long strides and a swinging, easy gait that seemed almost military, while his air of careless merriment as he laughed and joked, smoking the choice cigar which the man had handed to him in the hall just before our departure, gave him the aspect of an easy-going man-about-town.

"I fully expect, my dear fellow," he laughed—"I fully expect that you'll be falling in love with the pretty Mabel if you're in her company very much."

"You're chaffing," I protested, echoing his laugh.

"Not at all," he asserted. "Only take care. Love-making with her is a dangerous pastime—devilish dangerous, I assure you."

"Dangerous to the man's heart—eh?"

"Yes," he responded in a vague tone, glancing at me curiously; "if you like to put it in that way."

We had passed from the Fulham Road into the King's Road, Chelsea, and at that moment he halted suddenly at the corner of a street of high, regularly built houses, most of which were in darkness, saying—"I live down here. Come in and have a final whisky and soda with me; then you can take a cab back to the Strand. There are cabs all night on the rank in Sloane Square."

"I fear it's too late," I protested, glancing at my watch, and finding it past one o'clock.

"No, no, my dear fellow, come along," he urged. "You'll want a drink before you get home;" and, thus persuaded, I accompanied him up the street to one of the high houses, each exactly similar to its neighbour, with a flight of hearthstoned steps leading up to its front door, and a deep, grimy basement protected by a few yards of iron railings.

In the hall, although the gas had been extinguished, there remained a small hand-lamp alight, evidently placed there for his use. This he took, and conducted me to a front room, upon what the landlady of such a residence would term her "drawing-room floor." The house smelled close and stuffy; the furniture of the sitting-room was covered with plush which had once been crimson, but which was now sadly worn and badly moth-eaten; the threadbare carpet had been perforated in many places by hot cigarette-ends carelessly thrown down, and there was a general air of disorder about the place which seemed incongruous with my friend's smart air and general demeanour. I believed him to be a gentleman, yet found that he lived in a not over-clean lodging. To the practical Londoner, whose fate it is to live in "diggings," apartments in the neighbourhood of the King's Road are notable as being both dear and dirty.

He threw off his overcoat, tossed his hat aside, and pulled up a long, comfortable wicker-chair for me. Then he opened the buffet, and took therefrom a bottle of whisky and a couple of sodas, with which he proceeded to mix the drinks, his cigar-stump still in his mouth, even though he talked all the time, recounting some amusing stories which caused me to laugh.

I could not quite make him out. The remarks he let fall while, over our coffee, we had discussed the chances at roulette, led me to the suspicion that he was a practised gambler, and here in his rooms I detected evidence that he was fond of sport, of betting, and of other games of hazard.

We had lit fresh cigars from his own box, and as he sat in his big armchair he lifted his glass to me merrily, expressing pleasure at our meeting.

"I hope," he added, "that we shall meet very often. But take my tip, my dear fellow, and don't fall in love with Mabel Anson."

Why he should emphasise this warning just as Channing had done struck me as very curious. It might be, of course, that he was in love with her himself, and regarded me as a possible rival. This, indeed, was the impression conveyed to me by his words, and it aroused within me a vague feeling of distrust. That quick sinister glance when I had been introduced still lingered in my memory.

"I can't think why you should so repeatedly warn me," I remarked, laughing with affected amusement. "It really isn't likely that I shall fall in love with her."

He made no response. He only puffed slowly at his cigar, and smiled cynically through the veil of smoke he created.

I replaced my cigar in my mouth—for my friend was evidently a connoisseur of Havanas, and this was an excellent one—but at that instant my tongue, as I twisted it in my mouth, came in contact with the cut end of the weed, and I felt pricked as if by some sharp point. Quickly I removed it and examined it closely, exclaiming—

"Do they wrap up needles in your cigars? Look!" And I passed it across to him, indicating where, protruding from the end, which I had chopped off with the cutter on my watchguard, was the tiny point of either a needle or a pin.

"Extraordinary!" he exclaimed, taking it from my hand and examining it carefully.

But ere a few moments had elapsed I felt a strange sensation creeping upon me; a curious chilliness ran down my spine, my tongue seemed swelling until it filled my mouth, and my brain felt aflame.

"God?" I cried, springing to my feet in alarm. "Why, I believe I'm poisoned!"

"Nonsense!" he laughed. His voice seemed to sound afar off, and I saw his dog's face slowly assume an expression of evil as he sat opposite, intently watching me.

A sudden dizziness seized me; a spasm of sharp pain shot through all my limbs from head to toe; my senses reeled, I could see nothing distinctly. The man Hickman's ugly visage seemed slowly to fade in a blurred, blood-red mist.

At that same instant my blood was frozen by terror, for I felt convinced that this abrasion of my tongue had been planned by my companion's devilish ingenuity, and that upon that needle-point had been placed some baneful substance, the action of which was rapid and certain. I saw it all, now that it was, alas! too late.

With a wild cry I stretched forth both hands to steady myself, but, staggering, only clutched the air.

Then a strange and utterly unaccountable thing happened to me—stranger than has ever happened to any other living man.

XVII

THE MARBLE HAND

I approach this and the following chapters of my secret personal history with feelings of amazement and of thankfulness that I should still be alive and able to write down the truth freely and without fear, for the events were certainly most remarkable and utterly mystifying.

In no man's history has there ever been such a strange, bewildering page as the one I am about to reveal to you.

Reader, as I have taken you into my confidence, so also I tell you confidentially that I myself, an ordinary man, would never have believed that in this life of ours such things were possible, had I not myself experienced them, and personally endured the frightful agony of mind which they entailed. But I am writing down in black and white upon these pages the solid unvarnished facts, fearless of contradiction, so that the whole of the strange truth shall be known, and hat she who is dearest to me on earth may be adjudged by the world with fairness and with justice. For that sole reason I have resolved to relate this romance of real life, otherwise it would ever remain in that crabbed writing in that small portfolio, or secret dossier as it is called, numbered, docketed, and reposing in the archives of the Ministry of the Interior of a certain European Power.

Well, I have written the truth here, so that all who read may judge.

Immediately after the slight abrasion of my tongue, caused by the scratch of the needle so cunningly concealed in the cigar, I must have lost all consciousness. Of that I have no doubt. The recollections I have are only the faintest ones, blurred and indistinct, like shadows in a dream. I remember shouting in alarm and fighting fiercely against the drowsiness and general debility which seemed to overcome me, but all was with little or no effect. The last I remember was the ugly face of Hickman glaring evilly into mine. His hideous grin seemed to render his dog's face the more repulsive, and his laugh of triumph sounded in my ears harsh and discordant, showing plainly that the spirit of murder was in his heart.

At the same instant that I had made a movement towards him, I seemed to have received a stunning blow upon the top of the skull, which so dulled my senses that I was powerless to combat the curious giddiness that seized me, and sank senseless upon the floor of that shabby room, helpless as a log.

The last thought that surged through my brain was the reflection that I was powerless in the hands of an enemy. My first estimate of this man Hickman had been correct, and I regretted that I did not allow my instinctive caution to overrule my desire to become on friendly terms with him. He had enticed me to that place with an evil purpose— possibly that I might share the same fate as did that young man on the fateful night at The Boltons.

The prick of an ordinary needle upon the tongue would never have created such an electrical effect upon me, therefore it was certain that the point had been smeared with some powerful drug or poison. The ingenuity with which the cigar had been prepared was shown by the fact that a needle placed within would, as the tobacco became moistened by the saliva, gradually work downward towards the tongue, while the heat at the further end of the needle would, of course, render liquid any coating placed upon it. Without doubt I had been the victim of a deeply-laid plot, prepared with a cunning that seemed almost beyond comprehension.

The blank in my mind, caused by my sudden unconsciousness, did not appear to me to be of very long duration. All I know is that I was utterly ignorant of every event that transpired about me, and knew nothing whatever of any of the incidents which afterwards took place in that dark, obscure house, or elsewhere. And yet they must have been of a character absolutely unheard of.

I have said that the period of my benighted senses did not appear to be prolonged. Indeed, now on reflection in the calmness of the present, I am inclined to put down the lapse of time during which, in my estimation, I was lost to all knowledge of things about me at two, or perhaps three, hours. Of course, it is difficult to fix time when we awaken after sleeping, except by the degree of light in the heavens. If it is still dark, it is always difficult to gauge the hour. So it was with me when, with a heavy, bruised feeling about the top of my skull, I slowly struggled back to a knowledge of the world.

My first thought as I opened my eyes was of Hickman. My second was a feeling of surprise that I had been unconscious so long, for while it was about two o'clock in the morning when my tongue had, been pricked by the concealed needle, and my adversary had dealt me a crushing blow upon my skull as I had rushed upon him, yet straight before my eyes the sun was shining full upon the carpet, and the particles of dust were dancing in its golden rays.

Surely, I thought, I could not have remained unconscious for nearly twelve hours.

The pain in my skull was excruciating. I put my hand to the wound, and when I withdrew it found blood upon it. I felt a huge bump, but the abrasion of the skin was, I discovered, only slight.

At first my brain was confused and puzzled, as though my dulled senses were wrapped in cotton wool. At a loss to account for the time that had elapsed, I lay upon the carpet just as I was, in vague, ignorant wonderment. My eyes, dazzled by the bright sunlight, pained me, and I closed them. Perhaps I dozed. Of that I am not quite sure. All I know is that when I opened my eyes again the pain in my head seemed better, and my senses seemed gradually to recognise, appreciate, and perceive.

I was lying on my side upon the carpet, and slowly, with a careful effort involuntarily made by the march of intellect, I gazed around me.

The place was unfamiliar—utterly unfamiliar. I wondered if I were actually dreaming. I felt my head, and again glanced at my hand. No. There was sufficient proof that my skull had been injured, and that I was lying alone in that room with the bar of sunlight slanting straight before my eyes.

Gradually, and not without considerable difficulty—for I was still half-dazed—I made out the objects about me, and became aware of my surroundings.

My eyes were amazed at every turn. Whereas Hickman's apartment was a dirty, shabby lodging-house sitting-room of that stereotyped kind so well known to Londoners, the place wherein I found myself was a rather large, handsomely furnished drawing-room, the two long windows of which opened out upon a wide lawn, with a park and a belt of high trees far beyond. From where I was I could see a wealth of roses, and across the lawn I saw the figure of a woman in a white summer blouse.

The carpet whereon I was stretched was soft and rich, the furniture was of ebony, with gilt ornamentations—I think French, of the Empire period—while close to me was a grand piano, and upon a chair beside it a woman's garden hat.

I looked at that hat critically. It belonged to a young woman, no doubt, for it was big and floppy, of soft yellow straw, with cherries, and had strings to tie beneath the chin. I pictured its owner as pretty and attractive.

About that room there were screens from Cairo, little inlaid coffee-tables from Algiers, quaint wood-carvings of the Madonna beneath glass shades, fashioned by the peasants of Central Russia, Italian statuary, and modern French paintings. The room seemed almost a museum of souvenirs of cosmopolitan travel. Whoever was its owner, he evidently knew the value of *bric-a-brac*, and had picked up his collection in cities far afield.

The door was closed, and over it hung a rich *portiere* of dark-blue plush edged with gold. The sculptured over-mantel, in white marble, was, I quickly detected, a replica of one I had seen and admired in the Bargello, in Florence. One object, however, aroused my wonder. It was lying on the floor straight before me, an object in white marble, the sculptured arm of a woman with the index-finger outstretched. The limb was of life-size proportions, and had apparently been broken off at the elbow.

I staggered unevenly to my feet, in order to further pursue my investigations, and then I saw, upon a pedestal close to me, the marble figure of a Phryne with its arm broken.

In the centre of that handsome apartment I stood and gazed wonderingly around. My transition from that bizarre sitting-room in Chelsea to this house, evidently in the country, had been effected in a manner beyond comprehension. My surprising surroundings caused my weakened brain to reel again. I was without hat or overcoat, and as I glanced down at my trousers they somehow did not seem to be the same that I had been wearing on the previous night.

Instinctively I felt that only by some extraordinary and mysterious means could I have been conveyed from that close-smelling lodging in Chelsea to this country mansion. The problem uppermost in my mind was the identity of the place where I had thus found myself on recovering my senses, and how I got there.

My eyes fell upon the push of an electric-bell. My position, lying there injured upon the carpet, demanded explanation, and without further hesitation I walked across and pressed the ivory button.

I heard no sound. The bell must have rung far away, and this gave me the idea that the house was a large one.

Intently I listened, and a few minutes later heard a footstep. The door opened, and an elderly man-servant, with grey whiskers, appeared in the entry asking—"Did you ring, sir?"

"Yes," I answered. "Will you kindly inform me where I am?"

He regarded me with a strange, puzzled expression, and then, in alarm, he rushed forward to me, crying—"Why, sir! You've hurt your head! Look! You're covered with blood!"

His grey face was pale, and for an instant he stood regarding me open-mouthed.

"Can't you answer my question?" I demanded hastily. "I know that I've injured my head. I didn't call you in order to learn that. I want to know where I am."

The man's countenance slowly assumed a terrified expression as he regarded me, and then, without further word, he flew from the room as fast as his legs could carry him. I heard him shouting like a lunatic, in some other part of the house, and stood utterly dumbfounded at his extraordinary behaviour. He had escaped from my presence as though he had seen an apparition.

A few minutes later, however, he returned, accompanied by a dark-haired, well-dressed man of about thirty, tall, rather good-looking, and apparently a gentleman. The instant the latter saw me he rushed forward, crying, in a voice of distress—

"Oh, my dear sir, whatever has happened?"

"My head," I explained. "It was that ugly-faced scoundrel Hickman. Where is he?"

"Hickman?" echoed the new-comer. "Hickman? Who's he?"

"Oh, it's all very well for you to pretend to know nothing about it," I cried angrily. "But I tell you that as soon as I'm able I'll apply for a warrant for his arrest on a charge of attempted murder. Last night he tried to kill me."

"I don't understand you," the stranger responded. "I don't, of course, expect you to admit any complicity in the affair," I snapped. "You'd be a fool if you did. All I tell you is that an attempt has been made upon my life by a man to whom I was introduced as Hickman."

"Not in this room?"

I hesitated.

"No, not in this room," I admitted. "It was in a house at Chelsea."

The young man exchanged meaning glances with the man-servant.

"At Chelsea!" repeated the stranger. "In London?"

"In London."

"Well, that's very curious," he remarked. Then, turning to the servant, said—

"Gill, go and fetch Doctor Britten at once. Say nothing of this to any one in the house."

"Yes, sir," answered the servant, who instantly withdrew.

"I suppose you've sent for the doctor to bandage my head?" I remarked cynically. "I'm perfectly competent to do that if you'll kindly oblige me with a little warm water, a sponge, and some clean old linen."

"No, no," he urged. "Wait in patience until Britten comes. He'll be here in a moment. I saw him returning home only ten minutes ago."

"But how came I here?" I demanded.

He hesitated, regarding me with evident distrust, mingled with considerable alarm.

"I—I really don't know," he responded lamely.

"That's all nonsense," I cried, with more force than politeness. "I find myself here, in this room, wounded and weak through loss of blood, after having been half murdered, and then you have the cool impudence to deny all knowledge of how I came here. You're a liar—that's plain."

I had grown angry at this lame attempt of his to feign ignorance.

"You are extremely complimentary," he answered, colouring slightly.

"Well, perhaps you won't mind telling me the time. I find that that cunning scoundrel Hickman, not content with trying to poison me with a prepared cigar and striking me on the head in that cowardly way, has also robbed me of my watch and chain."

He glanced at his watch.

"It's half-past two," he answered abruptly.

"Half-past two! Then it happened more than twelve hours ago," I observed.

"I wish Britten would hurry," the young man remarked. "I don't like the look of that wound. It's such a very nasty place."

"Only a scalp-wound," I said lightly. "Properly bandaged, it will be all right in a few days. There's fortunately no fracture."

"Well, you're in a pretty mess, at any rate."

"And so would you be," I said, "if you had been entrapped as I've been."

His face seemed bloodless, as though the discovery of my presence there had caused him the utmost alarm. He fidgeted and glanced eagerly now and then towards the door.

At last I distinguished advancing footsteps, and there entered an elderly, dapper, white-bearded little man, whose general demeanour and buttoned frock-coat gave him the air of the medical practitioner. He held his silk hat in his hand, and as he placed it down I noticed that his stethoscope reposed cross-wise in the lining.

"My dear sir! My dear sir! What's this?" he began fussily. "Come, sit down;" and he drew me towards a chair, and seated himself upon the edge of another close to me.

"My head has been injured. Examine for yourself."

"Ah!" he exclaimed, first regarding me fixedly, and then rising and examining my head. "A nasty scalp-wound, I see." He felt it carefully with his fingers, causing me a sharp twinge of pain. "No fracture, no fracture. That's fortunate—very fortunate. It's not serious at all, I'm glad to tell you—nothing serious. How did it occur?"

"I was struck, that's all I remember," I answered, turning to him and looking into his face.

"With something sharp-pointed, evidently;" and he looked extremely puzzled.

"I don't know what it was."

"From what I can feel, I think you must have had a previous blow upon the same spot at some time or another. Do you remember it?"

"Not at all," I answered. "I once received a blow on the head by the kick of a horse, but it was at the side."

"Ah, perhaps this was a blow in infancy, and you don't recollect it."

Then, as he exchanged a strange look with the young man who stood eager and anxious at his side, his quick eyes suddenly fell upon the broken arm of the statue.

"Why, what's this?" he cried, a sudden light apparently dawning upon him. "Look here, there's blood and hair upon this marble finger. You've evidently struck your head against it in passing, and so violently as to break the marble. See!"

I looked, and there, sure enough upon the outstretched index-finger of the marble hand was a trace of blood, to which two or three hairs still clung.

"We've solved the mystery!" he cried. "I must dress your wound, and then, my dear sir, you must rest—rest. It will do your head good, you know."

"But I was struck down last night by a man named Hickman in his rooms at Chelsea. He attempted to murder me."

"Yes, yes," he said, as though intentionally humouring me. "We've heard all about that. But come with me upstairs and let me dress your wound at once. Gill," he added, turning to the servant, "get me some lukewarm water at once."

Then he took my arm and led me upstairs to a well-fitted dressing-room, where he fussily washed and bandaged my head, while I sat silent, dazed, and wondering.

XVIII

Mystery Inexplicable

B ritten was, I immediately detected, one of those men whose well-feigned air of fussy sympathy, whose unruffled good humour, and whose quick perception enabled him to gauge to a nicety his patient's character, and to thus ingratiate himself. By the younger people he was, no doubt, pronounced clever on account of his age and known experience, while old ladies—those whose very life depended upon regularly seeing the doctor—declared him to be "such a dear, kind man." Upon the family doctor's manner alone depends the extent of his popularity and the size of his practice. The most ignorant charlatan who ever held a diploma can acquire a wide practice if he is only shrewd enough to humour his patients, to take pains to feign the deepest interest in every case, and assume an outward show of superior knowledge. In medicine be the man ever so clever, if he has no tact with his patients his surgery bell will remain for ever silent.

Dr. Britten was a shrewd old fellow; a bit of a bungler, who made up for all defects by that constant good humour which people like in a medical man. "Don't worry, my dear sir; don't worry," he urged, when he had finished. "Rest well, and you'll be right again very soon."

"But the events of last night?" I said. "A man made a dastardly attempt upon my life, and I intend to secure his arrest."

"Yes, yes, I know," he answered, patting me on the shoulder with a familiarity curious when I reflected that I had never set eyes upon him till half an hour before. "But take my advice, and don't reflect upon it."

"If you know, then perhaps you'll kindly give me some explanation?" I said, resenting his manner. He was treating me as he would a child.

"I only know what you've told me," he responded. "It's a strange story, certainly. But don't you think that it is, greater part of it, imagination?"

"Imagination!" I cried, starting up angrily. "I tell you, Doctor Britten—or whatever your name is—that it is no imagination. The wound on my head is sufficient proof of that."

"The wound was inflicted by yourself," he answered calmly. "You accidentally ran against the statue."

"I don't believe it," I said, bluntly. "It's all a confounded conspiracy, and, moreover, you are staking your professional reputation by assisting in it."

He shrugged his shoulders and raised his grey eyebrows with an expression of regret.

"I have been called to you, my dear sir, because you have met with an accident," he said. "I have merely given you the best of my advice—namely, to remain quiet, and not trouble about anything that has passed. Your brain requires rest after the severe shock it has received."

"Doctor Britten," I said determinedly, "I quite understand the meaning of your vague words. You believe that I'm not quite right in my mind."

"No, no," he assured me quickly. "I did not say that. Pray do not misunderstand me. I merely advise rest and perfect quiet. Indeed, you would be far better in bed for a few days—far better."

"I know my own feelings best, thanks," I replied, for his manner, although it might impress nervous old ladies, aroused within me a strong resentment.

"Exactly. But surely you should, for your own sake, attend to the suggestions of your medical adviser?"

"You have formed wrong conclusions—entirely wrong conclusions," I laughed. "Is it likely that I shall take notice of anything you say when you believe that I'm not responsible for my actions?"

I had watched his face carefully, and I knew that, like the dark-faced young man and Gill, the servant, he believed my brain unbalanced.

"I assure you, my dear sir, you entirely misunderstand me," he protested. "I merely say—"

"Oh, enough!" I cried angrily, turning upon my heel and leaving the room abruptly. I was sick of the chattering old idiot, who evidently believed that I was not responsible for my actions.

Down the wide oak stairs I passed, and in the great hall, which seemed to run the whole length of the house, and was filled with stands of armour, tattered banners, and trophies of the chase, I encountered the pale-faced man who had sent for old Britten.

I was passing him by, intent upon exploring this strange house in which I found myself, when, approaching me, he said—

"Would you please come into the library for one moment?"

"The library?" I asked, looking at him, puzzled. "Where is it?"

He opened a door close by, and I followed him into a comfortable study, lined with books from floor to ceiling. In the centre was a large writing-table littered with papers, while close beside was another smaller table, very severe and business-like.

"Well?" I inquired. "What do you want?"

"This telegram has just arrived," he answered excitedly, unlocking a drawer in the smaller writing-table, and taking out a telegram, which he handed to me.

Puzzled, I took the flimsy paper and read the words written thereon, as follows:—

"We are to-day in receipt of following telegram from our Vancouver branch—'Inform Wilford Heaton that Charles Mawson, Dawson City, has struck it seven dollars to pan.' Bank of British North America, London."

Such a message was utterly unintelligible to me.

"Well?" I inquired, raising my eyes and looking at him, surprised. "I don't see why this Charles Mawson, whoever he is, need hasten to tell me that. What does it matter to me?"

"Matter? My dear sir? Matter?" he cried, staring at me, as though in wonder. "There must, I think, be something the matter with you."

"Well, perhaps you'll kindly explain what it means?" I said, "I have, I assure you, no idea."

"Why, it means," he said, his face betraying his intense excitement— "it means that Woodford's report is correct, that there is, after all, rich gold on the concession; in short, that, being owner of one of the most valuable placer concessions, you are a millionaire!"

"That's all very interesting," I remarked with a smile, while he stood staring at me in abject wonder.

"I fear," he said, "that you're not quite yourself to-day. The injury to your head has possibly affected you."

"No, it hasn't," I snapped quickly. "I'm quite as clear-headed as you are."

"Then I should have thought that to any man in his sane senses such a telegram as that would have been extremely gratifying," he observed.

"Now, tell me," I said; "do you know who I am?"

"I think I do. You are Mr. Wilford Heaton."

"And you tell me that I'm a millionaire?"

"I do, most certainly."

"Then, much as I regret to be compelled to say it, young man," I answered, "I am of opinion that you're a confounded liar."

"But Mawson has struck the gold seven dollars to the pan," he pointed out in protest.

"Well, what in the name of Fortune has it to do with me if he's struck it a thousand dollars to the handful?" I cried.

"I should be inclined to say it had a great deal to do with you as holder of the concession," he answered quite coolly.

"Oh, bother the concession," I said hastily. "I don't understand anything whatever about it, and, what's more, I don't want to be worried over any mining swindles." Then I added, sinking into the padded chair before the writing-table. "You seem to know all about me. Tell me, now—what's your name?"

"My name?" he echoed, staring at me blankly, as though utterly puzzled. "Well, I thought you knew it long ago. I'm Gedge—Reginald Gedge."

"And what are you, pray?"

"I'm your secretary."

"My secretary!" I echoed, gasping in amazement. Then I added, "Look here, you're trying to mislead me, all of you. I have no secretary—I've never had one. All this chatter about mines and concessions and such things is pure and simple rubbish."

"Very well," he answered with a slight sigh. "If you would have it so it must be. Britten has already said that you are somewhat confused after your accident."

"Britten be hanged!" I roared. "I'm no more confused than you are. All I want is a straightforward explanation of how I came here, in this house."

He smiled, pityingly I thought. That old medical idiot had apparently hinted to both the servant and this young prig, who declared himself my secretary, that I was not responsible for my actions; therefore, what could I expect?

"The explanation is one which I regret I cannot give you," he answered. "All I want is your instructions what to wire to Mawson."

"Oh, bother Mawson!" I cried angrily. "Wire him whatever you like, only don't mention his name again to me. I don't know him, and don't desire to make any acquaintance either with him or his confounded pans."

"I shall send him congratulations, and tell him to remain in Dawson City pending further instructions."

"He can remain there until the Day of Judgment, for all I care," I said, a remark which brought a smile to his pale features.

A brief silence fell between us. All this was absolutely bewildering. I had been struck down on the previous night in a street at Chelsea, to find myself next day in a country house, and to be coolly informed by a man who called himself my secretary that I was owner of a great gold concession and a millionaire. The whole thing seemed too utterly incredible.

I felt my head, and found it bandaged. There was no mistake about the reality of it all. It was no curious chimera of the imagination.

Before me upon the blotting-pad were some sheets of blank notepaper. I turned them over in idle curiosity, and found embossed upon them the address in bold, black characters: "Denbury Court, near Budleigh-Salterton."

"Is this place Denbury Court?" I inquired.

"Yes."

"And whose guest am I, pray?"

"You are no one's guest. This is your own house," was his amazing response.

I turned towards him determinedly, and in a hard voice said—

"I think, Mr. Gedge, that you've taken leave of your senses. I've never heard of this place before, and am certainly not its owner. Are you certain you are not confounding me with some one else—some one resembling me in personal appearance?"

"Absolutely certain," he replied. "Your name is Wilford Heaton, and I repeat that I am your confidential private secretary."

I shook my head.

"Well," he said quickly, "here is some further proof," and bending beside me he opened one of the drawers of the big writing-table, and took therefrom a number of blank memorandum forms, which he placed before me. In eagerness I read their printed heading. It was "From Wilford Heaton, 103A, Winchester House, Old Broad Street, London, E.C."

"Well, what are those used for?" I asked in wonder. "They are used at the City office," he answered, tossing them back into the drawer.

"And you tell me I am wealthy?" I said, with a cynical laugh.

"Your banker's pass-book should be sufficient proof of that," he answered; and taking the book from an iron safe let into the opposite wall, he opened it and placed it before me.

I glanced at the cover. Yes, there was no mistake. It was my own pass-book.

My eyes fell upon the balance, standing to my credit, and the largeness of the figures held me open-eyed in astonishment.

It was wealth beyond all my wildest dreams.

"And that is mine—absolutely mine?" I inquired, when at last I found tongue.

"Certainly," he replied, a moment later adding: "It is really very strange that I have to instruct you in your own private affairs."

"Why have I an office in the City?" I asked, for that point was puzzling.

"In order to carry on your business."

"What business?"

"That of financial agent."

I smiled at the absurdity of the idea. I had never been a thrifty man; in fact, I had never had occasion to trouble my head about finance, and, truth to tell, had always been, from a lad, a most arrant dunce at figures.

"I fear I'm a sorry financier," I remarked for want of something better to say.

"You are acknowledged to be one of the shrewdest and the soundest in the City of London," Gedge answered.

"Well," I remarked, closing the pass-book, securing the flap, and handing it back to him, "all I have to say is that this last hour that has passed has been absolutely replete with mystery. I can make nothing of all these things you tell me—absolutely nothing. I shall begin to doubt whether I'm actually myself very soon."

"It would be better to rest a little, if I might advise," he said, in a more deferential tone than before. "Britten suggested repose. That blow has upset you a little. To-morrow you'll be quite right again, I feel sure."

"I don't intend to rest until I've cleared up this mystery," I said determinedly, rising from the table.

At that moment, however, the door opened, and turning quickly, I was confronted by an angular, bony-faced, lantern-jawed woman, whose rouged and powdered face and juvenility of dress struck me as utterly ludicrous. She was fifty, if a day, and although her face was wrinkled and brown where the artificial complexion had worn off, she was nevertheless attired in a manner becoming a girl of twenty.

"Oh, my dear Wilford! Whatever has happened?" she cried in alarm, in a thin, unmusical voice, when she beheld the bandages around my head.

I looked at her in mingled surprise and amusement; she was so doll-like and ridiculous in her painted juvenility.

"Mr. Heaton accidentally struck his head against the statue in the drawing-room, madam," explained Gedge. "Doctor Britten has assured me that the injury is not at all serious. A little rest is all that is necessary."

"My dear Wilford! Oh, my dear Wilford! Why didn't you call me at once?"

"Well, madam," I answered, "that was scarcely possible, considering that I had not the honour of your acquaintance."

"What!" she wailed. "You—you can't really stand there and coolly tell me that you don't know me?"

"I certainly assert, madam, that I have absolutely no knowledge whatever of whom you may be," I said with some dignity.

"Is your brain so affected, then, that you actually fail to recognise me—Mary, your wife!"

"You!" I gasped, glaring at her, dumbfounded. "You, my wife! Impossible!"

XIX

My Unknown Wife's Story

"My dear Wilford!" exclaimed the thin-faced, angular woman. "I really think you must have taken leave of your senses."

"My dear madam," I cried excitedly, "I haven't the slightest notion of your name. To the best of my knowledge, I've never had the pleasure of meeting you before this moment. Yet you have the boldness to assert that you are my wife! The thing is absolutely preposterous!" I laughed cynically.

"You must be mad to talk like this!" the woman answered with some asperity.

"I tell you that I'm not mad, madam," I protested, "and further, I declare that I have never married."

"What rubbish you talk!" she said. "This accident to your head has evidently affected your intellect. You must rest, as Doctor Britten has ordered."

"The doddering old idiot thinks, like yourself, that I'm not quite responsible for my actions," I laughed. "Well, we shall see."

"If you were in your right senses you would never deny that I am your wife," answered the overdressed woman. "The thing's too absurd."

"My dear madam," I cried, growing angry, "your allegations are utterly ridiculous, to say the least. All this is either some confounded conspiracy, or else you mistake me for somebody else. I tell you that I am Wilford Heaton, of Essex Street, Strand, a bachelor who has neither thought nor inclination of marrying."

"And I tell you that you are Wilford Heaton, my husband, and owner of this house," she answered, her face growing redder with excitement.

The situation was certainly stranger than any other in which a man could possibly be placed. That it was no dream, but a stern reality, was entirely plain. I glanced around the comfortable library, and saw there evidences of wealth and refinement, while through the window beyond my gaze fell upon the wide park sloping away to a large lake glistening in the sunshine, and through the trees beyond could be seen a distant glimpse of the blue waters of the English Channel.

I stood utterly nonplussed by the startling declaration of this artificial-looking person, who aped youth so ridiculously, and yet spoke with such an air of confidence and determination.

"And you actually expect me to believe this absurd story of yours, that I am your husband, when only last night I dined at The Boltons, and was then a bachelor? Besides, madam," I added with a touch of sarcasm, for I confess that my anger was now thoroughly aroused, "I think the—well, the difference in our ages is sufficient to convince any one that—"

"No, no," she hastened to interrupt me, as though that point were very distasteful to her. "Age is entirely out of the question. Am I to understand that you distinctly deny having made me your wife?"

"I do, most decidedly," I laughed, for the very idea was really too ridiculous to entertain.

She exchanged a pitying look with Gedge, who stood at a little distance, watching in silence.

"Poor Wilford! poor Wilford?" she exclaimed in a tone of sympathy, and, addressing the man who called himself my secretary, said, "It seems quite true what the doctor has declared; the blow has upset the balance of his mind."

"Madam," I cried very determinedly, "you will oblige me by not adding further insult to your attempted imposture—for such sympathy is insulting to me."

She clasped her hands, turned her eyes upwards, and sighed in the manner of the elderly.

"You believe that I'm mad. Therefore you are trying to impose upon me!" I went on furiously. "But I tell you, my dear madam, that I am just as sane as yourself, and am fully prepared to prove that I am not your husband."

"Ask Mr. Gedge whether I speak the truth or not," she said, turning to the secretary.

"Certainly," answered the man addressed, looking straight into my face. "I have no hesitation whatever in bearing out Mrs. Heaton's statement."

"It's all humbug!" I cried, turning savagely upon him. "I don't know this woman from Adam!"

"Well," he laughed cynically, "you ought to know her pretty well, at any rate."

It was apparent from his tone that he had no very high opinion of her.

"I'm pleased to say that until this present moment we have been strangers," I said, for I was not in a humour to mince words.

"You are extremely complimentary, Wilford," she observed resentfully.

"It appears to me that compliments are entirely unnecessary in this affair," I said. "You are endeavouring to thrust yourself upon me as my wife, in order, I suppose, to achieve some object you have in view. But I tell you once and for all, madam, that any such attempt will be futile. To speak plainly, I don't know you, neither have I any desire to add you to my list of acquaintances."

"Well," she cried; "of all the stories I've ever heard, this is the most extraordinary!"

"I think, madam, I may say the same," I remarked coldly. "Your story is the wildest and most incredible that I've ever heard. Last night, as a bachelor, I dined with friends in Kensington, and left at a late hour, calling at a house in Chelsea on my way home to Essex Street. To-day I awake to be told that I am the owner of wealth beyond the dreams of avarice; master of this house—in Devonshire, I believe, isn't it; and your lawful husband. Now, if you think me capable of swallowing such a pack of palpable fictions as these, you must certainly consider me absolutely insane, for none but a madman would give credence to such a tissue of lies."

"Doctor Britten considers that your brain is unbalanced, because you do not know the truth," she said calmly. "I quite agree with him."

"He's a fool—a drivelling idiot," I cried, forgetting myself in the heat of the moment, and using an unwriteable word. Mention of that pottering old fossil's name was to me as a red rag to a bull. "I surely know who and what I am!" I cried.

"No, my dear Wilford, that's just it. You don't know who you are," the woman answered with a smile.

"Oh!" I exclaimed. "Then perhaps you'll kindly inform me. All this may be very amusing to you, but I assure you that to me it's the very reverse."

"I can only tell you who you are as I know you to be," answered the powdered-faced, doll-like old lady, whose attempts at juvenile coquetry sickened me.

"Go on," I said, preparing myself for more attempts to befool me.

"I ask you first whether you are not Wilford Heaton, of Heaton Manor, near Tewkesbury?"

"Certainly."

"And you were once stricken by blindness?"

"That is so, unfortunately."

"And you are now carrying on business as a financier in the City of London?"

"I know nothing of finance," I answered. "This Mr. Gedge—or whatever his name is—has told me some absurd fairy tale about my position in London, but knowing myself, as I do, to be an arrant duffer at figures, I'm quite positive that the story is all bunkum."

"Then how do you account for these memorandum forms?" inquired Gedge, taking some from the table, "and for these letters? Are they not in your handwriting?"

I glanced at the letters he held. They referred to some huge financial transaction, and were certainly in a hand that appeared wonderfully like my own.

"Some one has been imposing upon you, I tell you. This is a case of mistaken identity—it must be, my dear sir."

"But I tell you it isn't," protested Gedge. "All that your wife has said is the absolute truth."

"My wife!" I cried angrily. "I have no wife—thank Heaven!"

"No, no," whined the painted old woman, dabbing her eyes with her handkerchief, very lightly, however, so as not to disturb their artificiality. "No, don't say that, my dear Wilfred, don't say that! You know that you are my husband—you know you are!"

"I know, my dear madam, quite well that I do not occupy that distinguished position," I responded very firmly.

"But I can prove it—I can prove it!" she cried, with a futile effort at tears.

"Then I shall be most interested to see this extraordinary fiction proved," I said. "Perhaps we shall then get down to facts."

"The facts are as already stated," Gedge remarked.

"Then let me see proof. There must be a certificate or official entry somewhere if what this lady says is really correct. Where is it?"

"My certificate was stolen when my jewel-case was rifled in the train between Waterloo and Exeter," she answered. "But, of course, a copy can easily be obtained. Your solicitor in London can get a copy at once from Somerset House."

"Certificate stolen!" I cried. "A most ingenious excuse. I quite anticipated it, although it, unfortunately, exhibits no originality. Thieves don't usually steal marriage certificates. They can't pawn them, you know."

The woman before me glanced around the room with an air of bewilderment, and I then knew that I had cornered her.

"And where did this extraordinary marriage between us take place, pray?" I inquired, not without some bitter irony.

"At St. Andrew's, Wells Street."

"Wells Street, in London?"

"Yes. You surely remember it, don't you? The church is close by Oxford Circus."

"I know the church quite well," I answered. "But I most firmly and distinctly deny ever having been inside it in my life."

"If you examine the marriage register there you'll find your signature, together with that of your wife," Gedge observed, with a confidence that rather surprised me.

"I shall certainly take no trouble in such a matter," I declared. "It is alleged that I am the husband of this lady, therefore it is for her to bring proof—not for me to seek it."

"Very well, then," cried the woman who called herself Mrs. Heaton. "Within three days a copy of the certificate shall be placed in your hands."

"I'm not very partial to copies of documents," I observed very dubiously. "I always prefer originals."

"The original is, unfortunately, lost."

"Stolen, or strayed away of its own accord—eh?" I added with a doubtful laugh.

"Are you content to wait until the certificate can be obtained from Somerset House?" she inquired.

"No," I responded. "If you are actually my wife as you allege, madam, perhaps you will kindly explain the mystery of my presence here, in a house that until an hour ago I had never seen in all my life."

The woman and the secretary again exchanged glances. I saw they considered me an utterly irresponsible agent. They believed me to be demented.

"None of us can explain it," Gedge answered. "There is some mystery, but what it is we can't yet fathom."

"Mystery!" I echoed. "I should think there was some mystery—and devilishly complicated it must be too, when I find myself in this amazing position. Why, it's sufficient to turn the brain of any man to be told of one's marriage to a—to a woman one has never set eyes upon before, and—well, old enough to be his own mother!"

"Hush, hush!" said the secretary, who apparently wished to avoid a scene. He evidently knew that this angular woman, notwithstanding her affected juvenility, possessed a fiendish temper. I had detected it by the keen look in her eyes and the twitchings of her thin, hard lips.

"If I'm in my own house," I cried wrathfully, "I am surely permitted to say what I like. Am I master here, or not?"

"Certainly you are, sir," he responded, instantly humbled.

"Then listen," I said. "Until the arrival of the certificate from London I have no wish to meet this lady who alleges that she is my wife."

Then, turning to her, I made her a mock bow, adding, ironically—

"I think, madam, that it will avoid any further words of a disagreeable nature if we remain apart for the present."

"Certainly, Wilford," she cried, putting her hands out to me with an imploring gesture. "Go and rest, there's a dear, and carry out Doctor Britten's orders. You will soon be right again if you do. You've been puzzling your head too much over your figures, and the blow has affected you. Go and rest. But before you go I would ask you one favour."

"Well?" I inquired in a hard voice.

She drew nearer to me, and with that detestable artificial coquetry lifted her face to mine that I might kiss her.

"No!" I cried roughly, for I was beside myself with anger. "Let me remain in peace. I don't want to meet you again, my dear madam, until—until I know the worst."

"What have I done, Wilford, that you should treat me thus?" she wailed bitterly, bursting into a torrent of tears. "Oh, what have I done? Tell me."

"I don't know what you've done, and I'm sure I'm not interested in it," I responded. "All I know is that when you declare that you are my wife you tell a deliberate and downright lie."

For a moment she stood in hesitation, then, with tears flowing fast, she covered her face with her hands and staggered from the room.

Was she only acting the broken-hearted wife, or was that emotion real? Which, I could not decide.

If all this were part of some conspiracy, it was certainly one of no ordinary character. But what a confounded old hag the woman was! I shuddered. Surely she could not be my wife! The suggestion was too utterly preposterous to be entertained for a single moment, and within myself I laughed her allegation to scorn.

XX

How Many Yesterdays?

"N ow," I said, turning to Gedge, "perhaps you will show me over this new domain of mine. They seem to be pretty comfortable quarters, at any rate."

He looked at me strangely.

"You surely don't mean, sir, that you wish me to show you over your own house?" he said with incredulity.

"Of course I do," I answered. "I've never been over it yet, and I think I may as well embrace the opportunity now."

"But hadn't you better go to your room and rest? It will surely do you good. I'll ring for Rayner, the valet." He spoke as though solicitous of my welfare.

"I want no valets, neither do I require rest," I answered impatiently. "I mean to fathom this mystery."

"But pardon me," he said deferentially, "there is no mystery, as far as I can see. You accidentally struck your head against the statue while passing through the drawing-room, and were rendered unconscious. The blow has, according to the doctor, impaired your mental capacity a little. In a few days you'll be all right again. Poor Mrs. Heaton!—she's awfully upset."

"I will not have her called Mrs. Heaton!" I cried in indignation. "Understand that! I have no wife—and a hag like that I certainly would never marry." He raised his eyebrows with a gesture of regret, sighed, but hazarded no remark.

"Come," I said, "show me over the place. It will be a most interesting visit, I'm sure." And I laughed, reflecting upon my extraordinary position, one absolutely unparalleled in man's history.

"But before doing so will you not sign one or two cheques?" he urged, glancing at his watch. "The postman will call for the letters in half an hour, and they must be dispatched to-day."

"What cheques?"

"There are six," he answered, taking out a large cheque-book and opening it. "I've already made them out, if you will kindly sign them."

I glanced at them. All six were for large amounts, each considerably over a thousand pounds.

"They relate to business transactions, all of which are exceedingly good bargains," he explained.

"Well," I said, laughing again. "I've never before signed cheques for such big amounts as these. But here goes, if you wish. Whether they'll be honoured is quite another thing."

And I took up a pen and appended my signature to each, while he placed one by one in envelopes ready directed to receive them.

"Now," he said at last, "if you really wish me to take you round I'll do so, but the whole thing seems so droll and absurd that I hope, sir, you'll excuse my doubts as to your sanity."

"Well, why do you think I'm insane?" I asked, looking straight at him. "Do I look like a madman?"

"Not at all. With your head swathed in those bandages, you look like a man who's received a serious injury."

"Of course, that confounded old charlatan Britten put forward the suggestion that I'm not in my right mind!" I said. "But I tell you quite calmly, and without fear of contradiction—indeed, I could swear upon oath—that never in my life have I entered this place or set eyes upon you or upon that painted old girl before to-day. Now, if you were in my place, surely you would resent, being called husband by a woman whom you don't know from Adam; you wouldn't relish being condemned as a lunatic by an idiotic old country quack, and being imposed upon all round by persons in whom you have not the slightest interest."

His face relaxed into a smile.

"If I may be permitted to advise," he said, "I think it best not to discuss the matter further at present. A solution must present itself before long. Meanwhile your intellect will be rendered the clearer by repose."

"I've already told you that I don't intend to rest until I've extricated myself from this absurdly false position," I said determinedly. "I feel absolutely certain that I've been mistaken for some one of the same name."

He shrugged his shoulders. He was evidently a shrewd fellow, this man who said he was my secretary, and was apparently a very confidential servant.

"I'd like to know what to reply to Mawson's cable," he said. "You really ought to take some notice of such a marvellous stroke of good fortune. His discovery means fabulous wealth for you as holder of the concession."

"My dear sir," I said, "for mercy's sake don't bother me about this fellow and his confounded pans. Reply just as you like. You seem to know all about it. I don't—nor do I want to know."

"But in a case like this I do not care to act on my own discretion alone," he protested. "They are evidently awaiting a reply in Dawson City."

"Let them wait," I said. "I don't want to bother my head over matters in which I can have no possible concern. This alleged matrimonial alliance of mine is of far more importance to me than all the gold in the Klondyke."

"Well, the lady is your wife, so why worry further about it?" he said.

"And how do you know, pray?"

"Because I was present at the ceremony."

I looked at him for a moment, unable to utter further words.

"I suppose you'll tell me next that you were my secretary in my bachelor days?" I said at last.

"Certainly I was."

"And you say that you were actually present at the church, and saw me married?" I cried, absolutely incredulous.

"I was. You were married at St. Andrew's, Wells Street. It was a smart wedding, too, for Mrs. Fordyce was very well known in society, and had a large circle of friends."

"Fordyce?" I echoed, puzzled.

"Yes, that was Mrs. Heaton's name before her marriage with you."

"Then she was a widow?" I gasped.

He nodded in the affirmative.

I groaned. The affair grew more puzzling now that he declared himself an actual witness of my matrimonial misfortune.

But how could such a thing have taken place without my knowledge? It was impossible. The mystery, like the strange incidents which had preceded this remarkable situation in which I found myself, grew more and more inexplicable each hour.

We went forth, together, passing from room to room through the great country mansion. The place was handsome, of rather modern type, furnished glaringly in the manner which bespoke the parvenu. It possessed no mellow, time-worn appearance, as did the dear old Manor House beside the Severn. The furniture and hangings were too apparently of the Tottenham Court Road type, and the art displayed was that of the art furnisher given *carte blanche* to furnish with the newest and most fashionable fancies in the matter of wallpapers, dadoes, cornices, and art-pottery. There were art-carpets and art-curtains, art-cupboards and art-chairs, art-china and art-chintzes. Art was everywhere in painful enamel and impossible greens. There were pictures, too, but different, indeed, to the long row of noble faces with their ruffles and doublets and their arms painted on shields in the corners that looked down so solemnly in the great hall at Heaton. The pictures in that modern mansion were of the *queue-de-siecle* French school, daubs by the miscalled impressionists, some being rather too *chic* to be decent.

That a large amount of money had been expended upon the place I could not doubt, but the effect was that of dazzling the gaze by colour, and nowhere seemed there a good, comfortable old-fashioned sitting-room. All the apartments were arranged to please the eye, and not for personal comfort. The house was just the kind that a man suddenly successful in the city might set up in the vain endeavour to develop into a country gentleman; for to become such is the ideal of every silk-hatted business man, whether he trades in stocks or stockings.

"That I should be compelled to show you over your own house is, to say the least, very amusing," said Gedge, as we were passing up the grand staircase. "If people were told of this they wouldn't believe it possible."

"I myself don't believe what you tell me is possible," I remarked. "But who gave orders for this furniture?"

"You did."

"And who chose it—approved of the designs, and all that sort of thing?"

"You certainly did," he answered. "Some of the ideas were, of course, Mrs. Heaton's."

"I thought so. I don't believe myself capable of such barbaric taste as those awful blues and greens in the little sitting-room."

"The morning-room you mean."

"I suppose so. The whole place is like a furniture show-room—this style complete, thirty-five guineas, and so on. You know the sort of thing I mean."

He smiled in amusement at my words.

"Your friends all admire the place," he remarked.

"What friends?"

"Sir Charles Stimmel, Mr. Larcombe, Lady Fraser, and people of that class."

"I never heard of them in all my life. Who are they?" I inquired, interested.

"Friends of yours. They visit here often enough. You surely ought to know them. Lady Fraser is your wife's dearest friend."

"Fraser?" I said reflectively. "The only Fraser I know is a baker in Clare Market, who supplies my old servant, Mrs. Parker, with bread." Then, after a pause, I added, "And you say that these people are friends of mine? Have I many friends?"

"Lots. A rich man has always plenty of good-humoured acquaintances."

"They like to come down here for a breath of country air, I suppose, eh?" I laughed.

"That's about it," he answered. "A good many of them are not very sincere in their friendship, I fear. The man who has money, lives well, keeps a good table, and has choice wines in his cellar need never be at a loss for genial companions."

"You seem to be a bit of a philosopher, my friend." I remarked.

He smiled knowingly.

"I haven't acted as your secretary without learning a few of the crooked ways of the world."

"What?" I exclaimed. "Don't I always act honestly, then?" This was something entirely new.

"Nobody can be honest in finance."

"Well," I said, resenting his imputation, "I wasn't aware that I had ever swindled a person of sixpence in my life."

"Sixpences in such sums as they deal in at Winchester House don't count. It's the thousands."

We passed a couple of gaping maid-servants in long-stringed caps, who stood aside, looking me in wonder. No doubt the news that a demented man was in the house had reached the servants' hall. I was, in fact, on show to the domestics.

"Then you mean to imply that these financial dealings of mine—of which, by the way, I have no knowledge whatsoever—are not always quite straight?" I said, as we walked together down a long carpeted corridor. He looked at me in hesitation.

"It's, of course, business," he answered—"sharp business. I don't mean to imply that the dealings at Winchester House are any more unfair than those of any other financier in the City; but sometimes, you know, there's just a flavour of smartness about them that might be misconstrued by a clever counsel in a criminal court."

"What?" I cried, halting and glaring at him. "Now, be frank with me, Gedge. Tell me plainly, have I ever swindled anybody?"

"Certainly not," he said, laughing. "Why, it's this very smartness that has made you what you are to-day—a millionaire. If you had not been very wide awake and shrewd you'd have been ruined long ago."

"Then, I suppose, I'm well known in the city, eh?"

"Your name's as well known as Bennett's clock, and your credit stands as high as any one's between Ludgate Hill and Fenchurch Street."

"Extraordinary!" I said. "What you tell me sounds like some remarkable fairy tale."

"The balance at your banker's is sufficient proof that what I say is truth," he remarked. "There may be a good many fairy tales in certain prospectuses, but there certainly is none in your financial soundness."

We wandered on from room to room. There must, I think, have been quite thirty sleeping apartments, guests' rooms, etc, all furnished in that same glaring style, that greenery-yellow abomination miscalled art.

"The next room," explained my secretary, as we approached the end of the corridor, "is Mrs. Heaton's boudoir. I expect she's in there. I saw Dalton, her maid, enter a moment ago."

"Oh, for Heaven's sake, leave her alone!" I said, turning at once on my heel. I had no wish to meet that awful rejuvenated hag again.

I fancy Gedge smiled, but if he did he was very careful to hide his amusement from me. He was, without doubt, a very well-trained secretary.

The thought of Mabel Anson crossed my mind. All the recollections of the dinner on the previous night, and the startling discoveries I subsequently made recurred to me at that moment, and I felt dazed and bewildered. This painted and powdered person could surely not be my wife, when I loved Mabel Anson with all my soul! Only yesterday I had sat at her side at dinner, and had felt the pressure of her soft, delicate hand upon mine. No; it could not be that I was actually married. Such a thing was utterly impossible, for surely no man could go through the marriage ceremony without knowing something about it.

Hickman's treachery angered me. Why, I wondered, had he enticed me to his rooms in order to make that extraordinary attempt upon my life? The wound upon my head was undoubtedly due to the blow he had dealt me. The theory that I had accidentally knocked my head against the marble statue and broken it was, I felt assured, only one of that fool Britten's brilliant ideas with which he misled his too-confiding patients. If this were so, then all the incidents subsequent to my recovery of consciousness were part of the conspiracy which had commenced on the previous night with Hickman's attempt.

We descended the stairs, passing the footman Gill, who with a bow, said—

"I hope, sir, you feel better."

"A little," I answered. "Bring me a whisky and soda to the library."

And the man at once disappeared to do my bidding. "I suppose he think's I'm mad," I remarked. "This is a very remarkable *menage*, to say the least."

In the great hall, as I walked towards the library, was a long mirror, and in passing I caught sight of my own figure in it. I stopped, and with a loud cry of wonder and dismay stood before it, glaring at my own reflection.

The bandages about my head gave me a terribly invalid appearance, but reflected by that glass I saw a sight which struck me dumb with amazement. I could not believe my eyes; the thing staggered belief.

On the morning before I had shaved as usual, but the glass showed that I now wore a well cut, nicely reddish-brown beard!

My face seemed to have changed curiously. I presented an older appearance than on the day before. My hair seemed to have lost its youthful lustre, and upon my brow were three distinct lines—the lines of care.

I felt my beard with eager hands. Yes, there was no mistake. It was there, but how it had grown was inconceivable.

Beyond, through the open door, I saw the brilliant sunlight, the green lawn, the bright flowers and cool foliage of the rustling trees.

It was summer. Yet only yesterday was chill, dark winter, with threatening snow.

Had I been asleep like Rip Van Winkle in the legend? "Tell me," I cried excitedly, turning to the man standing behind me, "what's the day of the month to-day?"

"The seventeenth of July."

"July?" I echoed. "And what year is this?"

"Why, eighteen hundred and ninety-six, of course."

"Ninety-six!" I gasped, standing glaring at him in blank amazement. "Ninety-six?"

"Certainly. Why?"

"Am I really losing my senses?" I cried, dismayed. "*Yesterday was six years ago!*"

XXI

Gedge Tells the Truth

Yesterday six years ago!" he echoed, looking at me in blank bewilderment. "What do you mean?"

"I mean that if what you've told me is really the truth," I cried, agape in wonder, "then it is the most astounding thing I've ever heard of. Are you absolutely certain of the date?"

"Certain? Why, of course."

"Of the year, I mean?"

"Positive. It's eighteen ninety-six."

"For how long, then, have you been my secretary?" I inquired.

"Nearly five years."

"And how long have I lived in this place?"

"For nearly four."

"And that woman," I demanded, breathlessly—"is she actually my wife?"

"Most certainly," he answered.

I stood stupefied, stunned by this amazing statement.

"But," I protested, lost in wonder, "yesterday was years ago. How do you account for that? Are you certain that you're not deceiving me?"

"I've told you the absolute truth," he responded. "On that I stake my honour."

I stood aghast, glaring at my reflection in the mirror, open-mouthed, as though I gazed upon some object supernatural. My personal appearance had certainly changed, and that in itself convinced me that there must be some truth in this man Gedge's statement. I was older, a trifle stouter than before, I think, and my red-brown beard seemed to give my face a remarkably grotesque appearance. I had always hated beards, and considered them a relic of prehistoric barbarity. It was surprising that I should now have grown one.

"Then according to your account I must have spent yesterday here—actually in this house?"

"Why, of course you did," he responded. "We were engaged the greater part of the day over Laffan's affair. Walter Halliburton, the mining engineer, came down to see you, and we were together all the afternoon. He left for London at five."

"And where did I dine?"

"Here. With Mrs. Heaton."

"Don't speak of her as Mrs. Heaton!" I cried in anger. "She's not my wife, and I will not have her regarded as such."

He gave his shoulders a slight shrug.

"Now, look here, Mr. Gedge," I said, speaking for the first time with confidence. "If you were in my place, awakening suddenly to find that six years of your life had vanished in a single night, and that you were an entirely different person to that of twelve hours ago, what would you believe?"

He looked at me with a somewhat sympathetic expression upon his thin features.

"Well, I don't know what I should think." Then he added, "But surely such a thing can't be possible."

"It is possible," I cried. "It has happened to me. I tell you that last night was six years ago."

He turned from me, as though he considered further argument unavailing.

My head reeled. What he had told me was utterly incredible. It seemed absolutely impossible that six whole years should have passed without my knowledge; that I should have entered upon a business of which I had previously known nothing; that I should have rapidly amassed a fortune; and, most of all, that I should have married that powdered and painted woman who had presented herself as my wife. Yet such were the unaccountable facts which this man Gedge asked me to believe.

He saw that I was extremely dubious about the date, therefore he led me back to the library, where there hung upon the wall a large calendar, which quickly convinced me.

Six; years had really elapsed since yesterday.

In that vexing and perplexing present I reflected upon the puzzling past. That happy dinner with Mabel at the Boltons, the subsequent discoveries in that drawing-room where she had sat at the piano calmly playing; her soft words of tenderness, and the subsequent treachery of that dog-faced man Hickman, all passed before me with extraordinary vividness. Yet, in truth, all had happened long ago.

Alas! I was not like other men. To the practical, level-headed man of affairs "To-day" may be sufficient, all-engrossing; but to the very large majority—a majority which, I believe, includes also many of the practical, the business of to-day admits of constant pleasant excursions into the golden mists of "long ago," and many happy flights to the rosy heights of "some day." Most of those who read this strange story of my life will remember with a melancholy affection, with a pain that is more soothing than many pleasures, the house wherein they were born, or at any rate the abode in which they passed the earlier years of their lives. The agonising griefs of childhood, the disappointments, the soul-racking terrors, mellowed by the gentle touch of passing years, have no sting for our mature sensibilities, but come back to us now with a pathos that is largely tinctured with amusement.

I stood there reviewing the past, puzzled, utterly unable to account for it. Age, the iconoclast, had shattered most of the airy idols which my youth had set up in honour of itself. I had lost six of the most precious years of my life—years that I had not lived.

Yet this man before me declared most distinctly that I had lived them; that I had enjoyed a second existence quite apart and distinct from my own self. Incredible though it seemed, yet it became gradually impressed upon me that what this man Gedge had told me was the actual, hideous truth, and that I had really lived and moved and prospered throughout those six unknown years, while my senses had at the same time remained dormant, and I had thus been utterly unconscious of existence.

But could such a thing be? As a prosaic man of the world I argued, as any one in his right mind would argue, that such a thing was beyond the bounds of possibility. Nevertheless, be it how it might, the undisputed fact remained that I had lapsed into unconsciousness on that winter's night six years before, and had known absolutely nothing of my surroundings until I found myself lying upon the floor of the drawing-room of what was alleged to be my country house.

Six years out of a man's life is a large slice. The face of the world changes considerably in that space of time. I found myself living a life which was so artificial and incongruous to my own tastes as to appear utterly unreal. Yet, as I made further inquiry of this man Gedge, every moment that passed showed me plainly that what he had said was the truth.

He related to me the routine of my daily life, and I stood listening agape in wonder. He told me things of which I had no knowledge; of my own private affairs, and of my business profits; he took big leather-bound ledgers from the great green-painted safe, and showed me formidable sums entered therein, relating, he explained, to the transactions at the office up in London. Some documents he showed me, large official-looking sheets with stamps and seals and signatures, which he said were concessions obtained from a certain foreign Government, and opened my private letter-book, exhibiting letters I had actually written with my own hand, but without having any knowledge of having done so.

These revelations took away my breath.

It could not be mere loss of memory from which I was suffering. I had actually lived a second and entirely different life to that I had once led in Essex Street. Apparently I had become a changed man, had entered business, had amassed a fortune—and had married.

Assuredly, I reflected, I could never have been in my right senses to have married that angular person with the powdered cheeks. That action, in itself, was sufficient to convince me that my brain had been unbalanced during those six lost years.

Alone, I stood, without a single sympathiser—without a friend.

How this astounding gap in my life had been produced was absolutely beyond explanation. I tried to account for it, but the reader will readily understand that the problem was, to me, utterly inexplicable. I, the victim of the treachery of that man Hickman, had fallen unconscious one night, and had awakened to discover that six whole years had elapsed, and that I had developed into an entirely different person. It was unaccountable, nay, incredible.

I think I should have grown confidential towards Gedge were it not that he apparently treated me as one whose mind was wandering. He believed, and perhaps justly so, that my brain had been injured by the accidental blow. To him, of course, it seemed impossible that I, his master, should know nothing of my own affairs. The ludicrousness of the situation was to me entirely apparent, yet what could I do to avert it?

By careful questions I endeavoured to obtain from him some facts regarding my past.

"You told me," I said, "that I have many friends. Among them are there any persons named Anson?"

"Anson?" he repeated reflectively. "No, I've never heard the name."

"Or Hickman?"

He shook his head.

"I lived once in Essex Street, Strand," I said. "Have I been to those chambers during the time—the five years you have been in my service?"

Never, to my knowledge.

"Have I ever visited a house in The Boltons, at Kensington?"

"I think not," he responded.

"Curious! Very curious!" I observed, thinking deeply of the graceful, dark-eyed Mabel whom I had loved six years before, and who was now lost to me for ever.

"Among my friends is there a man named Doyle?" I inquired, after a pause.

"Doyle? Do you mean Mr. Richard Doyle, the war correspondent?"

"Certainly," I cried excitedly. "Is he back?"

"He is one of your friends, and has often visited here," Gedge replied.

"What is his address? I'll wire to him at once."

"He's in Egypt. He left London last March, and has not yet returned."

I drew a long breath. Dick had evidently recovered from fever in India, and was still my best friend, although I had had no knowledge of it.

What, I wondered, had been my actions in those six years of unconsciousness? Mine were indeed strange thoughts at that moment. Of all that had been told me I was unable to account for anything. I stood stunned, confounded, petrified.

For knowledge of what had transpired during those intervening years, or of my own career and actions during that period, I had to rely upon the statements of others. My mind during all that time had, it appeared, been a perfect blank, incapable of receiving any impression whatsoever.

Nevertheless, when I came to consider how I had in so marvellous a manner established a reputation in the City, and had amassed the sum now lying at my bankers, I reflected that I could not have accomplished that without the exercise of considerable tact and mental capacity. I must, after all, have retained shrewd senses, but they had evidently been those of my other self—the self who had lived and moved as husband of that woman who called herself Mrs. Heaton.

"Tell me," I said, addressing Gedge again, "has my married life been a happy one?"

He looked at me inquiringly.

"Tell me the truth," I urged. "Don't conceal anything from me, for I intend to get at the bottom of this mystery."

"Well," he said, with considerable hesitation, "scarcely what one might call happy, I think."

"Ah, I understand," I said. "I know from your tone that you sympathise with me, Gedge."

He nodded without replying. Strange that I had never known this man until an hour ago, and yet I had grown so confidential with him. He seemed to be the only person who could present to me the plain truth.

Those six lost years were utterly puzzling. I was as one returned from the grave to find his world vanished, and all things changed.

I tried to reflect, to see some ray of light through the darkness of that lost period, but to me it seemed utterly non-existent. Those years, if I had really lived them, had melted away and left not a trace behind. The events of my life prior to that eventful night when I had dined at The Boltons had no affinity to those of the present. I had ceased to be my old self, and by some inexplicable transition, mysterious and unheard of, I had, while retaining my name, become an entirely different man.

Six precious years of golden youth had vanished in a single night. All my ideals, all my love, all my hope, nay, my very personality, had been swept away and effaced for ever.

"Have I often visited Heaton—my own place?" I inquired, turning suddenly to Gedge.

"Not since your marriage, I believe," he answered. "You have always entertained some curious dislike towards the place. I went up there once to transact some business with your agent, and thought it a nice, charming old house."

"Ay, and so it is," I sighed, remembering the youthful days I had spent there long ago. All the year round was sunshine then, with the most ravishing snow-drifts in winter, and ice that sparkled in the sun so brilliantly that it seemed almost as jolly and frolicsome as the sunniest of sunlit streams, dancing and shimmering over the pebbles all through the cloudless summer. Did it ever rain in those old days long ago? Why, yes; and what splendid times I used to have on those occasions—toffee-making in the schoolroom, or watching old Dixon, the gamekeeper, cutting gun-wads in the harness-room.

And I had entertained a marked dislike to the place! All my tastes and ideas during those blank years had apparently become inverted. I had lived and enjoyed a world exactly opposite to my own—the world of sordid money-making and the glaring display of riches. I had, in a word, aped the gentleman.

There was a small circular mirror in the library, and before it I stood, marking every line upon my face, the incredible impress of forgotten years.

"It is amazing, incredible!" I cried, heart-sick with desire to penetrate the veil of mystery that enshrouded that long period of unconsciousness. "All that you have told me, Gedge, is absolutely beyond belief. There must be some mistake. It is impossible that six years can have passed without my knowledge."

"I think," he said, "that, after all, Britten's advice should be followed. You are evidently not yourself to-day, and rest will probably restore your mental power to its proper calibre."

"Bah!" I shouted angrily. "You still believe I'm mad. I tell you I'm not. I'll prove to you that I'm not."

"Well," he remarked, quite calmly, "no sane man could be utterly ignorant of his own life. It doesn't stand to reason that he could."

"I tell you I'm quite as sane as you are," I cried. "Yet I've been utterly unconscious these six whole years."

"Nobody will believe you."

"But I swear it to be true," I protested. "Since the moment when consciousness left me in that house in Chelsea I have been as one dead."

He laughed incredulously. The slightly confidential tone in which I had spoken had apparently induced him to treat me with indifference. This aroused my wrath. I was in no mood to argue whether or not I was responsible for my actions.

"A man surely can't be unconscious, while at the same time he transacts business and lives as gaily as you live," he laughed.

"Then you impute that all I've said is untrue, and is due merely to the fact that I'm a trifle demented, eh?"

"Britten has said that you are suffering from a fit of temporary derangement, and that you will recover after perfect rest."

"Then, by taking me around this house, showing me those books, and explaining all to me, you've merely been humouring me as you would a harmless lunatic!" I cried furiously. "You don't believe what I say, that I'm perfectly in my right mind, therefore leave me. I have no further use for your presence, and prefer to be alone," I added harshly.

"Very well," he answered, rather piqued; "if you wish I'll, of course, go."

"Yes, go; and don't return till I send for you. Understand that! I'm in no humour to be fooled, or told that I'm a lunatic."

He shrugged his shoulders, and muttering some words I did not catch, turned and left the library.

XXII

Broken Threads

He is a faint-hearted creature indeed who, while struggling along some dark lane of life, cannot, at least intermittently, extract some comfort to himself from the thought that the turn must come at last—the turn which, presumably, will bring him out upon the well-metalled high-road of happy contentment.

I do not know that I was exactly faint-hearted. The mystery of it all had so stunned me that I felt myself utterly incapable of believing anything. The whole thing seemed shadowy and unreal.

And yet the facts remained that I was alive, standing there in that comfortable room, in possession of all my faculties, both mental and physical, an entirely different person to my old self, with six years of my past lost and unaccountable.

Beyond the lawn the shadow of the great trees looked cool and inviting, therefore I went forth, wandering heedlessly across the spacious park, my mind full of thoughts of that fateful night when I had fallen among that strange company, and of Mabel, the woman I had loved so fondly and devotedly.

Sweet were the recollections that came back to me. How charming she had seemed to me as we had lingered hand-in-hand on our walks across the Park and Kensington Gardens, how soft and musical her voice! how full of tenderness her bright dark eyes! How idyllic was our love! She had surely read my undeclared passion. She had known the great secret in my heart.

Nevertheless, all had changed. In a woman's life half a dozen years is a long time, for she may develop from girl to matron in that space. The worst aspect of the affair presented itself to me. I had, in all probability, left her without uttering a word of farewell, and she—on her part—had, no doubt, accepted some other suitor. What more natural, indeed, than she should have married?

That thought held me rigid.

Again, as I strolled on beneath the rustling elms which led straight away in a wide old avenue towards where a distant village church stood, a prominent figure in the landscape, there recurred to me vivid

WILLIAM LE QUEUX

recollections of that last night of my old self—of the astounding discovery I had made in the drawing-room at The Boltons.

How was I to account for that?

I paused and glanced around upon the view. All was quiet and peaceful there in the mid-day sunlight. Behind me stood the great white facade of Denbury; before, a little to the right, lay a small village with its white cottages—the villages of Littleham, I afterwards discovered—and to the left white cliffs and the blue stretch of the English Channel gleaming through the greenery.

From the avenue I turned and wandered down a by-path to a stile, and there I rested, in full uninterrupted view of the open sea. Deep below was a cove—Littleham Cove, it proved to be—and there, under shelter of the cliffs, a couple of yachts were riding gaily at anchor, while far away upon the clear horizon a dark smoke-trail showed the track of a steamer outward bound.

The day was brilliant. It was July in Devonshire, that fairest of all counties—and July there is always a superb month. The air, warm and balmy, was laden with the scent of roses and honeysuckle, the only sounds that broke the quiet were the songs of the birds and the soft rustling of the trees.

I sat there trying to decide how to act.

For the first time it occurred to me that my position was one of a certain peril, for if I did not act with tact and caution, that woman who called herself my wife, aided by that idiot Britten, might declare that I was mad, and cause me to be placed beneath restraint. Therefore, to gain my freedom, it was evidently necessary that I should act with discretion and keep my own counsel.

I looked around upon the fair panorama of nature spread before me. The world was six years older than when I had known it. What national events had, I wondered, happened in that time? Place yourself in my position, and picture to yourself the feeling of bewilderment that overcame me when I reflected upon what might or might not have transpired.

There crept over me a longing to escape from that place, the habitation of that awful woman with the powdered cheeks, and to return to London. All my life and pleasure had been centred in the giant capital, and to it I intended now to go back and seek, if possible, the broken thread of my history, which might lead me to an elucidation of the marvellous mystery.

The world around me, the calm blue sea, the cloudless sky, the green grass-lands, the soft whispering of the foliage seemed so peaceful that I could scarce believe that so much evil, so much of human malice, could exist. The tranquillity of my surroundings induced within me a quieter frame of mind, and I set to planning carefully how I might escape and return to London.

To endeavour to do so openly would, I saw, be to draw upon me the spies of my hideous wife. Was I not believed by all to be insane? Then certainly I should not be allowed to go at large without some one at my side.

I wanted to be alone. The presence of a second person entertaining suspicions as to my sanity would seriously hamper me, and prevent me prosecuting the inquiries I intended to institute regarding my past. No. To escape successfully I should be compelled to fly to London, and once there alter my appearance and assume another name. Search would undoubtedly be made for me, but once in London I felt confident in being able to foil any efforts of my wife's agents.

Therefore I sat upon the stile and calmly matured my plans.

The chiming of a clock, apparently in the turret upon my own stables at Denbury, fell upon my ears. It struck one. Then the sharp ringing of a bell—the luncheon-bell—followed.

Gedge had told me that the place was near Budleigh-Salterton. Was it near enough, I wondered, for me to walk there, and was there a station? There might, I reflected, be a map in the library. I would be compelled to trace it out and seek my route, for I was absolutely ignorant of that corner of Devonshire.

Yes, my best policy, I decided, was to return to the house, act as indifferently as possible, and meanwhile complete my plans for escape.

I retraced my steps to the house by the path I had traversed, and upon the lawn was met by the man Gill, who announced—

"The luncheon-bell has rung, sir. I hope you feel a little better, sir."

"Oh, much better," I answered airily, and with an effort at self-possession followed him into the imitation old-oak dining-room, which Gedge had shown me during our tour of the place.

The woman with the powdered cheeks was already seated at the head of the table, erect and stately, with an expression of *hauteur* which ill became her.

"I hope you feel better after your walk," she said, as I seated myself.

"Oh, much better," I responded in a tone of irony. "The pain has practically passed."

"You should really rest," she said, in that squeaky, artificial tone which so jarred upon my nerves. "Do take the doctor's advice."

It was on the tip of my tongue to make a further unwriteable remark regarding the doctor, but I managed to control myself and reply—

"Yes, I think after luncheon I shall lie down for a little time. I have, however, some pressing letters to write first."

"Let Gedge attend to your correspondence for to-day," she urged, with that mock juvenility which rendered her so hideously ridiculous.

"No," I responded. "I have, unfortunately, to attend to several pressing matters personally. Afterwards I will rest."

"Do, there's a dear," she said.

I bit my lip. She nauseated me when she used that affectionate term. The only woman I loved was Mabel Anson, but whether she were still alive, or whether married, I knew not. The very thought that I was bound in matrimony to this woman sitting in the high-backed chair of carved oak was disgusting. I loathed her.

How I continued to eat the dishes Gill handed me I know not, nor do I remember what conversation passed between my pseudo-wife and myself as we sat there. Many were the abrupt and painful silences which fell between us.

She struck me as an ascetic, strong-minded woman, who, before others, fawned upon me with an affected devotion which in one of her age was ludicrous; yet when we were alone she was rigid and overbearing, with the positive air of one who believed me far beneath her alike in social station and in intellect. When Gill was absent she spoke in a hard, patronising tone, which so angered me that with great difficulty I retained my temper.

Yet it was my policy, I knew, to conceal my thoughts, and to lead her to believe that the words I had uttered, and my failure to recognise her, were owing to the blow I accidentally received, and that I was now, just as I had been before, her husband.

What a hollow sham that meal was! Now that I think of it I cannot refrain from smiling at my extraordinary position, and how I showed her delicate attention in order to the more impress her of my solicitude for her welfare.

When at last she rose it was with a hope that I would go to my room and rest.

I seized that opportunity.

"I shall," I answered. "But don't let them call me for dinner. I will have something when I awake. Britten has ordered perfect quiet."

"Very well," she answered. Then, turning to Gill, she said, "You hear. Mr. Heaton is not to be aroused at dinner."

"Yes, madam," answered the man, bowing as we both passed out.

At once I walked along to the library, shut the door, and locked it.

I had much to do to prepare for my flight.

Yes, as I had expected, there was an ordnance map of the Teignmouth district tacked to the wall; and searching, I quickly found Denbury marked upon it, standing on the Exmouth road over the High Land of Orcombe, halfway between that place and Budleigh-Salterton. The South-Western Railway ran; I saw, from Exmouth to London, by way of Exeter, and my first impulse was to walk into Exmouth, and take train thence. The fact that I was probably known at that station occurred to me, therefore I made up my mind to avoid the terminus and join the train at Lympston, a small station further towards Exeter.

Taking up my pen I made a rough sketch-plan of my route, which passed Littleham church, then by the left-hand road struck across country, crossing the high-road to Exmouth at right angles, continuing through the village of Withycombe Raleigh, and keeping straight on until it joined the main road to Exeter. At the commencement of the village of Lympston it was necessary, I saw, to turn sharp to the left, and at the end of the road I should find the station, close to the river Exe.

In order to avoid mistaking the road and entering the town of Exmouth, I made a full and careful plan, which when completed I placed in my pocket. The distance, I calculated roughly, was between five and six miles over a road rather difficult to find without a map.

Among the books on the table I found a Bradshaw, with the page of local trains turned down, and from it learned that a train with connexion from London stopped at Lympston at 7:55 P.M., while the train in connexion with the up-mail from Exeter stopped there at 8:20. The latter I decided upon taking.

The fact that I had expressed my desire to sleep would prevent Gill coming to call me at the dinner hour, and by the time I was missed I should be well on my way to London.

The question of money occurred to me. I had noticed some loose gold and a couple of five-pound notes in one of the drawers which

Gedge had opened, and having a duplicate set of keys in my pocket, I transferred the whole—a little under fourteen pounds—to my pocket.

Then I took out my cheque-book. It was too large to be carried in my pocket, therefore I tore out a couple of dozen or so, folded them, and placed them in an envelope.

I recognised that I could draw money with them, yet the bank need not know my whereabouts. If these people, who would, I suppose, call themselves "my friends," made active search to find the fugitive "madman," they would certainly obtain no clue from my bankers.

In the same drawer as the cheque-book I found a black leather portfolio, securely locked.

The latter fact impressed me. Everything else was open to my secretary, who possessed keys, both to writing-table and safe. But this was locked, apparently because therein were contained certain private papers that I had wished to keep from his eyes.

No man, whoever he may be, reposes absolute confidence in his secretary. Every one has some personal matter, the existence of which he desires to preserve secret to himself alone.

I drew forth the locked portfolio, and placed it upon the blotting-pad before me. It was an expansive wallet, of a kind such as I remembered having seen carried by bankers' clerks in the City from bank to bank, attached by chains to the belts around their waists.

Surely upon my ring I must possess a key to it. I looked, and found a small brass key.

It fitted, and a moment later I had unlocked the wallet and spread my own private papers before me.

What secrets of my lost life, I wondered, might not those carefully preserved letters and documents contain?

In eager, anxious wonder I turned them over.

Next instant a cry of dismay broke involuntarily from my lips, as within trembling fingers I held one of those papers—a letter addressed to me.

I could scarce believe my own eyes as I read it. Yet the truth was plain—hideously plain.

XXIII

I Make a Discovery

Reader, I must take you still further into my confidence. What you have already read is strange, but certain things which subsequently happened to me were even still stranger.

I held that astounding letter in my hand. My eyes were riveted upon it.

The words written there were puzzling indeed. A dozen times I read them through, agape with wonder.

The communication, upon the notepaper of the *Bath Hotel* at Bournemouth, was dated June 4, 1891—five years before—and ran as follows:—

Dear Mr. Heaton,

"I very much regret that you should have thus misunderstood me. I thought when we met at Windermere you were quite of my opinion. You, however, appear to have grown tired after the five months of our engagement, and your love for me has suddenly cooled; therefore our paths in life must in future lie apart. You have at least told me the truth honestly and straightforwardly. I, of course, believed that your declarations were true, and that you really loved me truly, but alas! it is evidently not so. I can only suffer in silence. Good-bye for ever. We shall never, never meet again. But I tell you, Wilford, that I bear you no malice, and that my prayers will ever be for your welfare and your happiness. Perhaps sometimes you will give a passing thought to the sorrowful, heart-broken woman who still loves you.

Mabel Anson

What could this mean? It spoke of our engagement for five months! I had no knowledge whatever of ever having declared the secret of my love, much less becoming her affianced husband. Was it possible that in the first few months of my unconscious life I had met her and told her of my affection, of how I worshipped her with all the strength of my being?

As I sat there with the carefully preserved letter in my hand there arose before my eyes a vision of her calm, fair face, bending over the piano, her handsome profile illumined by the candles on either side, the single diamond suspended by its invisible chain, gleaming at her throat like a giant's eye. The impression I had obtained of her on that night at The Boltons still remained indelibly with me. Yes, her beauty was superb, her sweetness unsurpassed by that of any other woman I had ever met.

Among the other private papers preserved within the wallet were four scraps of notepaper with typewriting upon them. All bore the same signature—that of the strange name "Avel." All of them made appointments. One asked me to meet the writer in the writing-room of the *Hotel Victoria* in London, another made an appointment to meet me "on the Promenade at Eastbourne opposite the Wish Tower"; a third suggested my office at Winchester House as a meeting-place, and the fourth gave a rendezvous on the departure platform at King's Cross Station.

I fell to wondering whether I had kept any of these engagements. The most recent of the letters was dated nearly two years ago.

But the afternoon was wearing on, therefore I placed the puzzling communications in my pocket and ascended to my room in order to rest, and thus carry out the feint of attending to old Britten's directions.

The dressing-bell awakened me, but, confident in the knowledge that I should remain undisturbed, I removed the bandages from my head, bathed the wound, and applied some plaster in the place of the handkerchief. Then, with my hat on, my injury was concealed.

The sun was declining when I managed to slip out of the house unobserved, and set forth down the avenue to Littleham village. The quaint old place was delightful in the evening calm, but, heedless of everything, I hurried forward down the hill to Withycombe Raleigh, and thence straight across the open country to Lympston station, where I took a third-class ticket for Exeter. At a wayside station a passenger for London is always remarked, therefore I only booked as far as the junction with the main-line.

At Exeter I found that the up-mail was not due for ten minutes, therefore I telegraphed to London for a room at the *Grand Hotel*, and afterwards bought some newspapers with which to while away the journey.

Sight of newspapers dated six years later than those I had last seen aroused within me a lively curiosity. How incredible it all seemed as in that dimly lit railway-carriage I sat gathering from those printed pages the history of the lost six years of my life!

The only other occupant of the compartment besides myself was a woman. I had sought an empty carriage, but failing to find one, was compelled to accept her as travelling companion. She was youngish, perhaps thirty-five, and neatly dressed, but her face, as far as I could distinguish it through her spotted veil, was that of a woman melancholy and bowed down by trouble. In her dark hair were premature threads of silver, and her deep-sunken eyes, peering forth strangely at me, were the eyes of a woman rendered desperate.

I did not like the look of her. In travelling one is quick to entertain an instinctive dislike to one's companion, and it was so in my case. I found myself regretting that I had not entered a smoking-carriage. But I soon became absorbed in my papers, and forgot her presence.

It was only her voice, a curiously high-pitched one, that made me start.

She inquired if I minded her closing the window because of the draught, and I at once closed it, responding rather frigidly, I believe.

But she was in no humour to allow the conversation to drop and commenced to chat with a familiarity that surprised me.

She noticed how puzzled I became, and at length remarked with a laugh—

"You apparently don't recognise me, Mr. Heaton."

"No, madam," I answered, taken aback. "You have certainly the advantage of me."

This recognition was startling, for was I not flying to London to escape my friends? This woman, whoever she was, would without doubt recount her meeting with me.

"It is really very droll," she laughed. "I felt sure from the first, when you entered the compartment, that you didn't know me."

"I certainly don't know you," I responded coldly—

She smiled. "Ah! I expect it's my veil," she said.

"But it's really remarkable that you should not recognise Joliot, your wife's maid."

"You! My wife's maid!" I gasped, recognising in an instant how cleverly I had been run to earth.

"Yes," she replied. "Surely you recognise me?" and she raised her veil, displaying a rather unprepossessing face, dark and tragic, as though full of some hidden, sorrow.

I had never seen the woman before in my life, but instantly I resolved to display no surprise and act with caution.

"Ah, of course!" I said lamely. "The light here is so bad, you know, that I didn't recognise you. And where are you going?"

"To London—to the dressmaker's."

"Mrs. Heaton has sent you on some commission, I suppose?"

"Yes, sir."

"You joined this train at Exeter, then?"

"I came from Exmouth to Exeter, and changed," she explained. "I saw you get in at Lympston." My heart sank within me. It was evident that this woman had been sent by my self-styled wife to keep watch upon my movements. If I intended to escape I should be compelled to make terms with her.

Those sharp dark eyes, with a curious light in them—eyes that seemed strangely staring and vacant at times—were fixed upon me, while the smile about her thin lips was clearly one of triumph, as though she had caught me in the act of flying from my home.

I reflected, but next moment resolved to take her into my confidence. I disliked her, for her manner was somewhat eccentric, and, furthermore, I had only her own word that she was really maid to that angular woman who called herself my wife. Nevertheless, I could do naught else than make a bargain with her.

"Now," I said at last, after some desultory conversation, "I want to make a suggestion to you. Do you think that if I gave you a ten-pound note you could forget having met me to-night? Do you think that you could forget having seen me at all?"

"Forget? I don't understand."

"Well, to put it plainly, I'm going to London, and I have no desire that anybody should know that I'm there," I explained. "When I am found to be missing from Denbury, Mrs. Heaton will do all in her power to discover me. You are the only person who knows that I've gone to London, and I want you to hold your tongue."

She smiled again, showing an even row of white teeth.

"I was sent by my mistress to travel by this train and to see where you went," she said bluntly.

"Exactly as I thought," I answered. "Now, you will accept this as a little present, and return to Denbury to-morrow after a fruitless errand—utterly fruitless, you understand?"

She took the ten sovereigns I handed her, and transferred them to her purse, promising to say nothing of having met me.

I gathered from her subsequent conversation that she had been maid to Mrs. Heaton ever since her marriage, and that she had acted as confidential servant. Many things she mentioned incidentally were of the greatest interest to me, yet they only served to show how utterly ignorant I was of all the past.

"But why did you disclose your identity?" I inquired, when the lights showed that we were entering the London suburbs.

"Because I felt certain that you didn't recognise me," she laughed; "and I had no wish to spy upon you, knowing as I do that your life is the reverse of happy."

"Then you pity me, eh?"

"I scarcely think that is the word that one of my position ought to use," she answered, with some hesitation. "Your life has, since your marriage, not been of the happiest, that's certain."

"And so you have no intention of telling any one where I've gone?" I asked eagerly.

"None in the least, sir. Rest assured that I shall say nothing—not a single word."

"I thank you," I said, and sat back pondering in silence until the train ran into Waterloo, where we parted, she again reassuring me of her intention to keep my secret.

I congratulated myself upon a very narrow escape, and, taking a cab, drove straight to Trafalgar Square. As I crossed Waterloo Bridge the long line of lights on the Embankment presented the same picture as they had ever done. Though six years had passed since I had last had knowledge of London, nothing had apparently changed. The red night-glare in the leaden sky was still the same; the same unceasing traffic; the same flashing of bright dresses and glittering jewels as hansoms passed and repassed in the Strand—just as I had known London by night during all my life.

The gold-braided porter at the *Grand* handed me out of the cab, and I ascended by the lift to the room allotted to me like a man in a dream. It hardly seemed possible that I could have been absent in mind from that whirling, fevered world of London for six whole years. I had given a false name in the reception bureau, fearing that those people who called themselves my friends—Heaven save the mark!—might make inquiries and cause my arrest as a wandering lunatic. I had no baggage, and I saw that the hotel-clerk looked upon me with some suspicion. Indeed, I threw down a couple of sovereigns, well knowing the rules that no person without luggage was taken unless he paid a deposit beforehand.

I laughed bitterly within myself. How strange it was!

Next morning I went forth and wandered down the Strand—the dear old Strand that I had once loved so well. No; it had in no wise changed, except, perhaps, that two or three monster buildings had sprung up, and that the theatres announced pieces quite unknown to me. A sudden desire seized me to see what kind of place was my own office. If, however, I went near there, I might, I reflected, be recognised by some one who knew me. Therefore I turned into a barber's and had my beard cut off, then, further on, bought a new dust coat and another hat. In that disguise I took a hansom to Old Broad Street.

I was not long in finding the business headquarters of my own self. How curious it all was! My name was marked upon a huge brass plate in the entrance-hall of that colossal block of offices, and I ascended to the first floor to find my name inscribed upon the door of one of the largest of the suites. I stood in the corridor carelessly reading a paper, and while doing so witnessed many persons, several of them smart-looking City men, leave, as though much business was being conducted within.

Fortunately, no one recognised me, and descending, I regained the street.

When outside I glanced up, and there saw my name, in big gilt letters, upon the wire blinds of six big windows.

If I were actually as well known in the City as Gedge had alleged, then it was dangerous for me to remain in that vicinity. Therefore I entered another cab and drove to my old chambers in Essex Street.

Up the thin-worn creaking stairs of the dismal, smoke-begrimed old place I climbed, but on arrival at my door a plate confronting me showed that Percival and Smale, solicitors, were now the occupants. From inquiries I made of Mr. Smale, it appeared that they had occupied the floor as offices for the past three years, and that the tenants previous to them had been a firm of accountants. He knew nothing of my tenancy, and could tell me no word of either old Mrs. Parker or of Dick Doyle, who had, it appeared, also vacated his quarters long ago. That afternoon I wandered in the Park, over that same road where I had lingered with Mabel in those cherished days bygone. Every tree and every object brought back to me sweet memories of her. But I remembered her letters reposing in my pocket, and bit my lip. Truly, in the unconscious life when I had been my other self, my real tastes had been inverted. My love for her had cooled. I had actually, when engaged to her, cast her aside.

It was incredible. Surely my experience was unique in all the world.

Unable to decide how to act in those puzzling circumstances, I spent fully a couple of hours in the Park. The Row was hot, dusty, and almost deserted, but at last I turned into the shady walks in Kensington Gardens, and wandered until I came out into the High Street by that same gate where she had once discovered the dead man's pencil-case in my possession.

As I stood there in the full light of that glaring afternoon, the whole scene came back vividly to me. She had known that man who had been so foully murdered in her mother's home. I must, at all costs, find her, clear myself, and elucidate the truth.

Hence, with that object, I hailed another cab, and, giving the man directions to drive to The Boltons, sat back, eager and wondering.

As the conveyance drew up my heart gave a leap for joy, for I saw by the blinds that the house was still occupied.

I sprang out and rang the visitors' bell.

XXIV

The Master Hand

A man-servant answered my summons.

"Mrs. Anson?" I inquired.

"Mrs. Anson is out of town, sir," answered the man. "The house is let."

"Furnished?"

"Yes, sir."

"Is your mistress at home?" I inquired.

"I don't know, sir," answered the man, diplomatically.

"Oh, of course!" I exclaimed, taking out a card. It was the first I found within my cigarette-case, and was intentionally not my own. "Will you take this to your mistress, and ask her if she will kindly spare me a few moments. I am a friend of Mrs. Anson's."

"I'll see if she's at home, sir," said the man, dubiously; and then, asking me into the entrance-hall, he left me standing while he went in search of his mistress.

That hall was the same down which I had groped my way when blind. I saw the closed door of the drawing-room, and knew that within that room the young man whose name I knew not had been foully done to death. There was the very umbrella stand from which I had taken the walking-stick, and the door of the little-used library, which I had examined on that night when I had dined there at Mrs. Anson's invitation—the last night of my existence as my real self.

The man returned in a few moments and invited me into a room on the left—the morning-room, I supposed it to be—saying:

"My mistress is at home, sir, and will see you."

I had not remained there more than a couple of minutes before a youngish woman of perhaps thirty or so entered, with a rather distant bow. She was severely dressed in black; dark-haired, and not very prepossessing. Her lips were too thick to be beautiful, and her top row of teeth seemed too much in evidence. Her face was not exactly ugly, but she was by no means good-looking.

"I have to apologise," I said, rising and bowing. "I understand that Mrs. Anson has let her house, and I thought you would kindly give me her address. I wish to see her on a most pressing personal matter."

She regarded me with some suspicion, I thought.

"If you are a friend of Mrs. Anson's, would it not be better if you wrote to her and addressed the letter here? Her letters are always forwarded," she answered.

She was evidently a rather shrewd and superior person.

"Well, to tell the truth," I said, "I have reasons for not writing."

"Then I must regret, sir, that I am unable to furnish you with her address," she responded, somewhat stiffly.

"I have been absent from London for six years," I exclaimed. "It is because of that long absence that I prefer not to write."

"I fear that I cannot assist you," she replied briefly.

There was a strange, determined look in her dark-grey eyes. She did not seem a person amenable to argument.

"But it is regarding an urgent and purely private affair that I wish to see Mrs. Anson," I said.

"I have nothing whatever to do with the private affairs of Mrs. Anson," she replied. "I merely rent this house from her, and, in justice to her, it is not likely that I give the address to every chance caller."

"I am no chance caller," I responded. "During her residence here six years ago I was a welcome guest at her table."

"Six years ago is a long time. You may, for aught I know, not be so welcome now."

Did she, I wondered, speak the truth?

"You certainly speak very plainly, madam," I answered, rising stiffly. "If I have put you to any inconvenience I regret it. I can, no doubt, obtain from some other person the information I require."

"Most probably you can, sir," she answered, in a manner quite unruffled. "I tell you that if you write I shall at once forward your letter to her. More than that I cannot do."

"I presume you are acquainted with Miss Mabel Anson?" I inquired.

She smiled with some sarcasm.

"The Anson family do not concern me in the least, sir," she replied, also rising as sign that my unfruitful interview was at an end. Mention of Mabel seemed to have irritated her, and although I plied her with further questions, she would tell me absolutely nothing.

When I bowed and took my leave I fear that I did not show her very much politeness.

In my eagerness for information, her hesitation to give me Mrs. Anson's address never struck me as perfectly natural. She, of course, did not know me, and her offer to forward a letter was all that she could do in such circumstances. Yet at the time I did not view it in that light, but regarded the tenant of that house of mystery as an ill-mannered and extremely disagreeable person.

In despair I returned to St. James's Street and entered my club, the Devonshire. Several men whom I did not know greeted me warmly in the smoking-room, and, from their manner, I saw that in my lost years I had evidently not abandoned that institution. They chatted to me about politics and stocks, two subjects upon which I was perfectly ignorant, and I was compelled to exercise considerable tact and ingenuity in order to avoid betraying the astounding blank in my mind.

After a restless hour I drove back westward and called at old Channing's in Cornwall Gardens in an endeavour to learn Mabel's address. The colonel was out, but I saw Mrs. Channing, and she could, alas! tell me nothing beyond the fact that Mrs. Anson and her daughter had been abroad for three years past—where, she knew not. They had drifted apart, she said, and never now exchanged letters.

"Is Mabel married?" I inquired as carelessly as I could, although in breathless eagerness.

"I really don't know," she responded. "I have heard some talk of the likelihood of her marrying, but whether she has done so I am unaware."

"And the man whom rumour designated as her husband? Who was he?" I inquired quickly.

"A young nobleman, I believe."

"You don't know his name?"

"No. It was mentioned at the time, but it has slipped my memory. One takes no particular notice of teacup gossip."

"Well, Mrs. Channing," I said confidently, "I am extremely desirous of discovering the whereabouts of Mabel Anson. I want to see her upon a rather curious matter which closely concerns herself. Can you tell me of any one who is intimate with them?"

"Unfortunately, I know of no one," she answered. "The truth is, that they left London quite suddenly; and, indeed, it was a matter for surprise that they neither paid farewell visits nor told any of their friends where they were going."

"Curious," I remarked—"very curious!"

Then there was, I reflected, apparently some reason for the present tenant at The Boltons refusing the address.

"Yes," Mrs. Channing went on, "it was all very mysterious. Nobody knows the real truth why they went abroad so suddenly and secretly. It was between three and four years ago now, and nothing, to my knowledge, has since been heard of them."

"Very mysterious," I responded. "It would seem almost as though they had some reason for concealing their whereabouts."

"That's just what lots of people have said. You may depend upon it that there is something very mysterious in it all. We were such very close friends for years, and it is certainly strange that Mrs. Anson has never confided in me the secret of her whereabouts."

I remembered the old colonel's strange warning on that evening long ago, when I had first met Mabel at his table. What, I wondered, could he know of them to their detriment?

I remained for a quarter of an hour longer. The colonel's wife was full of the latest tittle-tattle, as the wife of an *ex-attaché* always is. It is part of the diplomatic training to be always well-informed in the sayings and doings of our neighbours; and as I allowed her to gossip on she revealed to me many things of which I was in ignorance. Nellie, her daughter, had, it appeared, married the son of a Newcastle shipowner a couple of years before, and now lived near Berwick-on-Tweed.

Suddenly a thought occurred to me, and I asked whether she knew Miss Wells or the man Hickman, who had been my fellow-guests on that night when I had dined at The Boltons.

"I knew a Miss Wells—a very pronounced old maid, who was a friend of hers," answered Mrs. Channing. "But she caught influenza about a year ago, and died of it. She lived in Edith Villas, Kensington."

"And Hickman, a fair man, of middle age, with a very ugly face?"

She reflected.

"I have no recollection of ever having met him, or of hearing of him," she answered. "Was he an intimate friend?"

"I believe so," I said. Then, finding that she could explain nothing more, I took my leave.

Next day and the next I wandered about London aimlessly and without hope. Mabel and her mother had, for some unaccountable reason, gone abroad and carefully concealed their whereabouts. Had this fact any connexion with the mysterious tragedy that had been enacted at The Boltons? That one thought was ever uppermost in my mind.

A week passed, and I still remained at the *Grand*, going forth each day, wandering hither and thither, but never entering the club or going to places where I thought it likely that I might be recognised. I could not return to the life at Denbury with that angular woman at the head of my table—the woman who called herself my wife. If I returned I felt that the mystery of it all must drive me to despair, and I should, in a fit of desperation, commit suicide.

I ask any of those who read this strange history of my life, whether they consider themselves capable of remaining calm and tranquil in such circumstances, or of carefully going over all the events in their sequence and considering them with logical reasoning. I tried to do so, but in vain. For hours I sat within the hotel smoking and thinking. I was living an entirely false life, existing in the fear of recognition by unknown friends, and the constant dread that sooner or later I must return to that hated life in Devonshire.

That a hue-and-cry had been raised regarding my disappearance was plain from a paragraph which I read in one of the morning papers about ten days after my departure from Denbury. In the paragraph I was designated as "a financier well known in the City," and it was there stated that I had left my home suddenly "after betraying signs of insanity," and had not since been heard of.

"Insanity!" I laughed bitterly as I read those lines supplied by the Exeter correspondent of the Central News. The police had, no doubt, received my description, and were actively on the watch to trace me and restore me to my "friends."

For nearly a fortnight I had been in hiding, and was now on the verge of desperation. By means of one of the cheques I had taken from Denbury I succeeded in drawing a good round sum without my bankers being aware of my address, and was contemplating going abroad in order to avoid the possibility of being put under restraint as a lunatic, when one evening, in the dusky, sunset, I went forth and wandered down Northumberland Avenue to the Victoria Embankment. In comparison with the life and bustle of the Strand and Trafalgar Square, the wide roadway beside the Thames is always quiet and reposeful. Upon that same pavement over which I now strolled in the direction of the Temple I had, in the days of my blindness, taken my lessons in walking alone. That pavement had been my practice-ground on summer evenings under the tender guidance of poor old Parker, the faithful servant now lost to me. My eyesight had now grown as strong as that of other men. The great blank in my mind was all that distinguished me from my fellows. During those past fourteen days I had been probing a period which I had not lived, and ascertaining by slow degrees the events of my unknown past.

And as I strolled along beneath the plane trees over that broad pavement I recollected that the last occasion I had been there was on that memorable evening when I had lost myself, and was subsequently present at the midnight tragedy in that house of mystery. I gazed around.

In the ornamental gardens, bright with geraniums, some tired Londoners were taking their ease upon the seats provided by that most paternal of all metropolitan institutions, the London County Council; children were shouting as they played at ball and hopscotch, that narrow strip of green being, alas! all they knew of Nature's beauty outside their world of bricks and mortar. The slight wind stirred the dusty foliage of the trees beneath which I walked, while to the left river-steamers belched forth volumes of black smoke, and barges slowly floated down with the tide. On either side were great buildings, and straight before the dome of St. Paul's. Over all was that golden, uncertain haze which in central London is called sunset, the light which so quickly turns to cold grey, without any of those glories of crimson and gold which those in the country associate with the summer sun's decline.

That walk induced within me melancholy thoughts of a wasted life. I loved Mabel Anson—I loved her with all my soul. Now that marriage with her was no longer within the range of possibility I was inert and despairing, utterly heedless of everything. I had, if truth be told, no further desire for life. All joy within me was now blotted out.

At length, at Blackfriars Bridge, I retraced my steps, and some twenty minutes later, as I took my key from the hotel bureau, the clerk handed me a note, addressed to "Burton Lawrence, Esquire," the fictitious name I had given. It had been delivered by boy-messenger.

Then I was discovered! My heart leapt into my mouth.

I tore open the envelope, and read its contents. They were brief and to the point.

"The undersigned will be obliged," it ran, "if Mr. Burton Lawrence will be present this evening at eight o'clock, in the main-line booking-office of the Brighton Railway, at Victoria Station. An interview is of very pressing importance."

The note was signed, by that single word which had always possessed such mysterious signification, the word "Avel."

Hitherto, in my old life long ago, receipt of communications from that mysterious correspondent had caused me much anxiety of mind.

I had always feared their advent; now, however, I actually welcomed it, even though it were strange and unaccountable that the unknown writer should know my whereabouts and the name beneath which I had sought to conceal my identity.

I made a hasty dinner in the coffee-room, and went forthwith to Victoria, wondering whom I should meet. The last time I had kept one of those strange appointments on that summer evening long ago in Hyde Park, I had come face to face with the woman I loved. Would that I could meet her now!

I entered the booking-office, searching it with eager eyes. Two lines of persons were taking tickets at the pigeon-holes, while a number of loungers were, like myself, awaiting friends. Beyond, upon the platform, all was bustle as is usual at that hour, when the belated portion of business London is bound for the southern suburbs. From that busy terminus of the West End trains were arriving and departing each minute.

The big illumined clock showed that it was yet five minutes to the hour. Therefore I strolled out upon the platform, lounged around the bookstalls, and presently returned to the spot indicated in the letter.

As I re-entered the booking-office my eager eyes fell upon a figure standing before me—a well-dressed figure, with a face that smiled upon me.

An involuntary cry of surprise escaped my lips. The encounter was sudden and astounding; but in that instant, as I rushed forward to greet the new-comer, I knew myself to be on the verge of a startling and remarkable discovery.

XXV

The Person Who Knew

The encounter was a startling one.

At the moment when my eyes first fell upon the figure standing patiently in the booking-office awaiting me, I halted for a second in uncertainty. The silhouette before me was that of a youngish, brown-haired, and rather good-looking woman, neatly dressed in dead black, wearing a large hat and a feather boa round her neck.

By the expression of her face I saw that she had recognised me. I had, of course, never seen her before, yet her personal appearance—the grey eyes and brown hair—were exactly similar to those described so minutely on several occasions by West, the cab-driver. I regarded her for a moment in silent wonder, then advanced to meet her.

She was none other than the unknown woman who had saved my life on that fateful night at The Boltons—the mysterious Edna!

As I raised my hat she bowed gracefully, and with a merry smile, said: "I fear that, to you, I am a stranger. I recognise you, however, as Mr. Heaton."

"That is certainly my name," I responded, still puzzled. "And you—well, our recognition is, I believe, mutual—you are Edna."

She glanced at me quickly, as though suspicious. "How did you know that?" she inquired. "You have never seen me before. You were totally blind on the last occasion we met."

"I recognised you from your description," I answered with a light laugh.

"My description!" she echoed in a tone of distinct alarm.

"Yes, the description given of you by the cabman who drove me home on that memorable morning."

"Ah! Of course," she exclaimed in sudden remembrance. Then, for a few seconds, she remained in silence. It seemed as though the fact that I had recognised her had somewhat confused her.

"But I am extremely glad that we have met at last," I assured her. "I have, times without number, hoped to have an opportunity of thanking you for the great services you once rendered me."

"I find with satisfaction that although six years have gone by you have not forgotten your promise made to me," she said, her large serious eyes fixed upon mine.

"I gave you that promise in exchange for my life," I remarked, as, at her suggestion, we turned and walked out of the station.

"And as acknowledgement of the service you rendered by preserving secret your knowledge of the events of that terrible night I was enabled to render you a small service in return," she said. "Your sight was restored to you."

"For that, how can I sufficiently thank you?" I exclaimed. "I owe it all to you, and rest assured that, although we have not met until this evening, I have never forgotten—nor shall I ever forget."

She smiled pleasantly, while I strolled slowly at her side across the station-yard.

To me those moments were like a dream. Edna, the woman who had hitherto been but a strange ghost of the past, was now actually beside me in the flesh.

"I have received other notes making appointments—the last, I think, a couple of years ago," I observed after a pause. "Did you not meet me then?"

She glanced at me with a puzzled expression. Of course she knew nothing of those lost years of my life.

"Meet you?" she repeated. "Certainly not."

"Who met me, then?"

"I really don't know," she answered. "This is the first time I have approached you, and I only come to you now in order to ask you to grant me a favour—a very great favour."

"A favour! What is it?"

"I cannot explain here, in the street," she said quickly. "If you will come to my hotel I will place the facts before you."

"Where are you staying?"

"At the *Bath Hotel*, in Arlington Street."

I knew the place well. It stood at the corner of Arlington Street and Piccadilly, and was an eminently respectable, old-fashioned place, patronised by a high-class clientele.

"And you are alone?" I inquired, thinking it strange that she should thus ask me to her hotel.

"Of course. I have come to London expressly to see you," she responded. "I went down to Budleigh-Salterton two days ago, but I ascertained at Denbury that you had left suddenly."

"Whom did you see there?" I inquired, much interested.

"Your butler. He told me some absurd story, how that you had become temporarily irresponsible for your actions, and had disappeared, leaving no address."

"And you came to London?"

"Of course."

"And how did you find out where I was hidden, and my assumed name?"

She smiled mysteriously.

"It was easy enough, I assure you. A man of your influence in the City, and as well known as you are, has considerable difficulty in effectively concealing his identity."

"But who told you where I was staying?" I demanded.

"Nobody. I discovered it for myself."

"And yet the police have been searching for me everywhere, and have not yet discovered me!" I remarked, surprised.

"The police have one method," she said. "I have an entirely different one."

"Tell me one thing," I said, halting in our walk, for we were already at the commencement of Victoria Street—that street down which I had wandered blindly on that night long ago when I had lost myself—"tell me for what reason those previous appointments were made with me at Grosvenor Gate, at King's Cross, at Eastbourne, and elsewhere?"

"You kept them," she replied. "You surely know."

"No, that's just it," I said. "Of course, I don't expect you to give credence to what I say—it sounds too absurd—but I have absolutely no knowledge of keeping those appointments except the one at Grosvenor Gate, and I am totally ignorant of having met anybody." She paused, looking me full in the face with those grey eyes so full of mystery.

"I begin to think that what the butler told me contains some truth," she observed bluntly.

"No," I protested. "My mind is in no way unhinged. I am fully aware of all that transpired at The Boltons, of—"

"At The Boltons?" she interrupted, turning a trifle pale. "What do you mean?"

"Of the crime enacted at that house—in The Boltons." She held her breath. Plainly she was not before aware that I had discovered the spot where the tragedy had taken place. My words had taken her by surprise, and it was evident that she was utterly confounded. My discovery I had kept a profound secret unto myself, and now, for the first time, had revealed it.

Her face showed how utterly taken aback she was. "There is some mistake, I think," she said lamely, apparently for want of something other to say.

"Surely your memory carries you back to that midnight tragedy!" I exclaimed rather hastily, for I saw she would even now mislead me, if she could. "I have discovered where it took place—I have since re-entered that room?"

"You have!" she gasped in the low, hoarse voice of one fearful lest her secret should be discovered. "You have actually re-discovered the house—even though you were stone blind?"

"Yes," I answered.

"How did you accomplish it?"

I shrugged my shoulders, answering: "There is an old saying—a very true one—that 'murder will out.'"

"But tell me more. Explain more fully," she urged in an earnest tone.

I hesitated. Next instant, however, I decided to keep my own counsel in the matter. Her readiness to deny that the events occurred in that house had re-aroused within me a distinct suspicion.

"It is a long story, and cannot be told here," I answered evasively.

"Then come along to the hotel," she suggested. "I, too, have much to say to you."

I do not know that I should have obeyed her were it not for the mystery which had hitherto, veiled her identity. She had saved my life, it is true, and I supposed that I ought to consider her as a friend, yet in those few minutes during which I had gazed upon her a curious dislike of her had arisen within me. She was, I felt certain, not the straightforward person I had once believed her to be.

Not that there was anything in her appearance against her. On the contrary, she was a pleasant, smiling, rather pretty woman of perhaps thirty-five, who spoke with the air and manner of a lady, and who carried herself well, with the grace of one in a higher social circle.

After a few moments' hesitation my curiosity got the better of my natural caution, and I determined to hear what she had to say. Therefore we drove together to the *Bath Hotel*.

In her own private sitting-room, a cosy little apartment overlooking Piccadilly, opposite Dover Street, she removed her big black hat, drew off her gloves, and having invited me to a chair, took one herself on the opposite side of the fireplace. Her maid was there when we entered, but retired at word from her mistress.

"You, of course, regard it as very curious, Mr. Heaton, that after these six years I should again seek you," she commenced, leaning her arm lightly upon the little table, and gazing straight into my face without flinching. "It is true that once I was enabled to render you a service, and now in return I ask you also to render me one. Of course, it is useless to deny that a secret exists between us—a secret which, if revealed, would be disastrous."

"To whom?"

"To certain persons whose names need not be mentioned."

"Why not?"

"Think," she said, very gravely. "Did you not promise that, in return for your life when you were blind and helpless, you would make no effort to learn the true facts? It seems that you have already learnt at least one—the spot where the crime was committed."

"I consider it my duty to learn what I can of this affair," I answered determinedly.

She raised her eyebrows with an expression of surprise, for she saw that I was in earnest.

"After your vow to me?" she asked. "Remember that, to acknowledge my indebtedness for that vow, I searched for the one specialist who could restore your sight. To my efforts, Mr. Heaton, you are now in possession of that sense that was lost to you."

"I acknowledge that freely," I answered. "Yet, even in that you have sought to deceive me."

"How?"

"You told me you were not the writer of those letters signed with a pseudonym."

"And that is true. I was not the actual writer, even though I may have caused them to be written."

"Having thus deceived me, how can you hope that I can be free with you?"

"I regret," she answered, "that slight deception has been necessary to preserve the secret?"

"The secret of the crime?"

She nodded.

"Well, and what do you wish to tell me this evening?" She was silent for a moment, toying with her rings.

"I want to appeal to your generosity. I want you to assist me."

"In what manner?"

"As before."

"As before!" I repeated, greatly surprised. "I have no knowledge of having assisted you before."

"What?" she cried. "Is your memory so defective that you do not recollect your transactions with those who waited upon you—those who kept the previous appointments of which you have spoken?"

"I assure you, madam," I said, quite calmly, "I have not the least idea of what you mean."

"Mr. Heaton!" she cried. "Have you really taken leave of your senses? Is it actually true what your butler has said of you—that on the day you left Denbury you behaved like a madman?"

"I am no madman!" I cried with considerable warmth. "The truth is that I remember nothing since one evening, nearly six years ago, when I was smoking with—with a friend—in Chelsea, until that day to which my servant has referred."

"You remember nothing? That is most extraordinary."

"If strange to you, madam, how much more strange to me? I have told you the truth, therefore kindly proceed to explain the object of these previous visits of persons you have apparently sent to me."

"I really think that you must be joking," she said. "It seems impossible that you should actually be unaware."

"I tell you that I have no knowledge whatsoever of their business with me."

"Then if such is really the case, let me explain," she said. "First, I think you will admit that your financial transactions with our Government have brought you very handsome profits."

"I am not aware of having had any transactions with the British Government," I answered.

"I refer to that of Bulgaria," she explained. "Surely you are aware that through my intermediary you have obtained great concessions—the docks at Varna, the electric trams at Sofia, the railway from Timova to the Servian frontier, not to mention other great undertakings which have been floated as companies, all of which are now earning handsome profits. You cannot be ignorant of that!"

I remembered that Gedge had shown me some official parchment which he had explained were concessions obtained from Prince Ferdinand of Bulgaria. That this woman had been the means of securing to me the greater part of the enormous profits which I had apparently made within the past five years was certainly surprising.

"On the day I recovered consciousness—the day of my departure from Denbury—I was shown some documents, but took but little heed of them," I said.

"You admit, however, that the employment of British capital in Bulgaria has realised a very handsome profit, and that the greater part of it has gone into your own pockets?"

"I suppose that is so," I responded. "Is it to you that I am indebted for those concessions?"

"Certainly."

"Are you, then, an ambassadress of the Principality of Bulgaria?"

"Well, yes—if you choose to put it so."

"Then, as I understand, it is with some further financial object that you have sought me this evening?"

"Exactly."

This latest development of the affair was certainly most remarkable. I had never dreamed that to this hitherto unknown woman I had been indebted for the unparalleled success which had attended my career during those past six years. Yet, from the facts she subsequently placed before me, it would seem that it was at her instigation that I first dabbled in finance. She, or rather her agents, had obtained for me the negotiation of a substantial loan to Prince Ferdinand, and this had been followed by all sorts of concessions, not one of which had tuned out badly.

The mysterious Edna, whom I had always believed to be a typical blouse-and-bicycle girl of the true Kensington type, was actually a political agent of that most turbulent of all the European States.

I sat looking at her in wonderment. She possessed a superb carriage, a smart, well-dressed figure, a smiling, intelligent face, white, even teeth, a complexion just a trifle dark, but betraying no trace of foreign birth. Her English was perfect, her manner purely that of the patrician, while her surprising tact possessed all the *finesse* of an accomplished diplomatist.

"I confess that I have all along been in entire ignorance of my indebtedness to you," I said, after listening to her while she explained how obediently I had followed the instructions contained in the letters signed "Avel," and how I had so materially advanced the interests of the Principality that the thanks of the Bulgarian Parliament, or Sobranje had been tendered to me, and the Prince himself had a couple of years ago conferred upon me the highest distinction within his power.

Yet it was more than strange that while this shrewd grey-eyed woman, the possessor of the secret of that puzzling crime, held aloof from me, she had ingeniously contrived that I should become the unwitting catspaw of an unstable State.

I was thinking of Mabel—my thoughts were always of my lost love—and I was wondering how I might obtain from this woman the secret of her whereabouts.

XXVI

Edna Makes a Proposal

W ell," I inquired at last; "and your reason for seeing me this evening?"

She hesitated, as though uncertain in what manner to place her project before me. She moved uneasily, and, rising, drew forth a large dispatch-box from its leathern case and placed it upon the table. I noticed that the outer case bore a count's coronet with a cipher beneath.

Having opened the box with a tiny gold master-key which hung upon her bracelet, she drew forth some official-looking papers, and with them returned to her chair.

"You have already been entrusted with a secret, which you have not betrayed—the secret of that unfortunate occurrence on the evening when accident first brought us together," she commenced gravely. "Therefore I feel convinced that any further confidence placed in you will not be abused."

"I am honoured to think, madam, that you should entertain such an opinion of me," I said, not, however, without the slightest touch of sarcasm.

I did not forget that she had only rescued me from my enemies in return for my silence. She was not a woman to act without strong motives. Moreover, she had admitted knowledge of that strange midnight crime at The Boltons, and was, therefore, an accessory after the fact.

"You are the Prince's confidential agent here, in London, and I come to you on a mission direct from His Serene Highness."

"From Bulgaria?" I inquired.

"Yes. I left Sofia a week ago," she answered. "It was at first proposed to place the matter in the hands of Guechoff, our diplomatic representative at the Court of St. James's, but, on consideration, His Serene Highness, knowing that with the present state of high feeling in the Sobranje a single hint leaking out might prove disastrous, to the dynasty, and perhaps to the nation, resolved to place the matter unreservedly in my hands. The Prince did me the honour of referring in terms of praise to my previous dealings with you, and instructed me to lose no time in seeing you and invoking your aid."

"In what direction?" Was it not amazing that I should awake from my years of unconsciousness to find myself so powerful in the world of finance that reigning princes sought my assistance?

"I have here a letter from His Serene Highness;" and she handed me a note which bore the Bulgarian royal arms, and had apparently been written by the Prince's own hand. It was merely a formal note asking me to consider the secret proposals which would be placed before me by the bearer.

"Well?" I inquired, when I had read it. "Explain."

"Briefly," she said, "the facts are as follows: The throne of Bulgaria, never very safe owing to the eternal bickering between St. Petersburg and the Porte, is at this moment in imminent danger. The People's Party in the Sobranje have been defeated, and the police have learnt of a projected popular uprising against His Highness in favour of a republic, the agitation being, of course, caused by paid agents of Russia. It is an open secret that Russia, at the first sign of an outbreak, would endeavour to annex the country, hence the position of the throne grows each moment more perilous. Fear of giving offence to Russia prevents orders being issued for the arrest of the secret agitators, and it seems therefore as though a revolution cannot long be delayed. It is your aid His Serene Highness seeks—your aid to negotiate a loan of half a million sterling."

"Half a million!" I exclaimed. "A large sum! It seems incredible that I should be a dealer in millions."

"A large sum, certainly, but you can easily obtain it," she quickly assured me. "I have all the necessary preliminaries of the securities here;" and she pointed to the pile of papers at her side.

"I take it that the money is required for the Prince's private purse?"

"No; solely for defence—to purchase arms and ammunition; to pay the army the arrears due, so as to secure their support in case of an outbreak, and to pay certain heavy sums as secret-service money. All this is imperative in order to save the country from falling into the hands of Russia. But it must be done, of course, in strictest secrecy, His Highness, as I have already explained, hesitated to entrust the matter to his recognised minister here because the spies of Russia are everywhere, and if any knowledge of his intentions leaked out it would be fatal to his plans."

"And so he trusts me!" I said, smiling.

"He does, absolutely."

"And where does His Highness think that I am going to get half a million of money from at a moment's notice, pray?" I asked with a smile.

"With these in your possession there will be no difficulty," she responded coolly, indicating the papers. "There is not a financial agent in the City of London who would not be only too delighted to, without its intentions being known."

"But you say it is all a secret," I observed. "How do you think it possible that I can raise such a loan without its intentions being known?"

She laughed outright.

"The money, you will find from the documents here, is ostensibly for the construction of a new railway from Philippopolis, by the Shipka to Rustchuk. The plans are here, properly prepared, so that you need have no hesitation in showing them to any railway engineer."

I saw that she had been trained in a school of clever diplomacy.

"And you say that security will be given?"

"Certainly. The proposal is to give the customs receipts. They would be ample. Failing that, it is probable that the Princess's jewels, which, as you know, include some of the finest pearls in Europe, might be available. Of the latter, however, I am not sure."

I remained silent, turning over the papers she had passed across to me. They were mostly in French, and, therefore, easily understood. The documents related to "the long projected scheme of constructing a railway from Philippopolis to Eski Saghra, thence across the Shipka to Rasgrad, joining the line already in operation between Varna and Rustchuk." Appended were official declarations from the Bulgarian Minister of Finance, countersigned by the Prince himself.

The documents were certainly very ingeniously contrived so as to conceal the real purpose of the loan. I remarked this, and my companion, laughing lightly, said—

"Deception, to some extent, is always necessary in delicate diplomacy."

The discovery that the mysterious woman—whose name she had withheld from me—was actually a secret agent of the autonomous Principality created by the Berlin Treaty—that turbulent State mostly notable for the assassination of its Ministers—was entirely unlooked for. On the night when accident had thrown us together, and she had smoothed my brow with her cool hand, I had believed her to be a young girl who had taken pity upon me in my helplessness; but the revelations she had made during that half-hour showed that there had been some firm purpose underlying it all.

She alone knew the truth of that tragic occurrence at The Boltons, and I saw that in this matter I had to deal with a very clever and ingenious woman.

I had now a double purpose in life—to discover Mabel, and to elucidate the mystery of the crime. Towards that end I intended to strive, and as I sat with my glance fixed upon those mysterious grey eyes, I endeavoured to form some plan of action.

"Madam," I said gravely, at last, "as you appear not to place sufficient confidence in me to tell me your name, I regret that I can place no confidence in these documents."

"My name!" she laughed. "Ah, of course; I had quite forgotten. There is no secret about it;" and from her purse she drew forth a folded, much-worn blue paper, which she handed to me.

It was an English passport, bearing the name of "Lucy Edna Grainger."

"Grainger?" I repeated. "Then you are English?"

"Yes, I am legally a British subject, because my father was English. I was, however, born abroad."

A silence fell between us. The roar of the traffic in Piccadilly came up from below; the summer night was warm, and the window stood open. At last I determined upon a bold course.

"Now that we have met," I said, "I wish to ask you one or two questions. First, I am desirous of knowing the whereabouts of Mrs. Anson and her daughter."

I was watching her narrowly, and saw her give a distinct start at my mention of the same. Next instant, however, she recovered herself, and with marvellous tact repeated—

"Anson? Anson? I have no acquaintance with any person of that name."

I smiled.

"I think it unnecessary that you should deny this, when the truth is so very plain," I observed sarcastically. "You will, perhaps, next deny that a young man was foully murdered within that house in The Boltons; that you were present, and that you are aware of the identity of those who committed the crime?"

The pallor of her cheeks showed plainly that I had recalled unwelcome memories.

"The unfortunate affair is all of the past," she said hoarsely. "Why need we discuss it?"

"In the interests of justice," I answered, with firm determination.

"Have you not agreed to remain silent? Have you not, as recompense, received back your sight, and become enriched beyond your wildest dreams? Surely you, at least, should not complain."

"I complain of the manner in which the secret of the crime has been preserved," I said. "I have determined, however, that it shall remain secret no longer."

"You would inform the police!" she gasped, for the moment unable to conceal her alarm.

"If you have no knowledge of Mrs. Anson, then I intend to invoke the aid of Scotland Yard in order to discover her."

My words perplexed her. That she was acquainted with the Ansons I had no doubt, and I was likewise certain that she would never risk information being given to the police. More than once in the days long past I had entertained a shrewd suspicion that she herself was the actual murderer of that young unknown man. I looked at her pale face, and vaguely wondered again whether such were the truth.

The fact that she had secured my silence in return for my life as an outcome of that most ingenious conspiracy had seemed to me proof conclusive of her guilt, and now that we had met in those strange circumstances the idea became impressed upon me more forcibly than ever.

What might be her real position in the secret diplomacy of Bulgaria I knew not. It was evident that considerable confidence was reposed in her. She had come to me with a cool demand to raise a loan of half a million sterling, and it was plain from what she had explained that the money was urgently needed for the protection of the State against enemies both internal and external. My own position was unique. Had not Gedge shown me those official documents, which gave me concessions in the Principality of Bulgaria, I should have laughed this woman's curious story to scorn as a piece of impossible fiction. But I had glanced over some of those papers at Denbury, and was satisfied that I had actually had many dealings with that State during the six years of my unconscious but prosperous existence. There seemed every truth in her statement that to her had been due my success in the City in the first instance.

"And supposing you broke your promise and went to Scotland Yard?" she suggested at length, her eyes still fixed upon me. "What would you expect to find?"

"To find?" I echoed. "I should find traces of the crime within that room."

She nodded. I had expected my words to have some confusing effect upon her, nevertheless, on the contrary, she remained perfectly calm. Her self-control was extraordinary.

"And what would it profit you, pray?" she asked.

"I should at least know that I had endeavoured to bring to justice those responsible for the poor fellow's death."

"It would only be an endeavour—a vain one, I assure you."

"You mean that the secret is too well concealed ever to be revealed," I observed quickly.

"Yes," she said; "you have guessed aright."

"And, in other words, you defy me to discover the truth?"

"I have not said so. The word defy is scarcely one which should be used between us, I think, considering that our interests are to-day mutual—just as they were on the night of the crime."

"I fail to see that," I answered. "I have no interest whatever in keeping this terrible secret hidden, for while I do so I am acting the part of accessory."

"But surely you have an interest in preserving your own life?" she urged.

"Then you imply that if I were to lay information at Scotland Yard I should be in peril of my life?" I asked, looking straight into those calm eyes that ever and anon seemed full of mystery.

"Of that I cannot speak with any degree of certainty," she responded. "I would only warn you that in this matter continued silence is by far the best."

"But you have uttered a veiled threat!" I cried. "You are aware of the whole facts, and yet refuse to impart to me the simple information of the whereabouts of Mrs. Anson. Do you think it possible in such a case that I can entertain any confidence in you, or in your extraordinary story regarding the affairs of Bulgaria and its Prince?"

"I am unable to give you any information regarding the lady you mention," she replied, with a slight frown of annoyance.

"But you are acquainted with her?"

"I may be—what then?"

"I demand to know where she is."

"And in reply I tell you that I am in ignorance."

"In that case," I said angrily, "I refuse to have any further dealings whatsoever with you. From the first I became drawn into a trap by you, bound down and for six years held silent by your threats. But, madam, I now tell you plainly of my intentions. I mean to-morrow to lay the whole facts before the Director of Criminal Investigations, including this story of yours regarding the Prince and his people."

She rose slowly from her chair, perfectly calm, her dignity unruffled. Her manner was absolutely perfect. Had she been a princess herself she could not have treated my sudden ebullition of anger with greater disdain.

She gathered up the papers she had put before me, and, replacing them in the dispatch-box, locked it with the golden master-key upon her bangle.

Afterwards, she turned to me and said, in a hard distinct voice—

"Then I understand that I have to inform His Serene Highness that you refuse to assist him further?"

"Tell him whatever you choose, madam," I answered, rising and taking up my hat and cane. "I shall, in future, act according to my own inclinations."

"And at your own risk!" she added, in a harsh voice, as, bowing stiffly before her, I turned towards the door.

"Yes, madam," I answered; "I accept your challenge—at my own risk."

XXVII

More Scheming

The mellow summer twilight was fast deepening into night as I strode along Piccadilly towards the Circus, after leaving the grey-eyed woman who held the secret.

What she had revealed to me was startling, yet the one fact which caused me more apprehension than all others was the curious means by which she had discovered my whereabouts. If she had been enabled to do this, then the police would, no doubt, very soon find me and return me to my so-called "friends."

In despair I thought of Mabel. Long ago I had surrendered my whole heart to her. She had at first placed a strong and high-minded confidence in me, judging me by her own lofty spirit, but that unaccountable rupture had occurred, and she had gone from me crushed and heart-broken. In my pocket I carried her letter, and the more I thought over it the more puzzled I became. Daily, hourly, I lamented over the broken and shattered fragments of all that was fairest on earth; I had been borne at once from calm, lofty, and delighted speculations into the very heart of fear and tribulations. My love for her was now ranked by myself as a fond record which I must erase for ever from my heart and brain. Once I had thought to link my destiny with hers; but, alas! I could not now marry her, nor could I reveal to her, knowing them not, the mysterious influences which had changed the whole current of my life and purposes. My secret burden was that of a heart bursting with its own unuttered grief.

The whole of the events swept past me like a torrent which hurried along in its dark and restless course all those about me towards some overwhelming catastrophe. Tormented by remorseful doubts and pursued by distraction, I felt assured that Mabel, in her unresisting tenderness, her mournful sweetness, her virgin innocence, was doomed to perish by that relentless power which had linked her destiny with crime and contest in which she had no part but as a sufferer. It is, alas! the property of crime to extend its mischiefs over innocence, as it is of virtue to extend its blessing over many that deserve them not.

Plunged in that sea of troubles, of perplexities, of agonies, and of terrors, I reflected upon all that the woman Edna had told me. It seemed inconceivable that Bulgaria's ruler should demand assistance of me—and yet it was undoubtedly true.

Presently I turned down the Haymarket, still walking slowly, deep in reflection.

Should I inform the police? Very calmly I thought it over. My first impulse was to go to Scotland Yard and make a plain statement of the whole facts, laying stress upon the suspicion against the woman Grainger as an accessory. Yet when I came to consider the result of such action I saw with dismay that my lips were sealed. Such statement could only reflect upon myself. First, I should, by going to Scotland Yard, be compelled to reveal my own identity, which would mean my return to Denbury; secondly, I could give no account of those six lost years of my life; and, thirdly, the statement of one believed not to be exactly responsible for his actions must be regarded with but little credence.

No, circumstances themselves had conspired to hold me to silence.

I went on in blind despair towards my hotel.

Determined upon tracing Mabel and ascertaining from her own lips the reason that our engagement had been terminated, I travelled on the following day down to Bournemouth, and made inquiries at the hotel from which her letter had been dated.

After searching the books the hotel-clerk showed me certain entries from which it appeared that Mrs. Anson and her daughter had arrived there on May 12, 1891, and had occupied one of the best suites of rooms until June 5, when they paid their bill and left suddenly.

I glanced at Mabel's letter. It was dated June 4. She had left on the following day. I could learn nothing further.

In an excited, unsettled state of mind, unable to decide how to act, I returned to London, and then, out of sheer want of something to do, I travelled down to Heaton. The old place was the same: neglected and deserted, but full of memories of days bygone. Old Baxter and his wife were both dead, and the caretakers were fresh servants whom my agent had apparently engaged. I also learnt that Parker, the faithful old woman who had tended to my wants in Essex Street, had also passed away more than two years before.

I spent a dismal day wandering through the house and park, then drove back to Tewkesbury, and on the following morning returned to London. In the six years that had elapsed since my last visit to the Manor nothing had changed save, perhaps, that the grass had grown more luxuriantly over the gravelled drive, and the stone exterior was being gradually rendered grey by the lichen which in those parts overgrows everything.

The mystery of the crime, and of the singular events which had followed, formed an enigma which seemed utterly beyond solution.

My nerves were shattered. As the days went by an increasing desire possessed me to ascertain more of that woman who called herself Grainger and was the confidential emissary of a reigning prince. She alone knew the truth, therefore why should I not carefully watch her movements, and endeavour to discover her intentions? From the veiled threat she had muttered, it was evident that although she did not fear any revelations that I might make, yet she regarded me as a person detrimental to her interests. As long as I had acted as her agent in negotiating loans for the Principality, she had secured for me high favour in the eyes of Prince Ferdinand. But the fact that I had gained consciousness and refused to assist her further had taken her completely by surprise.

That same evening I called at the *Bath Hotel*, and ascertained that "Mrs. Grainger" had left some days before. She had not, it appeared, given any address where letters might be forwarded, but a judicious tip administered to a hall-porter caused him suddenly to recollect that a couple of days before her departure she had sent a dressing-bag to a trunk-maker's a little further down Piccadilly, to be repaired. This bag had not been returned to the hotel, therefore it was quite probable, thought the hall-porter, that the trunk-maker had forwarded it to her.

"You know the people at the trunk-maker's, of course?" I said.

"Yes, sir. Many visitors here want repairs done to their boxes and bags."

"The *Bath Hotel* is therefore a good customer?" I remarked. "They would certainly give you her address if you asked for it."

He seemed a trifle dubious, but at my request went along to the shop, and a quarter of an hour later returned with an address.

She had not moved far, it appeared. Only to the *Midland Hotel* at St. Pancras.

Late that night I myself left the *Grand*, and, assuming a name that was not my own, took a room at the *Midland*, in order to commence my observations upon her movements. It was certainly a risky business, for I knew not when I might encounter her in the vestibule, in the lift, or in the public rooms. As soon as my room was assigned to me, I glanced through the list eagerly, but it was evident that if she were there she, too, had changed her name. In the long list of visitors was one, that of Mrs. Slade. Slade? The name was familiar. It was that of the doctor who had given me back my sight. That name struck me as being the most probable. She occupied a room on the same floor as mine, numbered 406. The door of that room I intended to watch.

My vigilance on the morrow was rewarded, for about eleven o'clock in the morning I saw Edna emerge from the room dressed to go out. She passed my door and descended by the stairs, while I took my hat and swiftly followed her at a safe distance from observation.

The porter called her a hansom, and I saw her neat, black-robed figure mount into the conveyance. She had a letter in her hand, and read the address to the porter, who in turn repeated it to the driver.

Meanwhile, I had entered another cab, and telling the man to keep Edna's cab in sight, we drove along King's Cross Road and Farringdon Street to the City, passing along Gresham Street and Lothbury. Suddenly the cab I was following turned into Austin Friars, while my driver, an intelligent young fellow, pulled up at the corner of Throgmorton Street and said—

"We'd better wait here, sir, if you don't want the lady to notice us. She's going into an office at number 14, opposite the Dutch Church."

"Get down," I said, "and try and find out whose office she's gone into," and I added a promise to give him an extra gratuity for so doing.

"Very well, sir," he answered. I sat back, hiding my face in a newspaper for fear of being recognised in that great highway of business, while he went along Austin Friars to endeavour to discover whose offices she had entered.

Some ten minutes later he returned with the information that the lady had entered the office of a moneylender named Morrison.

The thought occurred to me that she was perhaps still endeavouring to raise the loan for Prince Ferdinand. If so, however, why had she left the *Bath Hotel* and endeavoured to conceal her identity under another name?

After twenty minutes or so she came out rather flushed and excited, stood for a moment in hesitation upon the kerb, and then giving her cabman an address was driven off. I, of course, followed, but judge my astonishment when the cab pulled up in Old Broad Street and she alighted at Winchester House. After a few moments she found the brass plate bearing my name, and ascending to my office, for what purpose I knew not, and, fearing to reveal my presence in London, I could not ascertain.

I sat there in the cab in full view of that row of windows, with their wire blinds bearing my name, an exile and a fugitive, wondering what might be the object of her visit. It was not, however, of long duration, but when she descended again she was accompanied by my secretary Gedge, who handed her into her cab and afterwards took his seat beside her. By his manner it was evident they were not strangers, and it became impressed upon me that, in those lost days of mine, I must have had considerable dealings with her and her princely employer.

They drove to the Liverpool Street Railway-Station, where she dispatched a telegram; then they lunched at Crosby Hall.

I feared, of courser to approach them sufficiently near to overhear their conversation, but I peered into the restaurant and saw them sitting at a table in earnest conversation, the subject of which was evidently myself.

It was a wearisome task waiting for her in Bishopsgate Street, but I lunched in a neighbouring public-house off a glass of sherry and a biscuit, while my cabman partook gladly of the homely "half-pint" at my expense, until at length they both came forth.

Gedge called her a cab, and then took leave of her, while I followed her back to the *Midland*, having successfully accomplished my first essay at watching her movements.

XXVIII

Two Words

For two days the woman I was watching did not go out. I learnt from the chambermaid who, like all her class, was amenable to half a sovereign in her palm, that she was unwell, suffering from a slight cold. Then I took the servant into my confidence, and told her that I was in the hotel in order to watch Mrs. Slade's movements, giving her to understand that any assistance she rendered me would be well paid for.

I had an object in view, namely, to enter her room in her absence, and ascertain the nature of any letters or papers which might be in her possession. This I managed to effect, with the connivance of the chambermaid, on the following afternoon. Indeed, the chambermaid assisted me in my eager search, but beyond a few tradesmen's bills and one or two unimportant private letters from friends addressed to her at the *Royal Hotel* at Ryde, I found nothing. The dispatch-box with the coronet was locked, and she carried the key upon her bangle. I made careful search through all her belongings, the chambermaid standing guard at the door the while, and in the pocket of one of her dresses hanging in the wardrobe I discovered a crumpled telegram.

I smoothed it out, and saw that it had been dispatched from Philippopolis, in Bulgaria, about three weeks before, and was addressed to "Mrs. Grainger, *Royal Hotel*, Ryde." Its purport, however, I was unable to learn, for it was either in cipher, or in the Slav language, of which I had no knowledge whatever.

Again baffled, I was about to relinquish my search, when, in the pocket of a long driving-coat of a light drab cloth, I found a letter addressed to her at Ryde, and evidently forwarded by the hotel-clerk.

I caught sight of my own name, and read it through with interest.

"I suppose you have already heard from your friend Gedge, who keeps you in touch with everything, all the most recent news of Heaton," the letter ran. "It appears that he was found on the floor of one of the rooms at Denbury, with a wound in his head. He had suddenly gone out of his mind. The doctor said that the case was a serious one, but before arrangements could be made for placing him under restraint he had escaped, and nothing since has been heard of him. The common idea is

WILLIAM LE QUEUX

that he has committed suicide owing to business complications. They are, to tell the truth, beginning to smell a rat in the City. The Prince's concessions have not turned out all that they were supposed to be, and by a side wind I hear that your friend's financial status, considerably weakened during the past few weeks, has, owing to his sudden and unaccountable disappearance, dropped down to zero. If you can find him, lose no time in doing so. Remember that he must not be allowed to open his mouth. He may, however, be still of use, for his credit has not altogether gone, and I hear he has a very satisfactory balance at his bankers. But find out all from Gedge, and then write to me."

There was neither signature nor address.

The words, "he must not be allowed to open his mouth," were, in themselves, ominous. Who, I wondered, was the writer of that letter? The postmark was that of "London, E.C.," showing that it had been posted in the City.

I read it through a second time, then replaced it, and after some further search returned to my own room.

When the maid brought my hot water next morning she told me that Mrs. Slade had announced her intention to leave at eleven o'clock; therefore I packed, and leaving slightly earlier, was enabled to follow her cab to Victoria Station, whence she travelled to Brighton, putting up at the *Metropole*. I pursued similar tactics to those I had adopted in London, staying in the same hotel and yet contriving never to be seen by her. She went out but seldom. Sometimes in the morning she would stroll beneath her pale mauve sunshade along the King's Road, or at evening take an airing on the pier, but she apparently lived an aimless life, spending her time in reading novels in her own apartment. As far as I could learn, she met no one there, and only appeared to be killing time and waiting. After a fortnight she moved along to Hastings, thence to Ilfracombe, and afterwards to Hull.

We arrived at the *North-Eastern Hotel* at Hull one evening towards the end of August, having travelled by the express from London. Through nearly a month I had kept close watch upon her, yet none of her movements had been in the least suspicious. She lived well, always having her own sitting-room, although she had no maid. Those days of watchfulness were full of anxiety, and I had to resort to all sorts of ingenious devices to prevent observation and recognition.

The station hotel at Hull is comfortable, but by no means a gay place of residence, and for several days I wondered what might be her object in visiting that Yorkshire port. The room adjoining her sitting-room on the second floor became vacant on the third day after our arrival, and I fortunately succeeded in obtaining it. She entertained no suspicion that I was following her, although I dogged her movements everywhere.

In Hull she only went out twice, once to a stationer's in Whitefriar-gate, and on the other occasion to the telegraph office. As at Brighton and Ilfracombe, she still appeared to be waiting in patience for the arrival of some one whom she expected.

About nine o'clock one evening, after she had remained nearly a week in Hull, always taking her meals in her own room and passing her time in reading, I had returned from the coffee-room, and was about to go forth for a stroll, when suddenly I heard a waiter rap at her door and announce a visitor.

A locked door separated her sitting-room from mine, and standing by it, listening eagerly, I heard the sound of rustling paper, the hurried closing of a box, and her permission to show the visitor up.

A few minutes passed in silence. Then I heard some one enter, and a man's voice exclaimed with a distinctly foreign accent—

"Ah, my dear Edna! At last! I feared that you would have left before my arrival."

"I expected you days ago," she answered, and I knew from the man's sigh that he had sunk wearily into a chair.

"I was delayed," he explained. "I had a narrow escape. Oustromoff has guessed the truth."

"What?" she gasped in alarm, "The secret is out?"

"Yes," he answered gruffly.

"Impossible!"

"I tell you it's the truth," he answered. "I escaped over the frontier by the merest chance. Oustromoff's bloodhounds were at my heels. They followed me to Vienna, but there I managed to escape them and travel to Berlin. I knew that there was a warrant out for me—Roesch sent me word that orders had been issued by the Minister of Police—therefore I feared to cross to England by any of the mail routes. I knew the police would be on the look-out at Calais, Antwerp, Ostend, Folkestone, and Dieppe. Therefore I travelled to Copenhagen, thence by steamer to Gothenburg, and rail to Christiania. I arrived by the weekly mail steamer from there only an hour ago."

"What a journey!" exclaimed the woman I had been watching so long and patiently. "Do you actually mean that you are unsafe—here, in England?"

"Unsafe? Of course. The Ministry have telegraphed my description to all police centres, with a request for my extradition."

"It is inconceivable," she cried, "just at the moment when all seemed safest, that this catastrophe should fall! What of Roesch, Blumhardt, and Schaefer?"

"Schaefer was arrested in Sofia on the day I left. Blumhardt escaped to Varna, but was taken while embarking on board a cargo-boat for England. I tell you I had a narrow escape—a very narrow escape."

"Then don't speak so loud," she urged. "Some one might be in the next room, you know."

He rose and tried the door at which I stood. It was locked, and that apparently reassured him.

"Whom do you think informed the Ministry of Police?"

"Ah! at present no one knows," he responded. "What do you think they say?"

"What?"

"That some of your precious friends in London have exposed the whole thing."

"My friends? Whom do you mean?"

"You know best who are your friends," he replied, with sarcasm.

"But no one is aware of the whole facts."

"Are you absolutely certain?"

"Absolutely."

"And the loan for the Prince?" he said. "Have you raised it?"

"No; the thing is too dangerous in these circumstances. I have made a full report. You received it, I suppose?"

"No; I must have left Sofia before it arrived. Tell me."

"That very useful fool named Heaton has suddenly gone out of his mind."

"Insane?"

"Yes," she responded. "At least, he seems so to me. I placed the matter before him, but he refused to have anything whatever to do with it. His standing in the City has been utterly shattered by all sorts of rumours regarding the worthlessness of certain of the concessions, and as far as we are concerned our hopes of successfully raising the loan have now disappeared into thin air."

"What!" he cried. "Have you utterly failed?"

"Yes," she answered. "Heaton assisted us while all was square, but now, just when we want a snug little sum for ourselves, he has suddenly become obstinate and refuses to raise a finger."

"Curse him! He shall assist us—by Heaven! I'll—I'll compel him!" cried her mysterious companion furiously.

"To talk like that is useless," she responded. "Remember that he knows something."

"Something, yes. But what?"

"He knows more than we think."

"Where is he now?"

"Nobody can discover. I saw him once, but he has disappeared. They say he's a wandering lunatic. He left Denbury suddenly after showing signs of madness, and although that terror of a woman, his wife, strove to trace him, she was unsuccessful. His insanity, coupled with the fact that financial ruin overtook him suddenly, apparently preyed upon her mind. She fell ill, and according to a letter I received from Gedge a few days ago, she died suddenly of an aneurism, and was buried last Thursday at Budleigh-Salterton. The announcement of her death was in yesterday's papers."

I listened to those words open-mouthed. My wife was dead! Then I was free!

With my strained ear close to the thin wood of the door I stood breathless, fearing that they might distinguish the rapid beating of my heart.

"Your ingenuity has always been extraordinary, madame," he said reflectively, "but in this last affair you have not shown your usual tact."

"In what manner?"

"His Highness places confidence in you, yet you sit idly here, and profess yourself unable to assist him."

"A warrant is out against you; nevertheless, you still consider the Prince your friend. That is curious!" she remarked, with a touch of sarcasm.

"Most certainly. It was Oustromoff's doings. His Highness is powerless to control the Ministry of Police."

"And you believe that you will be safe in England?" she inquired dubiously.

"I believe so, providing that I exercise care," he responded. "After to-night it is best that we should remain strangers—you understand?"

"Of course."

"And Mrs. Anson and her charge? Are they at a safe distance?"

"Yes. When I met Heaton he inquired after them. He particularly wished to discover them, and of course I assisted him."

They both laughed in chorus. But her words in themselves were sufficient proof that she feared the result of our re-union. They impressed upon me the truth of my suspicion, namely, that Mabel held the key to the enigma.

"What does he know?" asked the man, evidently referring to me.

"He is aware of the spot where the affair took place," she answered.

"What?" gasped her companion in alarm. "That can't be. He was stone blind, you said!"

"Certainly he was. But by some means—how I can't say—he has ascertained at least one fact."

"Did he make any remark to you?"

"Of course he did. He gave me to understand that he was acquainted with the details of the whole affair." A long silence fell between them.

The mention of Mrs. Anson and her charge held me breathless. The "charge" referred to was evidently Mabel. I only hoped that from this conversation I might obtain some clue to the whereabouts of my darling.

"I wonder how much Heaton really does know?" observed her visitor reflectively at last.

"Too much, I fear," she answered. No doubt she recollected how I had expressed my determination to go to Scotland Yard.

Again there was a prolonged pause.

"Roesch has arrived in London. I must see him," exclaimed the man.

"In London? I thought he was still at his post in the Ministry at Sofia," she said in a tone of surprise.

"He was fortunate enough to obtain early intimation of Oustromoff's intentions, and after warning me, escaped the same evening. He took steamer, I heard, from Trieste to London."

"Why associate yourself further with that man?" she urged. "Surely it will only add to the danger."

"What concerns myself likewise concerns him," he answered rather ambiguously.

"You have apparently of late become closer friends. For what reason?"

"You will see later."

"With some distinctly evil purpose, I have no doubt," she observed, "but remember that I have no further interest in any of your future schemes."

He grunted dubiously.

"Now that you think our fortunes have changed you contemplate deserting us, eh?" he snapped. "A single word to the Prince and you would conclude your career rather abruptly, I'm thinking."

"Is that intended as a threat?" she inquired in a calm voice.

"Take it as such, if you wish," the man responded angrily. "Through your confounded bungling you've brought exposure upon us. We have only you to thank for it. You know me quite well enough to be aware that when I make threats they are never idle ones."

"And you are sufficiently well acquainted with me to know that I never run unnecessary risks."

"I know you to be a devilishly clever woman," he said. "But in your dealings with that man Heaton you showed weakness—a coward's weakness. All that he knows is through your own folly. You attempted to mislead him by your actions and letters, but he has, it seems, been a little too shrewd for you."

"And if he does know the truth—even, indeed, if he dared to inform the police—what direct evidence can he give, pray?" she queried. "He was blind, and therefore saw nothing. He is now mad, and nobody will believe him."

"Even though he may be an idiot his mouth is better closed," her companion growled.

His words startled me. This unseen man's intention was apparently to make a further attempt upon my life. But I chuckled within myself. Forewarned is forearmed.

Just at that moment I heard the waiter tap at the door, and opening it, announce the arrival of another visitor—a Mr. Roesch.

"Why, I wonder, has he sought you here?" exclaimed the man when the waiter had gone. "He must have some important news!"

Next moment the door was again thrown open, and the new arrival entered.

All three spoke quickly together in a foreign tongue. The man Roesch then made a brief statement, which apparently held his two companions for some moments speechless in alarm. Then again they all commenced talking in low confidential tones in that strange language—Slav I believe it was.

Whatever it might have been, and although I understood no word of it, it brought back vividly to my memory the indelible recollection of the night of the tragedy at The Boltons.

I listened attentively. Yes, there was no mistake—those tones were familiar. That trio of voices were the same that with my sharpened ears I had overheard conversing in the inner room immediately before the commission of the crime.

I have said that my nerves were shattered. All the past was a torturing memory to me, but the quintessence of that torture was my failure to discover my love. I believed that she alone could supply the solution of the enigma, and what truth there was in that suspicion you shall duly see.

The three voices continued to speak in that foreign tongue for perhaps half an hour, during which period I was unable to form any idea of the trend of the new-comer's announcement.

Then I heard the visitors taking their leave, apparently with many of those gesticulated reassurances of respect which mark the shallow foreigner. I extinguished my light and opened my door cautiously. As they passed on their way down the corridor I succeeded in obtaining a very good view of the interesting pair. They were talking together, and I distinguished the man who had first called upon Edna by his deep voice. He was a short, thick-set, black-bearded man of forty, well-dressed in black, with a heavy gold albert across his ample vest. His companion, whose name was apparently Roesch, was considerably older, about fifty-five or so, of spare build, erect, thin-faced, with long grey whiskers descending from either cheek, and shaven chin. He wore a frock-coat and silk hat, and was of a type altogether superior to his companion.

The woman Grainger's coffee was brought to her as usual in the morning, but about ten o'clock she rang again, and when the chambermaid responded, said—

"Here are two letters. Post them for me in the box in the bureau, and tell them to send my bill at once. I leave at ten forty-five."

"Yes'm." And the girl departed to post the letters.

To whom, I wondered, were those letters addressed? Within my mind I strove to devise some plan whereby I could obtain a glance at the addresses. The box, however, was only at the foot of the stairs, therefore ere I could resolve upon any plan the girl had dropped them into it, and I heard her linen flounces beating along the corridor again. Those letters were in the post, and beyond my reach.

She had written those two missives during the night, and after the departure of her visitors. They had, no doubt, some connexion with the matter which the trio had so earnestly discussed in that tantalising foreign tongue.

In hesitancy I remained some little time, then a sudden thought occurred to me. I addressed an envelope to the hall-porter of my club, enclosing a blank sheet of paper, and then descending, posted it. The box was placed outside the bureau, and the instant I had dropped the letter in I turned, as though in anger with myself, and, entering the bureau, said to the clerk—

"I've unfortunately posted a letter without a stamp. Have you the key of the box?"

"The box belongs to the Post Office, sir," he answered. "But we have a key to it."

"Then I should esteem it a favour if you would recover my letter for me. It is most important that the addressee should not be charged for its postage. I regret that my absent-mindedness should give you this trouble."

The clerk took the key from a drawer at the end of the bureau, and opening the box, took out the half-dozen or so letters which it contained, and spread them upon the desk. Among them were two square, pale-faced envelopes. As I took my own letter and affixed a stamp I glanced eagerly at the address of both.

One bore the superscription: "Mr. P. Gechkuloff, 98, King Henry's Road, Hampstead, N.W."

Upon the other were words which caused my heart to leap joyfully within me. They were—

"Miss Mabel Anson, *Langham Hotel*, London."

I posted my letter, hurried upstairs and paid my bill. Edna had already packed her trunk, but had changed her mind, and did not intend leaving Hull that day. I heard her inform the chambermaid of her intention of remaining, then I left the hotel, and caught the ten-forty-five express for London.

XXIX

The Enigma

At five o'clock that same afternoon I alighted from a taxi before the *Langham Hotel*, and presenting my card at the bureau, inquired for Miss Anson. The clerk looked at me rather curiously, I thought, glanced at the card, and entering the telephone-box, spoke some words into the instrument.

I was shown into a small room on the first floor, where I waited until a gentlemanly, middle-aged, fair-headed man entered, with my card in his hand.

"Good afternoon," he said, greeting me rather stiffly. "Her Highness is at present out driving. Is there anything I can do? I am her secretary."

"Her Highness?" I echoed, with a smile. "There must be some mistake. I have called to see Miss Mabel Anson."

He regarded me with some surprise.

"Are you, then, unaware that Anson is the name adopted by Her Highness to preserve her *incognita*?" he asked, glancing at me in quick suspicion. "Are you not aware of her real rank and station?"

"No!" I cried, in blank amazement. "This is indeed a revelation to me! I have known Miss Anson intimately during the past six years. What is her true rank?"

"The lady whom you know as Miss Anson is Her Imperial Highness the Archduchess Marie Elizabeth Mabel, third daughter of His Majesty the Emperor Francis Joseph of Austria."

"Mabel! The daughter of an Emperor?" I gasped involuntarily. "Impossible!"

He shrugged his shoulders. He was a foreigner, although he spoke English well—an Austrian most probably.

"You are surprised," he laughed. "Many people have also been surprised, as the Archduchess, living in England nearly her whole life, has frequently been taken for an Englishwoman."

"I can't believe it!" I cried. "Surely there must be some mistake!"

I remembered those days of long ago when we had wandered together in Kensington Gardens. How charming and ingenuous she was: how sweet and unaffected by worldly vanities, how trustful was that look when she gazed into my eyes! Her air was never that of the daughter of the reigning House of Hapsbourg-Lorraine. She had possessed all the enchantment of ideal grace without the dignity of rank, and it seemed incredible that she was actually a princess whose home was the most brilliant Court of Europe.

"I can quite understand your surprise," observed the secretary. "But what is the nature of your business with Her Highness?"

"It is of a purely private nature."

He glanced at the card. "The Archduchess does not receive callers," he answered coldly.

"But at least you will give her my name, and tell her that I have something of urgent importance to communicate to her," I cried eagerly.

He hesitated. "If you are, as you allege, an old friend, I will place your card before her," he said at last, with some hesitation. "You may leave your address, and if Her Highness consents to receive you I will communicate with you."

"No," I answered in desperation; "I will remain and await her return."

"That is impossible," he responded. "She has many engagements, and certainly cannot receive you to-day."

I recollected that the letter I had found at Denbury made it plain that we had parted abruptly. If this man gave her my card without any word, it was more than likely that she would refuse to see me.

Therefore I entered into argument with him, but while I was speaking the door opened suddenly, and my love stood before me.

She halted there, elegantly dressed, having just returned from her drive, and for a moment we faced each other speechless.

"Mr. Heaton!" she cried, and then, in breathless hurry arising from the sudden and joyful surprise, she rushed forward.

Our hands grasped. For the moment I could utter no word. The secretary, noticing our mutual embarrassment, discreetly withdrew, closing the door after him.

Once again I found myself, after those six lost years, alone with my love.

"At last!" I cried. "At last I have found you, after all these months!" I was earnestly gazing into her great dark eyes. She had altered but little since that night long ago at The Boltons, when I had discovered the traces of that hideous tragedy.

"And why have you come back to me now?" she inquired in a low, strained voice.

"I have striven long and diligently to find you," I answered frankly, "because—because I wished to tell you how I love you—that I have loved you always—from the first moment that we met."

A grave expression crossed her countenance.

"And yet you forsook me! You calmly broke off the secret engagement that we had mutually made, and left me without a single word. You have married," she added resentfully, "therefore it is scarcely fitting that you should come here with a false declaration upon your lips."

"It is no false declaration, I swear," I cried. "As for my wife, I knew her not, and she is now dead."

"Dead!" she gasped. "You knew her not! I don't understand."

"I have loved you always—always, Princess—for I have only ten minutes ago ascertained your true rank—"

"Mabel to you—as always," she said, softly interrupting me.

"Ah, thank you for those words!" I cried, taking her small gloved hand. "I have loved you from the first moment that we met at the colonel's, long ago—you remember that night?"

"I shall never forget it," she faltered in that low tone as of old, which was as sweetest music to my ears.

"And you remember that evening when I dined with you at The Boltons?" I said. "Incomprehensible though it may seem, I began a new life from that night, and for six whole years have existed in a state of utter unconsciousness of all the past. Will you consider me insane if I tell you that I have no knowledge whatever of meeting you after that night, and only knew of our engagement by discovering this letter among my private papers a couple of months ago?" and I drew her letter from my pocket.

"Your words sound most remarkable," she said, deeply interested. "Relate the whole of the facts to me. But first come along to my own sitting-room. We may be interrupted here."

And she led the way to the end of the corridor, where we entered an elegant little salon, one of the handsome suite of rooms she occupied.

She drew forth a chair for me, and allowing a middle-aged gentlewoman—her lady-in-waiting, I presume—to take her hat and gloves, we once more found ourselves alone.

How exquisitely beautiful she was! Yet her royal birth, alas! placed her beyond my reach. All my hopes and aspirations had been in an instant crushed by the knowledge of her rank. I could only now relate to her the truth, and seek her forgiveness for what had seemed a cruel injustice.

I took her unresisting hand, and told her how long ago I had loved her, not daring to expose to her the great secret of my heart. If we had mutually decided upon marriage, and I had deliberately deserted her, it was, I declared, because of that remarkable unconsciousness which had blotted out all knowledge of my life previous to that last night when we had dined together, and I had accompanied the man Hickman to his lodgings.

"But tell me all," she urged, "so that I can understand and judge accordingly."

And then, beginning at the beginning, I recounted the whole of the amazing facts, just as I have narrated them to the reader in these foregoing chapters.

I think the telling occupied most part of an hour; but she sat there, her lovely eyes fixed upon me, her mouth half open, held dumb and motionless by the strange story I unfolded. Once or twice she gave vent to ejaculations of surprise, and I saw that only by dint of supreme effort did she succeed in preserving her self-control. I told her everything. I did not seek to conceal one single fact.

"And he was actually murdered in my house?" she cried, starting up at last. "You were present?"

I explained to her in detail the events of that fateful night.

"Then at last the truth is plain!" she exclaimed. "You have supplied the key to the enigma for which I have been so long in search!"

"Tell me," I said, in breathless earnestness. "All these years I have been striving in vain to solve the problem."

She paused, her dark, fathomless eyes fixed upon me, as though lacking courage to tell me the truth.

"I deceived you, Wilford, from the first," she faltered, "I hid from you the secret of my birth, and it was at my request Colonel Channing—who, of course, knew me well when he was British Attache at Vienna—refused to tell you the truth. You wonder, of course, that I should live in England *incognita*. Probably, however, you know that my poor mother, the late Empress, loved England and the English. She gave me an English name at my baptism, and when only five years of age I was sent here to be educated. At seventeen I returned to Vienna, but soon became tired of the eternal glitter of palace life, and a year or two later, as soon as I was of age and my own mistress, I returned to London, took into my service Mrs. Anson, the widow of an English officer well known to my mother, and in order to preserve my *incognita* caused her to pass as my mother. I took the house at The Boltons, and only Colonel and Mrs. Channing knew my real station. I was passionately fond of music, and desired to complete my studies, besides which I am intensely fond of London and of life unfettered by the trammels which must hamper the daughter of an Emperor."

"You preferred a quiet, free life in London to that at your father's Court?"

"Exactly," she answered. "At twenty-one I had had my fill of life at Court, and found existence in London, where I was unknown, far more pleasant. Besides Mrs. Anson, I had as companion a young Englishwoman who had been governess in a well-known family in Vienna. Her name was Grainger."

"Grainger?" I cried. "Edna Grainger?"

"The same. She was my companion. Well, after I had been established at The Boltons nearly a year I met, while on a visit to a country house, a young man with whom I became on very friendly terms—Prince Alexander, heir to the throne of Bulgaria. We met often, and although I still passed as Mabel Anson, our acquaintanceship ripened into a mutual affection. With a disregard for the *convenances*, I induced Mrs. Anson to invite him on several occasions to The Boltons. One morning, however, I received a private message from Count de Walkenstein-Trosburg, our ambassador here, saying that he had received a cipher telegraphic dispatch that my father, the Emperor, was very unwell, and his Excellency suggested that I should return to Vienna. This I did, accompanied by Mrs. Anson, and, leaving the woman Grainger in charge of the household as usual, I wrote to the young Prince from Vienna, but received no reply, and when I returned a fortnight later searched for him in vain. He had mysteriously disappeared. A few days before, in my dreams, I had seen the fatal raven, the evil omen of my House, and feared the worst."

"Then the man who was murdered at The Boltons on that night was none other than Prince Alexander, the heir to the throne of Bulgaria!" I cried.

"Without a doubt," she answered. "What you have just told me makes it all plain. You took from the dead man's pocket a small gold pencil-case, and you will remember that I recognised it as one that I had given him. It was that fact which caused me to suspect you."

"Suspect me? Did you believe me guilty of murder?"

"I did not then know that murder had been committed. All that was known was that the heir to the throne had mysteriously disappeared.

The terrible truth I have just learnt from your lips. The discovery that the little gift I had made to him was in your possession filled me with suspicion, and in order to solve the mystery I invoked the aid of the police-agent attached to our Embassy, and invited both of you to dine, in order that he might meet you. You will remember the man you met on that night?"

"Hickman!" I cried. "Was he really a police-agent?"

"Yes. He induced you, it appears, to go to a lodging he had taken for the purpose, and without my knowledge gave you a drugged cigar. You fell unconscious, and this enabled him to thoroughly overhaul your pockets, and also to go to your chambers during the night, either with your latch-key, and make a complete search, the result of which convinced us both that you had no hand in the missing man's disappearance, in spite of the fact that his dress-stud and pencil-case were in your possession. On the following morning, however, when you were but half conscious—Hickman having then returned from making his search at Essex Street—you accidentally struck your head a violent blow on the corner of the stone mantelshelf. This blow, so severe that they were compelled to remove you to the hospital, apparently affected your brain, for when I met you again a month later you seamed curiously vacant in mind, and had no recollection whatever of the events that had passed."

"I had none, I assure you," I said.

"It seems marvellous that you should be utterly in ignorance of what followed," she went on, her sweet eyes still gazing deeply into mine. "You told me how you loved me, and I, loving you in return, we entered upon a clandestine engagement that was to be secret from all. A few summer months went by, happy, joyous months, the most blissful in all my life, and then your love suddenly cooled. You had embarked in financial schemes in the City—you were becoming enriched by some concessions in Bulgaria, it was whispered—but your love for me slowly died, and you married a woman twice your age. Can you imagine my feelings? I was heart-broken, Wilford—utterly heart-broken."

"But I knew not what I was doing," I hastened to declare. "I loved you always—always. My brain had been injured by that blow, and all my tastes and feelings thereby became inverted."

"I remained in England a few weeks longer, wandering aimlessly hither and thither, and then at last returned to Vienna and plunged into the vortex of gaiety at Court, in order to forget my sorrow."

"And that woman Grainger? What of her?"

"She left my service about a month after that night when you met with your accident at The Boltons. I have not seen her since."

I then related how for the past month I had been closely watching her, and repeated the conversation I had overheard at Hull between her and her visitors on the previous night.

"The woman, after leaving my service, has, it seems, somehow become an agent of the Bulgarian Government. She knows the truth," she said decisively. "We must obtain it from her."

"It was a woman who struck the young Prince down!" I exclaimed quickly. "Of that I am certain."

My wife reflected for a brief instant.

"Perhaps," she said. "That woman was jealous of the attention he paid me."

XXX

Conclusion

"Mrs. Slade is still in her room, sir, but she's not alone; her maid arrived from London last night," answered the chambermaid at the *North-Eastern Hotel* at Hull, when on the following morning, I made inquiry.

I had been accompanied from King's Cross by Mabel and the police-agent, Hickman, and we stood together in the hotel corridor prior to entering the woman's room. Hickman, whom I had all along believed to be deeply implicated in the plot, if not the actual murderer, was, I found, a clever detective of English birth, who had for some years been an officer of the Prefecture of Police in Vienna, but who had latterly been attached to the Austro-Hungarian Embassy in Belgrave Square, and entrusted with the personal safety of the Emperor's daughter. The revelations I had made utterly amazed him. By the last post on the previous night Mabel had received the letter written from Hull which merely asked for an interview, and we had all three set forth, determined to secure the arrest of the writer.

With that object we entered her sitting-room without a word of warning.

She was sitting at the table writing, but in an instant sprang to her feet, with a cry of profound alarm. When her eyes wandered from Mabel to Hickman and myself, her cheeks blanched. She apparently guessed our purpose.

"You have expressed a desire to meet me," Mabel said determinedly. "So I have come to you."

"And—and these gentlemen?" Edna inquired, glancing at us, puzzled.

"They are present to hear what you have to say to me."

She was taken aback.

"I—I have nothing to say to your Highness," the woman faltered. "I merely wished to know whether, when in London, I might call."

"Then listen," exclaimed Mabel. "The truth is known, and it is useless for you to further conceal it. If you have nothing to say, Mr. Hickman will at once call in the police, and I shall charge you with the murder of the Prince."

"The murder of the Prince!" she gasped, white to the lips. "I—did not commit the crime. I can prove that I didn't!"

Her hands were trembling, and she stood beside the table, steadying herself by it. There was a haunted look in those cold grey eyes. Our sudden descent upon her had taken her utterly by surprise.

"Then let us hear your statement," my love said in a hard voice quite unusual to her. "Let it be the truth, or I shall charge you now, at once, with the capital offence. The Prince was murdered in my house, and with your knowledge. Do you deny that?"

"No," she cried hoarsely, "I do not deny it."

A long silence ensued. The woman Grainger—or Slade, as she was known there—hung her head.

Hickman spoke authoritatively, demanding full explanation, but she maintained a dogged silence. A sudden fire flashed in her eyes—the fire of defiance and hatred.

"Then, as you refuse to speak," said Mabel at length, "you will have no further opportunity until you stand in the criminal dock."

"No, no!" cried the wretched woman quickly. "Hear me! I will tell you all—everything. Listen," she implored. "Do not call the police ere I have explained my exact position, and how the tragedy occurred."

"Proceed," Mabel said harshly. "We are all attention."

"You will remember that three days before the tragedy your Highness left London suddenly because of the illness of the Emperor, and I remained in charge of the household. It was on a Sunday you left, and you had invited the young Prince to dine on the following Wednesday evening. On the afternoon following your departure a visitor was announced. His name was Petrovitch Gechkuloff, a Bulgarian gentleman whom I knew slightly, he having been a visitor at the house in Vienna where I had previously been in service as English governess. He asked me whether I wished to earn a thousand pounds, and then, under promise of strictest secrecy, unfolded to me an ingenious and extraordinary scheme. He was acting, he said, together with Danilo Roesch, the Bulgarian Minister of Finance, whom he would later introduce to me, in the interests of the People's Party in the Sobranje, and they desired the young Prince Alexander to sign a certain deed. He told me nothing of the contents of the document, but asked me to assist them. I was to send no notice of your Highness's departure to the Prince, but, on the contrary, when he arrived on the Wednesday evening I was to entertain him, make some excuse for your Highness's absence, and afterwards introduce the Minister Roesch and his friend. There was nothing risky about the proceedings, he declared most emphatically. The pair merely wished to obtain the young Prince's signature."

"But did not this request strike you as extraordinary?" asked Mabel. "You knew the Prince quite well."

"It was the money which tempted me," the wretched woman cried. "I hesitated for some time, and at last yielded. The Prince arrived, and although greatly surprised and disappointed to find your Highness absent, remained and dined with myself and the man Gechkuloff, of whom he, of course, knew nothing save that he was one of his father's subjects. Near the conclusion of dinner we witnessed a cab accident opposite the window, a blind gentleman—Mr. Heaton—being run over, and I ordered the people to carry him into the drawing-room. Dr. Slater was fetched, and having bandaged his head, told us to let him remain quiet for an hour or so, then left. In the meantime the Bulgarian Minister, Roesch, arrived, apparently in a great hurry, was introduced, and had a long interview with the Prince in private. Afterwards we adjourned into the library. Some champagne was drunk, and the three men smoked, speaking often in their own language, so that I might not understand all that was said. Subsequently the deed was produced, and after a considerable amount of hesitation and many promises on the part of the Minister of Finance, his Highness signed it. Then a witness was required. Gechkuloff whispered to me the suggestion that the signature of Mr. Heaton, who was lying in the adjoining room half conscious, should be obtained, and having made him believe that he was signing a birthday book I got from him the desired signature. Shortly afterwards, while sitting at the piano playing I felt a heavy blow, which for a few moments stunned me. Then gazing through into the adjoining room I saw two figures struggling—the Prince and a woman. For a few seconds he held her tightly, but with a furious twist she freed herself and struck him full in the chest with the small dagger in her hand. He staggered and fell backward upon the couch dying. The scene struck terror into the hearts of all of us, the two men standing near me rigid in amazement. The woman closed and locked the door communicating between the two rooms, and left the house, while a few minutes later we also followed."

"You saw the woman's face?" inquired Hickman.

"Most certainly," she answered. Then, continuing, said, "The tragic *denouement* was so unexpected and startling that at first neither man

WILLIAM LE QUEUX

appeared to know how to act. Quickly, however, they saw that suspicion of the murder must fall upon them, owing, I suppose, to the part they had played in Bulgarian politics, and they at once made it imperative that I should join in and carry out their scheme. As together we hurried along Gilston Road, they confessed to me how they had contemplated the assassination of the young Prince after he had signed the document, in order to remove the heir to the throne, and thus strengthen the hands of the People's Party. They explained how they had discovered a cellar beside the Thames, close to the Turpentine Factory at Battersea Bridge, and had intended that on the Prince emerging from the house at The Boltons he should be accosted by a man in police uniform, and asked to walk to the police-station, only to find himself entrapped. Now they pointed out that the witness to the crime was the blind gentleman who had met with the accident, and as his signature was upon the document executed, it was necessary that he should be silenced."

"They intended to kill me!" I cried.

"Most assuredly," she responded, turning towards me. "When you emerged from the house you were met by the man who acted the part of police-constable, a London ruffian, and being blind, at once fell into the trap. I saved you, for I saw that by securing your silence in exchange for your life I should also secure you as an agent who might be useful to the two men into whose clutches I had so suddenly and hopelessly fallen. This proved correct, for ere long your assistance became of greatest use. On the morning when we parted, accompanied by Gechkuloff, I visited your chambers, and made a search there to ascertain who and what you were. Having once embarked on the conspiracy with these two men, whom I found were powerful factors in Bulgarian politics, I was compelled to assist them in disposing of the body—which was placed in the cellar beside the Thames, and allowed to float out with the tide. Then, having sent the servants on holiday, I removed the blood-stains, and worked the crochet cover for the couch."

"You told me that those stains were of coffee that you had spilled there," Mabel said.

"True," she answered. "But I was compelled to deceive you. I left you soon afterwards, for by Roesch's influence I became appointed English governess to the two youngest children of Prince Ferdinand, and it was while at Sofia that I suggested to the Minister of Finance the scheme for placing the concessions in the hands of Mr. Heaton, whom I had heard was now suffering from an unaccountable loss of memory, and recollected nothing of the past. The subject was mooted to Prince Ferdinand, who in all good faith empowered me to treat with Mr. Heaton, and before long several formidable concessions were floated in the City. The most remarkable thing was Mr. Heaton's absolute ignorance of all the past. He was as wax in the hands of the two men who had become my masters. Only at the last coup, when they desired to raise a loan of half a million sterling, intending to appropriate it to their own uses, did he refuse to render us further assistance. It was as though his memory had suddenly returned to him, and he suspected."

"My memory had then returned," I said briefly, marvelling at her remarkable narrative. "But what reason had the men in making those elaborate preparations for the assassination of the Prince?"

"There were two reasons. One was that by the execution of the deed they were empowered to raise upon post-obits large sums, repayable when the young Prince came to the accession, and, secondly, they had found out that he had, by some means, discovered the huge defalcations which had been made in the Ministry of Finance at Sofia, and feared that he might expose them."

"But you say that, although they had intention of assassinating him, they did not actually do so?" Hickman observed.

"No. They were not the actual assassins."

"Then who was?" demanded Mabel.

The woman stood in silence, her lips hard-set, her face drawn.

"The truth must be told," she said at last. "It is, I suppose, useless to try and conceal it now."

And with a sudden movement she flung open the door leading to a small ante-chamber, crying in a hoarse, desperate voice—

"Enter! The guilty one is there?"

We pressed forward, and there saw a thin grey-haired woman who had guilt written plainly upon her drawn white face. She had overheard all our conversation, and had been compelled to remain in that chamber, there being no outlet.

"Joliot!" gasped Mabel, amazed. "My maid!" Then, addressing the cowering, trembling woman, she demanded the truth.

We stood there astonished. There was a silence, long and painful. The contortions of the guilty woman's features were horrible; in her black eyes burned a fierce light, and she trembled in every limb.

"Yes," she cried hoarsely, after the question had been repeated, "I killed him! I killed him because I was jealous! I thought that instead of coming to visit your Highness he, in reality, came to visit Miss Grainger. Therefore without knowing why I did it, I dashed into the room where Miss Grainger was at the piano and attacked her. The Prince rose quickly and stretched out his arm to save her. Then rushing upon him I stabbed him to the heart! Since that day," she added, in her low voice, scarcely audible, "since that day I have lived upon the meagre charity of Roesch, and yesterday came here to take up a position as Miss Grainger's maid."

"Your interests were mutual in the preservation of your secret, therefore you resolved to adjust your differences and live together, eh?" remarked Hickman.

She gave vent to a shrill peal of hideous laughter, as though there were something humorous in that grim and terrible tragedy. It jarred upon our nerves, but it also explained to us the ghastly truth.

The woman Natalie Joliot was hopelessly insane.

"Your Highness recognises the state of the wretched woman's mind," observed Edna Grainger, with a pitying look. "She has been so ever since the homicidal frenzy which seized her on that fatal night, and I have now taken her beneath my charge, for with me she is as docile as a child."

The truth was a startling one. We all three stood by in wondering silence. The crime had been committed in a sudden access of madness by that miserable creature who could not be held responsible for her actions.

"Roesch and Gechkuloff, with their elaborate preparations for the assassination of the heir to the Bulgarian throne, were murderers at heart, but, by that strange combination of circumstances which so often render truth stranger than fiction, their work was accomplished by another hand," I remarked.

"There seems no doubt," said Edna, "that large sums were raised in London and in Paris upon the deed executed by the young Prince, who evidently had no knowledge of its true nature, and during the first six months before the hue-and-cry as to his disappearance all was plain sailing. When, however, suspicion arose that the heir had met with foul play they feared to continue using the deed, and hit upon the expedient of the concessions which I induced you to negotiate."

"And these two men, Roesch and Gechkuloff, where are they?" inquired Hickman.

"They were in England yesterday. The mystery surrounding the whereabouts of Prince Alexander has been used for political purposes in Bulgaria, with the result that the Ministry has been forced to resign. The defalcations of the head of the Treasury and his assistant being discovered, they were both forced to fly. They are, I believe, on their way to Australia."

"We must arrest them," said Hickman briefly. "Such a pair of villains must, not be allowed to go scot free."

"And to you," exclaimed Mabel, turning to me with the bright light of unshed tears in her fine eyes, "to your patience and careful watchfulness is due the unravelling of this extraordinary mystery, which might otherwise have remained an enigma always."

She took my hand. I saw in her beautiful countenance that love-look as of old. But I bent over her bejewelled fingers as a courtier would over those of a princess of an Imperial House, my heart too full for words.

The madwoman railed at us, shrieking and hurling imprecations interspersed with all sorts of rambling sentences, while Edna held her tightly by the wrist and strove to calm her.

The scene was a hideous one. Neither of us could bear it longer, therefore we withdrew, leaving Hickman with Edna and her charge.

The chronicle of this strange chapter of my life's history is finished.

There is no more to tell, save perhaps to explain—as Sir Henry Blundell, the specialist on mental diseases, explained to me in his consulting-room in Harley Street—the cause of my six lost years. Such an experience, it seemed, was not unknown in medical science, and he made it clear to me that the blow I had accidentally dealt myself in Hickman's rooms had so altered the balance of my brain—already affected by the cab accident during my blindness—that my intellect stopped like a watch. I lost all knowledge of the past, and from the moment of recovering consciousness commenced an entirely new life. This extended through the long period, nearly six years, until I had struck my head against the marble statue in the drawing-room at Denbury, when my brain, restored again to its normal capacity, lost all impression of events which had occurred during its abnormal state. This, of course, accounted for my extraordinary unconscious life, my inverted tastes, and my parting with the woman I loved so fondly.

And what of her, you ask?

She had, during that period of my unconsciousness, become satiated by the gaiety of the brilliant Court at Vienna, and the tragic death of her devoted mother, the Empress, at the hand of Luccheni, the anarchist, caused her to prefer a life quiet, free, and untrammelled. Knowing her royal birth, however, I dared not ask her hand in marriage, and it was not until many weeks later, after the woman Natalie Joliot had been confined as a homicidal patient in Woking Asylum, Edna Grainger had, owing to Mabel's clemency, escaped to the continent, the ex-Minister Roesch and his companion Gechkuloff had been extradited from Bow Street to Sofia to take their trial for their gigantic defalcations upon the State Treasury, and I had sold Denbury and made an end of the financial business which stood in my name, that she complained to me of her loneliness.

With eager, trembling heart I took her white hand in mine and put to her the question. I knew it was presumptuous, almost unheard of. But, reader, you may readily imagine what overwhelming joy arose within me when she threw her arms passionately about my neck, and as answer raised her face and gave me a warm fond kiss.

Our life to-day is very even, very uneventful, idyllically happy. Under her second title of Countess of Klagenfurt we were soon afterwards married. We spent part of our time at Heaton, with which she is charmed now that it is swept and garnished, and the remainder at her own mediaeval Castle of Mohaes, one of the great ancestral estates of the Hapsbourg-Lorraines in the Tyrol, not far from Innsbruck, which was presented to her as a marriage gift by the Emperor.

Her Imperial Highness the Archduchess Marie-Elizabeth-Mabel no longer exists. At the outset I made it quite plain that I had not written here my true name. I did so at my wife's suggestion, for although my real name is probably known to most of those who read this record of my strange adventures, yet the world is still in ignorance of Mabel's actual social position. She said that she had no desire to be pointed at as a Princess who married a commoner, and I have, of course, respected her wish.

She sacrificed all for my sake, and peace and joy are ours at last. With a fond and devoted love she gave up everything in order to become my wife, and as such has renounced for ever that world in which she was born—the world of Purple and Fine Linen.

The End

A Note About the Author

William Le Queux (1864–1927) was an Anglo-French journalist, novelist, and radio broadcaster. Born in London to a French father and English mother, Le Queux studied art in Paris and embarked on a walking tour of Europe before finding work as a reporter for various French newspapers. Towards the end of the 1880s, he returned to London where he edited *Gossip* and *Piccadilly* before being hired as a reporter for *The Globe* in 1891. After several unhappy years, he left journalism to pursue his creative interests. Le Queux made a name for himself as a leading writer of popular fiction with such espionage thrillers as *The Great War in England in 1897* (1894) and *The Invasion of 1910* (1906). In addition to his writing, Le Queux was a notable pioneer of early aviation and radio communication, interests he maintained while publishing around 150 novels over his decades long career.

A Note from the Publisher

Spanning many genres, from non-fiction essays to literature classics to children's books and lyric poetry, Mint Edition books showcase the master works of our time in a modern new package. The text is freshly typeset, is clean and easy to read, and features a new note about the author in each volume. Many books also include exclusive new introductory material. Every book boasts a striking new cover, which makes it as appropriate for collecting as it is for gift giving. Mint Edition books are only printed when a reader orders them, so natural resources are not wasted. We're proud that our books are never manufactured in excess and exist only in the exact quantity they need to be read and enjoyed.

Discover more of your favorite classics with Bookfinity™.

- Track your reading with custom book lists.
- Get great book recommendations for your personalized Reader Type.
- Add reviews for your favorite books.
- AND MUCH MORE!

Visit **bookfinity.com** and take the fun Reader Type quiz to get started.

Enjoy our classic and modern companion pairings!

Printed in the USA
CPSIA information can be obtained
at www.ICGtesting.com
JSHW022332140824
68134JS00019B/1439